LOST GIRLS

The Cellar Series, book II

http://coolgus.com

LOST GIRLS
The Cellar Series, book 2
COPYRIGHT © 2007 by Bob Mayer, Updated 2011

ISBN: 9781621250661

LOST GIRLS

The Cellar Series, book II

Bob Mayer

ONE YEAR AGO

IN THE NIGHT THERE IS DEATH.

It was one of the first lessons they had taught the Sniper and he had never forgotten it. Night is a common denominator regardless of terrain, enemy or mission. It will always come with the movement of the planet. He knew how to move unobserved, like a ghost, in daylight, but the night was his special friend.

He was dressed in a one-piece flight suit dyed black, underneath the full body ghillie suit, which consisted of burlap strips woven into green elastic. The natural color and uneven surface of the ghillie suit allowed him to blend in perfectly with his surroundings. He'd been in the same position for three days. His urine smelled of the jungle as he'd eaten only local food procured from it for a month prior to this mission. He'd had no need to defecate because he'd stopped eating two days before being infiltrated by covert Nightstalker helicopter into this Operational Area along the Caribbean coastline of Colombia close to the border with Panama. On one mission he'd gone eight days without the need. It wasn't just the lack of food either.

His cheek was pressed against the stock of the sniper rifle, his shooting eye closed and resting on the rubber, his other, free eye, open. It was a position he could hold for a very long time.

The other two members of his team were within ten meters of his position. His Spotter was to his left and slightly upslope with a better view of the road that approached the village across the valley. His Security was located on the back slope of the ridge-line, covering him and the Spotter from the rear. He had neither seen nor heard them since they'd settled into

1

position. That ended as the small earpiece crackled with static, a signal from the Spotter.

The Sniper's open eye spotted the headlights along the narrow mountain road on the ridgeline across from him, over a mile away. Three sets which agreed with the intelligence. Another unusual thing as the intelligence had come from the CIA, a source he'd found to be notoriously unreliable. Working with any of the alphabet soup organizations always entailed a certain degree of carefulness and there were a tangle of them operating here in South America.

He twisted the on knob for the satellite radio in his backpack. The small dish it was attached to was twenty feet over his head, set in the branches of the tree covering his position, with a clear uplink. It was the first thing he had done upon arriving at the site after determining it was secured. He had not moved since climbing down, winding the thin green connecting wire around a vine.

"Falcon, this is Hammer. Over." He knew his two teammates could hear the transmission also as he radioed back to their superior, as everything he said was picked up by his throat mike and transmitted over the short range FM radio they all had.

The reply was instantaneous. "This is Falcon. Go ahead. Over."

"Three vehicles moving in. Over." He closed the non-shooting eye as he turned on the thermal sight bolted on top of the rifle. He slowly opened his left eye and blinked, as it was flooded with a spectrum of colors. He could see the hot engines of the vehicles on the road. Shifting right, he noted the dull red glows of cooking fires damped low in the village. Orange forms indicated people sleeping inside of huts. He'd counted seventy-six the previous night.

His earpiece came alive. "Close to dawn. Over."

He knew what the Colonel meant. In less than thirty minutes they'd lose their friend, the darkness. He also knew what that sentence implied. They could pull out and leave the mission if they felt they couldn't accomplish it without being compromised.

The Sniper didn't move. "Do I still have green? Over."

"Still green. Over."

People were stirring in the village as the sound of the approaching vehicles reached them.

The Sniper wrapped his left hand around the stock, forefinger inside the trigger guard. The heavy barrel was supported by a bipod. His right hand was on the scope, adjusting the sensitivity. He'd zeroed in the thermal sight just before infiltration. He'd fired the weapon in many different situations so he knew how the bullet would act with the drop to the village. His nostrils flared as he sniffed and his eyes scanned the nearby vegetation for the slightest movement. No wind.

Two trucks flanked a Land Rover as they pulled into the center of the village and came to a stop. He watched as a dozen men piled out of the back of each truck and began herding the people out of their shacks and into the common area. At this distance there was no noise from the village, just the sound of the jungle all around.

They were efficient. In less than ten minutes all the villagers were corralled like cattle into a dark red blob in the center of the village. Except for two. He watched the heat signatures making their way through the village away from the crowd. Strange. One was human. A child from the size. The other was smaller, lower to the ground and leading the child.

A dog. A half-smile crossed his lips as he realized that. And moving smart. Not dashing. Slinking, hiding, like a ghost leading a ghost. The kid was smart too, mimicking the dog. The Sniper visually followed them as they worked their way, avoiding the men with guns running around.

"Good dog," he mouthed, the sound not even heard by a rat five feet away or picked up by the throat mike.

Very smart. It must be a very smart dog. And a very trusting boy. The Sniper tightened his left hand around the grip. His finger lightly touched the trigger as one of the men with guns was on an intercept course, but he held back as the dog paused, the boy right behind freezing, and the danger passed. They moved again.

They were in the jungle.

He abruptly shifted back to the village, the heat images getting blurred with the first rays of sun cutting horizontal lines across the scope.

"Time," Spotter said.

The voice in the Sniper's ear was flat, apparently without concern, but an unsolicited transmission like that from one of his teammates, the first word spoken since they'd settled into position, indicated the concern.

"Hold," he ordered.

Three figures were at the forefront of the men holding automatic weapons, facing the villagers. The sniper pulled back from the rubber eyepiece and opened his other eye. There was no more than just the tint of dawn to the east. He pushed a button on the bulky sight on top of the weapon, shifting from thermal to telescopic.

The gun was large, almost six feet long and weighed over thirty pounds. Thirty-two point five pounds without bullets to be exact. He had the number memorized along with many other strange facts that the vast majority of people walking the face of the planet had never been exposed to. A ten round box magazine was fitted into the receiver, holding bullets that matched the gun in size, each round a fifty caliber—half inch in diameter, over six inches long—shell. A round that had been designed in the early part of the twentieth century for anti-tank use. Tanks were smaller and lightly armored then. Flesh and blood was still the same.

Modern science had been applied to the weapon system though. These rounds were specially designed around a very hard, depleted-uranium core that gave them the capability to punch through lesser metal. On one mission he'd fired through a quarter inch steel plate taking out a thermal image on the other side.

He pressed his eye against the rubber and waited as his pupil adjusted and the sun rose, accepting that he had lost the advantage of darkness.

"Time," Spotter repeated.

The Sniper knew he was violating what they had agreed upon in mission planning, but he was in command and circumstances had changed. Spotter was simply doing his job with the reminder. The Sniper ignored the radio. He could see the three now. The center man was the target. The one on the right was also Colombian, but the face didn't register. With a twitch he shifted left to the third. An American. He knew it as surely as the weight of his gun. Wearing khakis and a light bush jacket. LL Bean visiting the jungle.

Mercenary?

He'd served with men who'd gone for the green, flag be damned. His right hand twisted the focus, closing the visual distance until he was next to the man.

The man reached inside his jacket and pulled out a cigarette. A flash of gold. A badge.

The Sniper pulled back from the sight. "ID the man on the left?"

"He has a badge," the Spotter replied. "But I don't recognize him. I think the badge is DEA but hard to tell at this range."

The Sniper keyed the satellite radio. "Falcon."

"Roger?"

"I've got an American agent here in the village with the target. Possibly DEA. Over."

"Wait one."

A minute passed. The Sniper leaned forward and looked. Two of the armed men had pulled an old man forward, forcing him to kneel in front of the center man. The Sniper knew what was coming. It was as inevitable as the sun coming up. The silence in his ear stretched out.

"Falcon?"

Silence.

The fact that neither of his teammates spoke either was a testament to their training as they dealt with a situation that was deteriorating with every passing minute.

In the village, the center man pulled out a pistol, pressed it against the old man's forehead and pulled the trigger all in one movement without hesitation.

The blossom of blood and brain was highlighted in the scope as the body slowly fell backwards, landing awkwardly, the knees still tucked under. The Sniper had seen much death and it was never dignified.

"Red."

The word from the satellite radio hit the Sniper almost as hard as the shot had the old man. "Say again. Over."

"Red. I repeat. Red. This is no longer your Operational Area. I say again, not your OA. Over."

A woman was dragged forward. The Sniper could see her mouth open, screaming. The center man put the muzzle of the gun against her forehead. The Sniper could see her speaking quickly, telling the gunman whatever it was he wanted to know.

After a minute the man turned to a couple of his cohorts. Two came forward, grabbed an arm each and dragged the woman into a hut. Again, what was going to happen was almost pre-ordained.

"Sir?" The Sniper said the word as if it were a question.

"Command Authority says red. They've redrawn the lines. DEA has this area. Over."

The Sniper watched as a young man broke from the cowering group running toward the hut and was gunned down with a burst of automatic weapon fire. "You know what's happening, sir?"

"I can imagine."

"This is our mission. We owe these people. They did what was asked of them."

"Somebody's running something. Something high level. This mission is the DEA's now with no interference. Politics."

"That's bullshit," the Spotter said, the voice picked up by the satellite radio and transmitted. "People are dying. People who trusted you."

"Orders," the Colonel repeated. "The line has been drawn. You're out of your area of operations. Exfiltrate immediately. Out."

Other women were being dragged into huts to be raped. Sunlight glinted off a machete as one of the invaders brutally beheaded a cowering old man. That released them all like sharks smelling chum and the blood flowed.

"We need to go," Spotter said.

The Sniper shifted the scope away from the rape and carnage to the far hill. He adjusted the thermal sight to accommodate the growing sunlight and then turned it on. He searched, the sight penetrating the jungle until he spotted the two small red dots. He scanned the space between the escapees and the village, freezing when he saw three men moving in the jungle. Professionals. He knew that. Making sure there were no witnesses to the massacre. These were a different caliber from the men raping and hacking in the village.

"Hammer?" The Colonel's voice had an edge to it. "Are you pulling back? Over."

"In a second," the Sniper replied.

"Damn it, Hammer. Don't screw this up. This is bigger than you."

"Let's go," the Spotter said, echoing Spotter.

The Sniper centered the reticules on the trail man's head. He then adjusted ever so slightly for the lateral movement. He let out his breath, didn't inhale, felt the rhythm of his heart. In between beats he squeezed the trigger. The round was just out of the muzzle as he shifted to the second, waited as his heart surged once, became still, pulled the trigger, shifted, heart-beat and then fired for the third time.

"Pulling back now. Send in our ride. Out." The Sniper tugged on the antenna wire and the satellite dish toppled out of the tree into his hands. He folded it and slid it into his rucksack with one practiced movement. He could hear yells and knew the men below were heading his way, reacting to the shots. He pulled the ghillie suit off and shoved it into a stuff sack, which went inside the rucksack. He placed the three bullet casings in the sack.

His fingers were steady as he knelt and unscrewed two butterfly nuts holding the bulky barrel to the gun's receiver. He slid the two parts into padded plastic containers on either side of his rucksack, and then retrieved an MP-5 sub-machinegun that had been strapped to the top. There was nothing left at the site as he threw the sixty pound pack holding gun, radio and other gear over his shoulders and set off into the jungle at a controlled sprint, the Spotter and Security falling in beside him without a word.

They could hear shots as the mercenaries fired wildly while giving chase.

The Sniper's right hand held the MP-5, finger resting on the trigger guard, the safety off. "Falcon, this is Hammer. Over."

The helicopter pick up zone was less than a kilometer ahead. The chopper was supposed to be on station just over the border in Panamanian airspace. Less than five minutes flight time. If the Colonel, who was on board the chopper, had ordered the pilot to move when the Sniper had asked, it should be in FM range.

He heard only the slight hiss of static indicating the radio was on.

"Falcon, this is Hammer. Over."

"You screwed up, Hammer, damn-it."

The sniper abruptly stopped. The other two men came to a sudden halt also. They heard some more shots. Closer now. And from the noise they could tell a large group was moving through the jungle about three hundred meters to their left.

"Say again? Over."

"I ordered you not to take action. We can't cross the border now. Orders. We're returning to base. You're on your own. Out."

"Falcon? Falcon, this is Hammer. Over."

There was no reply.

The Sniper considered their options. The pickup zone was no longer a viable destination. The mercenaries were between his team and the border. But any other direction took the three of them further into Colombia.

Both men were watching him, waiting.

"North," he ordered.

They turned to the right, for the sea, and began running.

The 5.45 mm round hit the Sniper just behind his left temple at such an angle that the bullet ricocheted along the skull and exited off the back of his head without penetrating.

The Sniper fell to the jungle floor, blood pouring from the wound just as a Claymore mine exploded, knocking the other two men down.

CHAPTER ONE

THE PRESENT

EMILY CRANSTON WAS TIRED. It was the last night of spring break, and even returning to class seemed bearable as long as she could get some sleep. She watched her friends, and wondered again where they got the energy. All three of them were dancing in what appeared to be a huge conga line of pressed bodies. You couldn't have slid a toothpick between any of the dancers, except the occasional couple of guys who had poorly timed their rush to join, and found themselves without a female buffer. Emily noticed Lisa waving her over, but she pretended not to see. Lisa was sweet, really the best one of her friends, but even she couldn't inspire Emily now.

The week had been a disappointment, and Emily wasn't sure of the reason. She had tried hard the last few nights to join in the dancing and drinking, but there was something wrong. She felt separate and alone, even in this crowded room. She watched her friends gyrate with abandon, their slender tanned bodies, and their shiny navel rings proof that they had done their vacation homework. They had endured the months in spin classes, the endless stomach crunches and the hours sweltering in a tanning bed. At the time, Emily had been too depressed to bother with the fifteen pounds she had gained eating cafeteria food.

It seemed as soon as she left for college her parents announced that they had been separated for some time, and were getting a divorce. Emily had been shocked. She had always believed they were the happiest of families. Apparently, she had been happy alone. Her mother had even admitted their problems were longstanding, and that they had waited for Emily to leave home before separating. She, the last child of three, had postponed the split by a few years. It was a horrible thought. She tried not to dwell on it, but occasionally the odd memory would pop up, and she would wonder how she could have been so naive.

All the trauma aside, Emily found herself much more accepting of her parental situation. The problem now was that she felt like a huge, pale lump especially with her three perfect friends. They got asked to dance. They got handed the beers, and the promotional t-shirts and key chains. It was hard to be so ignored. Lisa thought she was full of crap and insisted she looked great. That made Emily feel worse knowing she had to look pretty bad for Lisa to tell her she looked great.

The song was thudding to a finale, and she waited for her friends to join her hoping that they were ready to go. The extra pounds she was carrying seemed to be just the amount that would hold her back from the fun. What she found perplexing was the question of whether guys were truly affected by those pounds. She suspected it might be the other way around if she waited long enough. She glanced at her watch and noticed it was almost one. She yawned into her cupped hand and waited as Lisa fought her way through the crowd.

"You can't be that tired."

Emily stared at Lisa noting her sweaty, lanky hair and the dark mascara circles around her eyes. "Please, you look a little wiped yourself."

Lisa licked her finger and tried to wipe the biggest smudges from her eyes. "OK, I'm tired but there's plenty of time for sleep later."

"I'm not like you guys, I can't store up sleep and then stay awake for three days"

Lisa lifted the hair off her neck in a vain attempt to cool down. "Look the place is closing in an hour; just find a nice quiet seat and then we'll go."

"I can't wait an hour. I'm taking the car. You guys can take a taxi." Emily hoped that Lisa was sober enough to see the logic in that.

Lisa shrugged and dropped her hair back onto her sweaty shoulders. "Whatever. Just remember to hide the key."

The idea made Lisa cringe. She hated the thought of hiding the key outside—kind of defeated the purpose-- and was still pissed that the condo company had issued only one key to four paying guests. "No way. Ring the bell. I'll wake up."

Lisa laughed. "Yeah, right. I've seen you sleep." Her voice took on a more plaintive tone. "Come on, just another hour?"

Emily shook her head. "Sorry, I gotta get out of here."

Lisa realized her friend meant what she said and knew further discussion was pointless. A small part of her was mildly put out. Emily wasn't one to suck it up. "You better be at that door as soon as I start banging."

Emily felt a wave of relief. She could take off and she didn't have to hide the key for some nut to find. "Thanks. I'll be a lot better tomorrow if I can get some sleep."

The look on Lisa's face made Emily realize that it was time to shut up.

She watched as Lisa, obviously the one chosen to deal with her, ran back to their friends.

As she dug around in her purse feeling for the car keys, she thought of sleep. She knew Lisa was upset and by extension so was everyone else. Screw it. They were all supposed to be adults. And someone had to be awake enough to begin the drive back to college later in the day.

The parking lot was still packed, and as she wandered across the crushed shells that served as gravel, she thought of the traffic jam to come. It really was best to get the car out of here now, and let them take a taxi. She edged her way to the side of the narrow lane as she heard a car coming up behind her. It was moving slowly, but she decided it was time to cut across the lot instead of remaining a target for some drunk. There were two rows of cars parked head to head off to the left, and as she turned the big SUV passed by her on the right.

She never even noticed the van. She did hear the door start to open, but by then she was right next to it. The man didn't even bother stepping out. He grabbed her neck, and yanked her into the van so suddenly; she didn't have time to scream. Like a tiny ripple on a still pond the van slowly pulled away and left no trace of Emily Cranston. All that remained were two slips of paper the man slid out the driver's window, floating to the ground like the first two leaves of fall.

CHAPTER TWO

THE SUN ROSE SLOWLY, fighting through the mist to send warm fingers to the wide beach left exposed by the inevitable cycle of the tide. High above, the trade winds blew thin cloud contrails against the last vestiges of night. The sounds of the thick swamp beyond the beach shifted from the occasional outbursts of predators and prey to the more serene symphony of daytime activity. Palmettos, old oaks gray-bearded with Spanish Moss, and tall pines rose high, competing for the coming sunlight.

Between swamp and beach is a thin stretch of grass-covered sand-dunes where storms had heaped all they picked up as they thundered toward the coast, and the ocean in calmer weather could never quite reach to pull away. It is called Pritchards Island, but at high tide it really is several islets as the seawater filled canals like blood into the island's veins, bringing fish, turtles, gators and birds. It is one of thousands of islands that dot the coast of South Carolina. The Marine Corps base at Parris Island is to the west, and to the south, separated by the Broad River, is Hilton Head Island, a vacation destination along the east coast. Just north, Fripps Island was following the same fate of Hilton Head as developers moved in and seized prime ocean front property.

The man sat on the crumbling concrete portal of a long-abandoned Coast Guard station. He'd heard that a beach front lot on Hilton Head went for a couple of million. As far as he could see left and right, the beach was clear and open. Of course, he didn't own any of it. He didn't own any land. He considered himself a visitor, even though he'd been here for just under a year and a half, except for his few trips. He'd learned the island was privately owned, but perpetually deeded to the University of South Carolina for research. He'd often seen the students and their professors making forays out of the bungalow on the north side of the island in their small boats and ATVs, but they had never seen him. The island was a preserve for sea turtles and the visitors were focused on that.

As he sat, watching the sun rise, he lifted his entire body off the concrete by virtue of pressing the fingertips of his right hand down and keeping his legs extended straight out in front. He would do this ten times with each hand, staying balanced on those five fingertips for the space of two breaths on each lift, then shift to the other hand. He did it almost without noticing, a monotony born of long practice. The fact he was lifting one hundred and eighty pounds with each thrust was displayed only by the veins on the down arm pulsing full of blood, much like the canals of the island at high tide. He breathed slowly, forcing the tensed muscles of his stomach holding up the legs to ripple with the exertion.

He'd come to the Low Country for simple reasons for a man who lived a complex life. He'd read Pat Conroy's tales of the land while at the Military Academy and he thought it was about as far as one could get from the mountains and the deserts of the world he'd spent the previous decades fighting in. And before that the streets of New York where he'd spent his childhood. He particularly enjoyed the mornings, watching the sun come up out of the ocean. It made him feel small and insignificant, as if his actions mattered little. That gave him comfort.

He'd also come to the south because he'd always been fascinated by the Civil War, and he'd already walked all the battlefields of the North— Gettysburg, Antietam and the others-- and most of the rest were south of the Mason-Dixon line. The previous month he'd gone to the site of Andersonville Prison in Georgia, not exactly a battlefield, but a place of significance in that war and he still hadn't shaken off the depression and despair still emanating from that small patch of South Georgia despite the years that had passed since it had been home to so many Yankee prisoners.

While the occasional students and professors knew nothing of the long time visitor to their island, there were those who had known of his presence within a few days of his arrival. The Gullah, the descendants of freed slaves who'd lived on these islands for generations, had noticed him almost immediately but left him in peace. He'd returned the courtesy, only gradually getting to know these people with their own language as he met them hunting and fishing around the island. It took six months of passing nods across the water and marsh before one of them pulled close enough to speak to him and then it was only a brief greeting and a warning of a storm coming despite the deceptive blue sky.

He'd always found that there were those who had their senses attuned to the pulse of the land and saw more than most. In Germany, the local forest-meister always knew when a Special Forces team had parachuted into their woodlands to conduct training exercises. In the desert the Bedouins could also sense a sand-storm on the clearest day and were aware of who traversed their lands. In Afghanistan the mountain villagers knew who walked the high trails and when. As a child in the Bronx he'd seen the men in white undershirts who sat in front of the small store on the street corner watching with half-lidded eyes whenever unknown cars turned into the block. Territoriality seemed to be genetic in men, but he must have missed out on that particular chromosome. He had no yearning to return to the Bronx from the day he escaped there to go fifty miles up the Hudson to West Point at seventeen. He considered wherever he currently slept to be his home.

He'd been told by an old Gullah man named Goodwine that a house had once stood at this spot, built by pirates in the late eighteenth century. And that the pirates had been caught by the fledgling American Navy and massacred to a man, refusing to give up the location of their treasure even under the painful incentive of the blade. Goodwine said the sailors burned the house and then dug through the ashes searching for the gold and, finding none, filled the hole with the bodies of the pirates. It was not a place of bad spirits Goodwine insisted, but of discontented spirits. The man liked that story. He didn't share with Goodwine his own belief that the pirates had not had any treasure, which explained why they couldn't point out where it was buried. The man knew the difference between fact and fiction and the fact was, in his experience, that everyone talked under enough pain and in fear of death.

The Coast Guard station had been built on the spot during the early days of World War II when German submarines had hunted the coast, sinking ships within sight of the shore, the flames observed by a civilian populace who thought themselves safe. It had been abandoned after the war and slowly gave in to the weather and vegetation. The man had constructed a cozy shelter inside, one that kept the rain off in winter and gave him shade in summer.

There was no bed. He had forsaken beds years ago as they were a place where one could be expected to be found, usually in a vulnerable state. He had a thin therm-a-rest pad that he rolled out when he was tired. Sometimes he slept on the beach above the high water mark, sometimes in the dunes, and if the weather threatened, in the station. He had a small battery powered radio with which he listened to National Public Radio twice a day. The portal to the station had been made for smaller men, set at an even six feet, so he had to duck slightly to come and go.

The biggest issue was fresh water. He made a run in his kayak over to Parris Island once a week and filled up two five-gallon cans at the dock. He had a solar shower, simply a clear bladder of water resting on top of a shelf, under which he quickly bathed when needed. The green-colored kayak he kept hidden up one of the waterways, tucked behind a cluster of thick palmetto bushes.

He knew what time it was very accurately according to some inner coding he'd never bothered to examine. In the same manner he'd never used an alarm clock. Even at the Academy during Beast Barracks. He always rose when he determined he needed to wake before he went to sleep.

Done with that exercise, he walked onto the beach and began his katas, the ritualized movements that were part of martial arts training. His specific form would not have been recognized in any dojo as it was an amalgamation of various techniques from a spectrum of disciplines. The moves were focused on those that incapacitated and killed as quickly as possible.

He heard the tinny murmur of a small outboard and came to a halt in mid-kata. He walked down to the beach as a small flatboat came around the headland.

Goodwine saw the strange white man waiting on the beach. He was always up. Goodwine had passed by the island late at night or hours before dawn and it seemed the man was always around, like a ghost, often simply sitting in his strange way on one hand, or moving slowly along the beach or through the swamp. The first time he'd spotted the *buckra*--white man--Goodwine had thought he was a lost hunter or fisherman as few came to Pritchards, but the man had shown no sign of distress nor did he seem interested in what Goodwine was up to, so the two had noted each other with a simple nod but said nothing.

So it went for months before one day Goodwine saw the man out on the sand-bar a hundred yards from the shore, simply walking, paralleling the shore at low tide, the water up to his waist. It was February and the water was cold, but the man had not seemed to notice. It wasn't until he got home that Goodwine realized that the man had been working his body against the water, building up his legs.

Goodwine had paused to tell the man a storm was coming and the tide would be up higher than had been seen for a while. The man had simply thanked Goodwine and continued on his way. What had impressed Goodwine more than the man's taciturn manner was his skin. He was a *buckra*, but the sun had burned him brown, except the lines and craters that marked the impact of violence on his flesh. There were dark tales written in those scars but the man said nothing of it, not even after they spent more time together. Goodwine had a similar crater on his right thigh where a North Vietnamese bullet had punched a hole many years ago. He didn't like talking

14

of that so he respected the man's silence. It had been Goodwine's only time away from the Low Country and he had been glad to return, even though the leg had never quite been the same.

After several more months of gradually longer exchanges, Goodwine offered to take the man deep into the swamp. He was unlike any white man Goodwine had ever met. The man had blue eyes that constantly moved yet always seemed to be focused on something. The thing that Goodwine told his wife as soon as he was back home was that the man had the patience of the 'gator. This was indeed a high Gullah compliment as Goodwine had seen alligators submerged, eyes and nostrils only showing, in the same place for days on end. The 'gator knew it needed just one good meal, a nice fat buck coming too close to the water's edge, to last it for months, so it was willing to be still for days in exchange. It was the epitome of disciplined violence.

The man had spoken only in response to something Goodwine said. He'd helped with the hunting in silence. And when the tide went out, he'd assisted in pushing the boat across the mud barriers while mosquitoes feasted on his blood without a word or sign of protest or inconvenience. They'd efficiently butchered the deer Goodwine had shot and the man had accepted a portion of the meat with thanks.

The man raised his hand in greeting as the flat bow grated on the sound and Goodwine tilted the engine forward. The man put the hand down and held the boat still as Goodwine carefully stepped over the gunwale onto the sand. The man then pulled the boat above the tide line with ease.

The man let go of the boat, then turned to face Goodwine. He saw the envelope in the old man's hands and was not anxious to know its contents. He pulled a cigar he'd bought on his last trip to Parris Island out of his shirt pocket and offered it to Goodwine who accepted it with a nod of thanks.

"*Yuh.*" Goodwine held out the envelope.

The man took it. He glanced at the return address. New York City. Addressed to Major Jack Gant. He found it interesting that his Uncle used his rank and that name. An appeal to loyalty and to forgive the past, he realized.

Goodwine had cut the end of the cigar and fired it up, inhaling deeply and letting out a puff of smoke that was borne away by the off-shore breeze. "Be good news?"

Goodwine spoke the white man's English as well as any on the coast when he wanted to. Gant had listened to Goodwine enough to have a basic understanding of Gullah, but he felt it would be insulting to try to carry on a conversation in the old man's native tongue.

Gant opened his Uncle's letter and looked at the thin, spidery writing. He read the first line and then lifted his eyes and looked out to sea.

"Is ya all right?" Goodwine asked.

"My brother is dead."

"I am sorry." Goodwine hung his head, his lips moving as he said a prayer for the dead.

"I knew it," Gant said, when the old man was done. He tapped his chest. "I felt something a few weeks ago. I felt something go. He was my twin."

Goodwine tapped his own chest. "His spirit be taken."

Gant shrugged, uncertain. "Something."

"Were you close?"

"Once. Not for a long time." Gant looked at the rest of the letter. "My Uncle would like me to come back to New York for a visit with my mother," he finally said.

Goodwine nodded. "Will ya be going?"

"No."

Gant heard a sound in the distance, one that brought mixed emotions on the top of the news of his brother. Today it brought a feeling of utter weariness. He wondered if it was connected to the letter, but doubted it. The man who had sent the helicopter didn't deal in sentimentality, if Gant's guess about the chopper's mission was correct.

"You shoulda get home," Goodwine said. His voice deepened as he shifted to Gullah. *"Mus tek cyear a de root fa heal de tree."*

Gant mentally translated the words—must take care of the root to heal the tree. The helicopter was getting closer. He looked along the shoreline to the south. Goodwine also turned in that direction, the old man's stomach fluttering a little also at the sound, decades old memories of a faraway land threatening to come back. A Coast Guard chopper appeared just above the surf line, coming in fast. Gant hoped it kept on going, but it was too early in the morning for the first shark patrol.

The helicopter slowed and came to a hover fifty feet away. It settled down onto the sand and a crew chief jumped out, sliding open the cargo bay door. A man dressed in a blazer and tie got out. There was a metal briefcase chained to the man's wrist. He stood underneath the rotating blades and waited. The man was bland looking, portly, with thinning blond hair and a broad face. Someone people would pass on the street and never give a second glance to.

There was nothing in the old station Gant needed. He stuck out his hand to Goodwine. "Keep an eye on everything. I'll be back."

Goodwine simply shook his hand and nodded.

Gant walked to the waiting man. He did not shake his hand, but jumped into the cargo bay and took a seat. He picked up a helmet and put it on. The man got on and did the same so they could talk over the intercom. Gant nodded. "Mister Bailey."

"Mister Gant. Mister Nero needs you."

Gant leaned back against the red cargo webbing as the chopper lifted and turned back to the south. "When did you know about my brother?"

Bailey reached into his suit jacket and pulled out a piece of gum, which he carefully unwrapped. He rolled the pink rectangle into a tight cylinder and then popped it in his mouth. "Three weeks."

"How did he die?"

"A natural death."

That earned Bailey a sharp look from Gant.

"I dug up his grave," Bailey said. "He was buried outside his cabin in Vermont."

"Who buried him?" Gant asked.

"Neeley."

Gant nodded. One bright spot in a sea of black. Gant had never met Neeley but he knew his brother had excellent taste in women. "What did he die of?"

"Cancer," Bailey continued. "I re-buried him."

Gant didn't ask why Bailey had dug his brother up and he recognized that Bailey wasn't offering an explanation so he changed the subject to the future. "Is this a Sanction?"

"We don't know yet." Bailey pulled a picture out of his pocket. Gant took it. A girl smiled up at him.

"And?"

"Emily Cranston is the daughter of Colonel Samuel Cranston."

The name sounded vaguely familiar. "And Cranston is?"

"The commander of the Special Warfare Center at Fort Bragg."

Gant wondered why Bailey was dragging this out and didn't hand over the file. Gant glanced down at the titanium case on the floor next to Bailey's sand covered shoes.

"I only want to brief this once," Bailey said, catching the glance.

Gant frowned. He worked alone. "Who else do you have to brief?"

"We're picking someone up."

"Who?"

"A shrink."

"Why do we need a shrink?"

Bailey took the photo back. "Because we think the girl is still alive."

Gant wasn't sure what that had to do with a shrink but he was used to Bailey being evasive. "Why do you think that?"

Bailey reluctantly opened the briefcase and removed a piece of paper. "That's a copy of what was left at the site she was taken from."

17

Gant glanced at the paper. "It's part of a cache report." Gant had first learned to make such a report at Fort Bragg, as a student at the center the father of the girl now ran. He knew now why Bailey had come for him.

Bailey nodded. "We think Emily Cranston is the cache."

The lifeguard was setting out the beach chairs as the woman came by, right on schedule. He saw her every morning he worked and he assumed she came by on the days he didn't, not being so self-centered to imagine her walks revolved around him in some way. The tide was going out, water giving way to gently sloping beach. The woman appeared to be in her late thirties, in good shape, but the skin on her face was stretched tight, not from a lift as many of the rich women on the island did, but from some inner tension that the lifeguard instinctively sensed he didn't want to know the reason for.

She walked at a steady rate, not with the frenzy of the 'power walkers', nor the idle stroll of the tourists looking for shells. She walked as if she were on her way to some place she had to be, but didn't want to get to. The lifeguard paused in his chair unfolding and raised a hand in greeting as was the way here on Hilton Head, where everyone acted friendly, especially to locals.

Susan Golden forced herself to acknowledge the lifeguard's wave with a flutter of her right hand. It was more out of habit than anything else, but years ago she had allowed herself to accept that habit was important. Indeed, she had built a large portion of her professional life on the principle that people were predictable.

Passing marker number fourteen, she turned right, heading inland toward the house she rented. As she walked up the thin concrete beach access path, she noted that the off-shore breeze had stopped and the air was still and hot. She too came to a complete halt when she saw the Beuafort County Sheriff's car parked in her drive. A young deputy was standing next to the car, looking decidedly nervous. His apparent discomfort paled in comparison to the surge of emotion that raced through Golden. He saw her and straightened, one hand unconsciously running down the front of his khaki shirt, straightening the folds.

"Dr. Golden?"

She could only nod at first as she struggled to find her voice. "Did you find him?"

"Excuse me?"

"Did you find him?"

"Who, ma'am?"

"My son. Jimmy."

"I'm not sure--" he paused and regrouped. "I was sent here to escort you to the airport."

"The airport?" Golden repeated dully.

"Yes, ma'am." He awkwardly opened the door to his patrol car and pulled out a clip board, and held it out to her.

She didn't take it, afraid to see what was on it.

The deputy continued to hold the clipboard out as if that would relieve him of his discomfort. "It's a request from the Department of Defense. Asking us to help you get to the airport as quickly as possible. A plane will be there shortly for you. Apparently someone needs you."

Golden's shoulders slumped. A mixture of relief and anger replaced her fear. "Why?"

The deputy pulled back the clipboard and glanced at the faxed letter, and then shrugged. "It doesn't say, Ma'am. It's signed by a Mister Nero if that means anything to you."

"It doesn't."

Golden still didn't move as the deputy shuffled his feet.

"There's a number you can call?" the deputy suggested.

Golden didn't want to call but she knew she had to. It could be about Jimmy.

She took the cell phone the deputy offered and the clipboard. She punched in the number.

It rang once and a woman's voice answered.

"Yes?"

"This is Doctor Golden and I--

"Hold please."

The voice that came next wasn't human, that was Golden's first reaction even before the words hit home. The voice was metallic, words sliding over steel and adjusted to be legible.

"Doctor Golden, my name is Mister Nero. A young girl is missing and we need your help in trying to resolve the issue. The girl is Colonel Cranston's daughter. Please go with the deputy to the airfield. There will be a plane there shortly to pick you up. All will be explained then. Thank you."

The phone went dead.

Sam Cranston. Golden remembered seeing a photograph on his nightstand. A young girl, pretty in a clean, freshly scrubbed way, slightly overweight. Golden felt faint and her body slumped, the deputy reaching out a protective hand, placing it on her shoulder.

"Are you all right, ma'am?"

"Please stop calling me ma'am," Golden said. "And take me to the airport immediately.

CHAPTER THREE

ONE OF THE children had spotted a snake earlier in the morning so the caregiver's eyes were constantly going toward the line at the edge of the play area where manicured lawn met palmettos, shrub brush and pine trees. Cathy Svoboda hated snakes and she was responsible for a half-dozen twelve year olds who ran about the park. She was thin, in a nervous pale way, with dark hair cut short in the latest Hollywood fashion according to the magazine she bought off the rack at the checkout counter. Twenty-four, she'd worked at the Chez Petite daycare center in Enterprise, Alabama for two years.

Cathy was seated on a wrought iron bench, giving her a clear view of all six, the playground and the tree line. She kept bringing her left hand up to her chin, resting on it, then sliding a hidden finger into her mouth, teeth gnawing at an already chewed down nail. She was counting days.

Three weeks late. Twenty-two days actually. That she knew from the marks on the calendar taped to her old refrigerator. It was the extra math back from that marked day which bothered her. Mark, her fiancé, had done his reserve duty thing over a month ago, spending two weeks with the other boys pretending to be men. Mark's friend Sean had shown up at her door with a twelve pack a day after Mark had gone off. She didn't mean for it to happen. She could admit to herself now that she'd just been stupid and drunk.

She closed her eyes and her forehead crinkled as she pictured both Mark and Sean in her mind. They looked a lot alike. Same color eyes and hair. Roughly the same height. Could one really tell? She wasn't sure. She opened her eyes and blinked.

How long had he been there? Cathy was startled, her eyes fixing on the man standing in the shadows under the wide oak near the swings. She didn't remember seeing him before. He was looking at the children. The man wore a long black leather coat, unusual for the area and weather, and a cap with a bill pulled down low over his eyes, putting his face in a shadow. She should have been paying closer attention, she chided herself. Her head swiveled as she quickly did a visual head count. Her heart slowed toward a more normal cadence as she accounted for all.

But Brandon, the little tow-headed kid who always had to push things, was on one of the swings. Cathy stood abruptly as Brandon turned when the man said something to him. She began walking across the closely-cut grass as Brandon stopped his swing and said something in reply. The man knelt down so that his head was at the same height as the boy's. He whispered something that Cathy couldn't hear as she arrived. He put a piece of paper in Brandon's hand. Cathy reached them and grabbed Brandon's other hand, pulling him off the swing.

"What are you doing?" she demanded, staring at the man.

"I was just asking him if he liked his teacher." The man gave a slight smile as he got to his feet. "He said yes."

His face was scarred as if it had been head on in a wind of slicing rain. She'd never seen anything like it and she could tell Brandon was nervous. Cathy leaned over to pick up Brandon, thinking the stranger was—

Her thoughts stopped, as there was a glint of sunlight off something metal in the man's hand as it flashed forward. She felt like she'd been slapped in the neck and her eyes opened wide as she saw blood on Brandon's hair. Had the man hurt him she wondered? How? She hadn't seen him touch the boy. She looked up—the man was gone. So quickly. Cathy blinked, hearing Brandon screaming as if from a distance, but he was right in front of her. More blood, soaking his blue t-shirt.

Cathy tried to hush Brandon, to calm him, but no words came. She felt sick, faint. Brandon fell backward into the sand under the swing, his hands up, protecting his face, both palms covered in blood, still wailing. Too much for a little boy, Cathy thought in panic.

She saw a jet of red spurt from her onto Brandon. Stunned she reached up toward her own throat—Brandon must have be scared.

She sunk to her knees as warm liquid splattered onto her hand. She looked down and saw that her new sundress was completely soaked in thick red. She looked at Brandon once more. She wanted to tell him he wasn't hurt. That he was just scared. But no words would come. So tired. She pressed her hand against her neck, feeling another pulse of blood come out, along with bubbling air. That was so strange. But no pain. Stranger more.

Her baby. She'd never thought of it in any way beyond the numbers. She tried to scream and red froth bubbled out of the deep six-inch smooth incision in her throat. Cathy fell forward into the sand and the last surge of arterial blood barely trickled out of her neck into the sand.

* * *

Emily opened her eyes and tried to remember where she was and what had happened to her. Before she remembered anything, she felt a wave of panic so strong she felt sick with its intensity. She could see nothing, hear nothing, and she couldn't move. For a terrible moment, she thought she had been in an accident and was paralyzed. Too quickly came the terrifying realization. A hospital room would never be this dark. That thought forced her to accept that her situation was much worse than an accident. Suddenly she was rolled to her left side by centrifugal force, and became aware that she was moving, or rather she was in something moving.

She tried to swallow, but her mouth was too dry. Then she knew. She remembered the sound of metal slamming; she remembered hitting her shoulder hard as a rough arm had tossed her down. It was so fast. Emily was astonished that it had been so fast. A piece of tape had been slapped over her mouth. There had been no way to stop what had happened. For a moment she felt anger. An anger blossoming from her sheer inability to prevent what had happened to her. That lasted as long as her second futile attempt to swallow.

The fear found her once more, and she felt her stomach begin to heave. She was alone with a madman. Emily fought panic at the thought of being completely at this man's mercy. She knew it was a man, and for the first time in her short life she understood with a deep clarity that she could die. She had felt the strength in his arms, and though his face had been covered, she'd had a brief glimpse of his powerful body. She tried to think. What exactly had happened? Had he hit her? Was she hurt? Then she remembered the stinging pain in her arm. He had given her some kind of a shot. That must be why she was so disoriented and thirsty.

She could still feel the van moving, and hear the roar of the tires beneath her. It felt like they were going fast and that the road was smooth. She thought they must be on an interstate. Emily was overcome with fear and nausea once more. He was taking her far away.

Nobody knew where she was. Maybe nobody even knew she was missing. Maybe Lisa and the girls hadn't even bothered to see if she was home. She could feel the tears well up at the thought that no one knew she was missing. She cried silently, the tears hot and biting against the skin around her eyes, trapped by the blindfold covering her face. She could see nothing, not even a trickle of light around the edge of the cloth wrapped tightly around her head.

Shaking her head as if to toss out the sadness, she decided to take stock of her position. She could cry later.

Her legs were tied together at the feet and also the knees. She could move them from side to side, but that was about all. Her arms were pulled behind her back and tied at the wrist. Her shoulder hurt from slamming onto the floor of the van, but there wasn't much painful tension, yet. Either her kidnapping had been recent, or she had recently been tied up. She felt ill at the thought of being handled while she was unconscious. This thought forced her to wonder if she had been assaulted. She relaxed for a moment, willing herself to calm her thinking and to calm her body. Did she feel anything? Suddenly the van slowed abruptly and made a sharp turn. She rolled violently to the right and felt her shin hit something sharp and unyielding. The van began to slow down. As it came to a stop, Emily began to pray. Not a real prayer as in church but the truest she had ever uttered: oh please, oh please. She just wanted to live. She could handle anything as long as she got away.

The screech of the door sliding open reminded her of the beginning of this nightmare. It also forced her to remember the van in more detail. She had paid no attention to it in the parking lot, but she now remembered that it had been dark and had no windows in the rear.

Emily knew the door was open. She could feel the fresh air, and smell freshly cut grass. She thought she heard something. She concentrated. In the second Emily strained to hear, she felt a hand on her shoulder and the needle puncture the bare flesh of her arm. The door slammed and she immediately knew she was passing out. She had to remember this. The air had felt cooler, less humid than the beach. The grass had just been cut. As she lost consciousness, she realized what the sound had been. She would have smiled, but she had already fallen into a deep well of darkness.

CHAPTER FOUR

THE WALK ACROSS the Parris Island airfield from the Coast Guard chopper to the jet tarmac had been all of fifty yards. The plane was a Gulfstream, modern and swift, but the inside was decorated by a government bureaucrat with a mind toward expenditures and budget without a single concession to luxury. Cheap plastic paneling covered the bulkhead and standard airline seats were bolted to the thinly carpeted floor. Near the rear were four seats, in pairs of two facing each other with a plastic table between them. That was where Gant and Bailey headed. The exterior of the plane was painted flat black, the only marking a tail number that was on file with the FAA, but didn't reveal the true operators of the aircraft.

In the open space behind the four seats was a large plastic case, which Gant had opened upon entering. It held Gant's deployment gear and he'd quickly inventoried it. Satisfied all was as it should be, he pulled out a pair of black khaki pants and slipped them on, replacing the worn shorts he'd been wearing. Then he took a black polypropylene undershirt and put it on. Over it he shrugged on a body armor vest, securing it in place with sew-in straps of Velcro. It was a thin vest and once he put a black, long sleeve shirt over, it was practically impossible to tell he had it on. The vest was slightly uncomfortable but Gant thought the trade-off was more than worth it.

Done with clothing and protection, he weaponed up. First a leather belt that had a wire garrote hidden on the inside curve, held in place by a few threads that could easily be parted. Then he strapped a sheath holding a slim dagger to his left ankle, underneath the pants cuff.

He velcroed a pistol in a waist holster to the body armor in the small of his back, hidden under the bottom of the shirt, which he left un-bloused. The pistol was a Glock Model 20, holding 15 rounds of 10mm ammunition. It had an integrated laser sight built into the gun itself, replacing the recoil spring guide assembly, just below the barrel. Touching the trigger activated the laser. With no external hammer, the gun could smoothly be drawn from under his shirt without catching, and the safety was built into the trigger, allowing rapid fire.

Gant had used many handguns over the years. While he liked the Glock, he also knew that the gun was only half the issue. The other important component was the bullets. At the Cellar armory, he'd taken standard load 10mm rounds, customized and reloaded them for high muzzle velocity and disintegration upon impact with a target for maximum damage. He slid two spare magazines into holders on either side of the gun.

There were other weapons in the case, but since Gant had little idea what was to be expected or what was going to happen next, he shut the lid and retook his seat, the gun pressing up against the small of his back and the body armor tight around his torso, both familiar feelings.

The two men had yet to exchange another word. Not out of any dislike but because neither saw the need for conversation at this point. The sound of the engines filled the silence as the plane taxied and then took off.

Gant didn't like the idea of someone else being part of this. He worked alone, Nero knew that. The fact that Bailey was bringing in some shrink meant Nero didn't want him to work alone on this. Thus there was no point in protesting a decision Nero made or even asking for an explanation.

The pilot's voice echoed tinnily out of a speaker informing them that the plane was on approach for Hilton Head Airfield, less than two minutes after taking off from Parris Island. The wheels locked down and thirty seconds later they were on the ground.

Gant glanced out the small round window and saw a deputy sheriff's patrol car next to the runway. A tall woman with dark hair pulled back tight got out. To Gant it seemed that not only was her hair pulled tight but every muscle in her body. He guessed her age to be mid-30s give or take. She reminded him in a way of a post-assassination, pre-Onassis, Jackie, both in looks and because she appeared to be bearing some kind of burden. She looked around, checking everything, before walking toward the plane.

Bailey opened the door and helped her in, shutting it immediately. Gant watched his lips and saw that Bailey was introducing himself to the shrink, which meant she was new to the Cellar. The plane was taxiing before they claimed their seats.

"Doctor Susan Golden meet Jack Gant."

She stuck her hand out and Gant took it briefly without rising. She was directly across from him, Bailey to her left. The small table was between them. There was no one else in the rear of the plane and the door to the cockpit had not opened, nor would it. The engines peaked as they raced down the runway, the nose was up and they were airborne.

Gant leaned back in the seat and waited as Bailey opened the metal briefcase. He could sense the woman's gaze on him but he ignored her.

Bailey tossed a photo on the table. The same young girl smiling at whoever was taking the picture.

"You know her?" Bailey asked Golden.

"I've seen her picture but never met her. Sam Cranston's daughter. What happened to her?"

Gant clasped his hands together in his lap and waited.

Bailey glanced at a piece of paper. "Emily Cranston was leaving a bar in Panama City, Florida by herself at approximately one twenty yesterday morning. Two men in an Explorer say they passed close by a girl who fit her description. They noticed her because she was alone. She ducked between two cars to get out of their way. They didn't see her again. When they came around again they noticed an empty space close to where they saw her, because the lot was full. They figured she just left.

"Her roommates arrived back at their condo at about four am. They couldn't get in because Emily had the only key and wasn't there to open the door as they'd arranged. They got the rental company to let them in. She wasn't inside. That afternoon after she didn't show and they were due to head home, they went back to the club and found her car. One of them called the cops. Who checked the parking lot of the bar and found not only her car but two other things."

Gant leaned forward.

Bailey put the paper he'd shown Gant on the table.

"What's this?" Golden asked.

Bailey glanced at Gant.

"An incomplete cache report," Gant said. He put his finger on the first line. "This is the immediate reference point, the IRP. Then an azimuth and direction to the cache."

"I don't understand," Golden said.

Bailey cleared his throat. "We think that someone has cached Emily Crantson."

"Why do you think that?" Golden pressed. "How do you even know it's regarding Emily?"

"As you know," Bailey said, "Emily's father is the commander of the Special Warfare Center at Fort Bragg. Where they teach this format as a cache report. Mister Nero is not a fan of remarkable coincidence."

Golden turned to Gant. "You said it was incomplete?"

"It's missing four things," Gant said. "There's no area designation, far reference point, and azimuth and direction to the immediate reference point.

Area gets you in the right part of the world. Say a country or a state. Then far reference point is a specific spot you can find on a standard one to fifty thousand geographic map. A bridge. A road intersection. A mountain top. Without those two, the IRP is worthless because it could be anywhere in the world."

The report was typed:

IRP: Stone chimeny
A/D: 274 DEGREES, TWO HUNDRED AND SIX METERS

Gant now realized the report was missing a fifth part. "It also doesn't say how the actual cache is put in."

"Put in?" Golden asked.

"Usually a cache is buried."

Golden looked slightly stunned at this piece of information.

"So she could be dead already?" Bailey asked.

Gant shrugged. "Normally the idea of a cache is to be able to recover what you put in it in a usable condition."

"But this isn't normal," Golden said.

"I've never heard of a person being cached," Gant said.

"He's taunting us," Golden said.

Gant ran a hand across his chin. It had been a couple of days since he'd shaved. "Taunting?"

"If this—" Golden tapped the cache report—"is about Emily and was left by whoever abducted her, if she was abducted, then it was left deliberately to give us incomplete information. To make us feel the lack of that information. A tease."

The only lack Gant felt at the moment was the loss of his brother, which he was forcing himself not to dwell on, and whatever Bailey had yet to brief them on. Some of the pieces were falling into place. This shrink apparently knew Colonel Cranston. Whether that was a good thing or bad, Gant had no idea.

"How do you know it's a he?" Gant asked.

"I'm not positive, but my research indicates it almost certainly would be a man who did this."

Gant wondered what her research was on. He looked at Bailey. "You said there were two things found."

Bailey reached in the briefcase and brought out a second piece of paper. "There were two pieces of paper left in the parking lot." He placed it on the table.

Gant looked at it. Another cache report. An almost complete one.

FRP: NORTHERN TIP LAKE
A/D TO IRP: 46 DEGREES, 8,620 METERS
IRP: ROAD JUNCTION
A/D TO CACHE: 203 DEGREES, 546 METERS

"Still missing the area and condition of the actual cache," Gant noted, "so it's almost as worthless as the other one."

"I know," Bailey said.

"So where are we going now?" Gant asked.

"The Cellar to wait. The Auxiliary have been alerted. We'll hear if anything happens."

Golden's eyes were dancing back and forth between Gant and Bailey, trying to keep up. "Who exactly are you? And what is the Cellar and who is this Nero fellow? And what is the Auxiliary?"

"Mister Nero is in charge of the Cellar," Bailey said. "We work for him."

"And the Cellar is?" Golden pressed.

Instead of answering, Bailey opened the case and pulled out a half-inch thick stack of plastic coated identification cards. He pulled one out and handed it to Gant, along with a leather case holding a silver shield. Gant checked the card. It had his photo and indicated he worked for the National Security Agency.

"Who are you people?" Golden demanded.

Bailey handed her a similar leather case with an official looking card with her photo and a shield. "You are now officially a consultant to the National Security Agency."

"So you're NSA?" Golden pressed.

Bailey shook his head. "As I said, we're with the Cellar."

"And the Cellar isn't the NSA?"

"No," Bailey said.

Gant could tell Golden was getting frustrated. "So what is the Cellar? Who does it work for? Why pretend to be NSA?"

Gant leaned back and closed his eyes. Rest when you could was a lesson he'd learned early in his Special Forces career. He'd had the same questions as Golden years ago when he'd first been recruited by Bailey to work for the Cellar. He really didn't know that much more after all that time. And Tony, his brother. How much more had he known? Tony had already worked for the Cellar for several years before they came calling for Jack. And by that time, Tony had 'retired' from the organization, disappearing with Neeley. Jack had always wondered what leverage his brother had had to allow him to escape the Cellar's clutches. And why had Bailey dug his brother's grave up?

"The Cellar," Bailey began, "was formed by presidential decree in 1947. Have you ever heard of Majestic-12?"

"The alien thing?" Golden asked. "Roswell? Area 51?"

"Disinformation," Bailey said succinctly. "Majestic-12 was a group formed by President Truman after the Second World War to bridge the gap between domestic and international security and intelligence and, in reality, be an overseeing agency. As you know the FBI is responsible for domestic crime and intelligence and the CIA for international intelligence. Then you have the military and their various covert units and intelligence services. And the National Security Agency. The alphabet soup of federal agencies with very little coordination. The Cellar was the part of Majestic that was formed to police all those agencies."

"The cops for the cops," Golden summarized.

"Roughly," Bailey agreed.

"How come I've never heard of it?" she asked.

Bailey stared at her with a blank face. "We do not advertise our presence. Only those who have a need to know are aware of the Cellar's existence."

"What legal powers does the Cellar have?"

Gant perked up slightly, waiting for the answer to Golden's question, one he himself had never asked. He realized that coming from the Army, he had just fit into the Cellar's domain without much question. Of course, when he'd been recruited, he hadn't been in the mood or place to ask questions.

Bailey seemed to be considering how to answer. "The Cellar exists under a direct Presidential order. It operates outside of what you would consider the law. It is a law unto itself and unto those in the covert world cross the line into activities harmful to our country and its citizens."

"So it's illegal?" Golden summed up.

"You're not listening," Bailey said. "It is not possible to apply common law, whether Federal or local, to those we hunt."

"Not possible or not prudent?" Golden asked.

Gant almost enjoyed watching Bailey get grilled. Nero's right hand man, Bailey was rarely ever challenged.

"Both," Bailey said. "Sometimes the transgressions involve classified operations. In all cases they involve people with security clearances. Additionally, it would not be smart to put on trial or incarcerate these types of personnel. Yes, the publicity would not be good, but most prisons would have a hard time holding people trained to get out of prisons."

Gant remembered his own SERE—survival, evasion, resistance and escape--training at Fort Bragg years ago. He knew that Golden couldn't envision all the training these people went through and why that made them so extremely dangerous if they went rogue.

Apparently Bailey also felt the same. He leaned forward toward the woman. "Doctor Golden, you need to appreciate that we are talking about people—and an environment—that is very different from who the normal citizen is and what they experience in day to day life."

Gant thought the most interesting aspect of this conversation was what Bailey wasn't telling her. He also thought it intriguing that as far as he knew, Golden had yet to ask why she had been brought in on this. He could feel the air pressure changing and the plane slowing. Silence reigned once more as they landed in Maryland. A military Bell Jet Ranger helicopter was waiting for them, blades already turning to take them to Fort Meade and the Cellar.

CHAPTER FIVE

THE FIRST THING Emily noticed was that the van was not moving. She had no idea how long she had been unconscious, but she thought she had been given another shot sometime during the drive. Everything from the bar parking lot to this moment was a blur. She knew there were things she had wanted to remember, but her mind seemed to be a muddled canvas of sounds and smells and bumps. The only consistent feeling was the fear and she did not like that all. The fear was making her weak and she couldn't afford to be weak.

She wondered how long the van had been stopped. As if in answer to her thought, the door began to slide open. She could see nothing. Rough hands grabbed her and started pulling her toward the door. She had planned to fight, but her limbs felt useless, and beyond her control. She could do nothing, but allow herself to be lifted like a baby, out of the van.

She immediately felt the cooler air. She had worn only a short skirt and sleeveless top since she had only planned for a night of sweaty dancing. She couldn't tell if her thin denim shirt was still tied around her waist. She remembered knotting it when the bar had become impossibly warm. She thought it must be daylight because even though the air was cool, she could feel heat on her bare skin.

The man was very strong. He seemed to have no difficulty carrying her. At first she thought he would set her down as soon as he took her from the van. Instead he seemed to be walking somewhere with her.

Emily suddenly became terrified that he was carrying her to the edge of a cliff. What if he just extended her over space and let go? Tied as she was she could do nothing, but squirm in his arms. Then she began to scream. The screaming must have affected him, because suddenly she felt him bend down and dump her to the ground. She fell painfully onto her tied wrists and began to cry. She was thirsty and exhausted. She was ready to face whatever this freak had in mind. She just wanted to be left alone.

He pushed her head toward her chest and began to fiddle with the blindfold. Suddenly it was off, and she clamped her eyes shut as the sunlight painfully hit her sensitive eyes. It took a few moments for her to tentatively try to lift her eyelids. When she did, she looked around. She was in a forest; a thick forest, by the look of it. Her abductor had dumped her in a little clearing made by the collapse of a couple of the older trees. He was standing behind her, and she almost couldn't turn her head to look. She knew enough about men like him to guess that her death was probably imminent.

When she did turn, she was surprised. He was wearing a baklava. His entire head was covered in black, except his eyes and a cruel-looking slit for his mouth. He looked huge and terrifying, but Emily suddenly felt a flash of hope. He was keeping his face covered; that must mean something.

"What are you going to do to me?" Her voice surprised her. It was a harsh rasp.

He said nothing. He merely pulled a short lead that you would use to train a dog from his pocket, and fastened it around her neck. Silently, he began pulling, indicating she should follow. Emily tried to get up. She had been drugged for hours, if not days. She felt dizzy with panic and dehydration. He tried to pull her to her feet again, but she simply couldn't move. He kept pulling.

"I can't. I can't get up. I need something to drink. I'm going to be sick if you don't stop pulling me." She felt the lead go slack. Relieved, she let her body drop back to the ground.

He was carrying a large backpack, which Emily had tried to ignore. She hated to think what it contained. Now, he bent to pull it off. She watched powerful muscles move under his shirt and as he crouched over the pack she noticed the same strength in his legs. He bent over and began rummaging.

Her jacket was still tied around her waist. For some reason that made her happy. Then she remembered the ID in her pocket. She hated carrying a purse into a bar, so she kept it minimal with ID and a lipstick. The lipstick and ID should be in the pocket of her skirt. She reached behind her as if to push herself up. She knew it was risky, but she had to take the chance. Emily slowly pulled her driver's license from her back pocket and dropped it. She scooted back and hoped it was hidden.

He was holding a bottle of water and motioned for her to take some. She was desperate to drink. He let her have only a little and when she seemed all right he gave her some more. Evidently her capturer didn't want her sick.

She sat for a few minutes, and when the lead again grew tight around her neck she attempted to stand up. She was wobbly, but she managed to get to her feet. As soon as she was up he pulled and she began to follow. "You know it's going to be really hard for me to walk with my hands tied around my back, if you're going to pull me. I can't keep my balance."

There was no answer and no change, so she started walking. At first she tripped a lot and she tried to fall to her knees. They were on a narrow trail that was relatively flat. The first couple of times she fell, it was jarring and irritating but she didn't hurt herself. As the trail became rockier, it became more difficult because she knew any fall here could really hurt her. She followed along like this for a long time before she realized that he wasn't stupid. She had been concentrating so intently on not falling that she had paid no attention to her surroundings. She thought they had changed direction a few times but she wasn't sure. She could have kicked herself.

They walked for hours, and Emily was so exhausted she no longer cared about her feet or her surroundings. She fell hard a couple of times; once cutting her leg on a sharp rock. The blood had dried on her shin but she ignored it along with the gnats that hovered around the wound as she focused on trying to stay upright. The trees formed a canopy above them, but even with that thick covering she could feel the strength of the sun slipping as the day grew late.

Emily couldn't understand what was happening to her. Why was he dragging her into these godforsaken woods? Surely if it were about rape and murder, she would be dead by now. She couldn't believe that the torture of this forced march could just end with a simple bullet. There was something else going on. She forced herself to abandon those thoughts, and focus instead on remembering any details of her abduction. It didn't make her feel any better, but it certainly felt more productive.

Suddenly they walked into a clearing. The sun, though brighter, was waning in the late afternoon. There was a single, large oak tree in the center of the open meadow. Emily's first thought was that it was pretty.

In continued silence he walked her to the solitary tree and pushed her down to a sitting position on the ground. She closed her eyes and thought of her parents. She didn't want to die. Strangely, she wasn't afraid now. She just hoped it would be quick. Nothing happened and when she heard him rustling around in the backpack she opened her eyes just in time to see him drag out a heavy chain.

She wanted to cry, but her eyes refused to tear. They had long ago dried past the point of tears. He stood up with the chain in one hand, and a bottle of water in the other. He dropped the bottle in her lap and Emily stared at it with true lust. He reached into his pocket and pulled out a small knife. Before she could react, he had leaned behind her, and cut her hands free. The feeling of release was wonderful and painful, as the circulation kicked in to her numb arms. She grabbed the bottle and drank greedily. She paid little attention to the man as she drank. She let the water run over her lips and down the front of her torn and dirty t-shirt. She drank too fast and as the cramps tore through her stomach she had to twist quickly to her side and vomit. There was little for her stomach to give up and she lay on her side panting until the nausea passed. When she sat up he was closing a lock on the chain, which he had wound round the base of the tree. She stared at the lock for a moment and then followed the other end of the chain. With growing horror she saw that it ended at a shackle. The shackle encircled her ankle.

He was staring at her when she looked up at him. The sound of his voice was almost as terrifying as her chained ankle. "I'm not going to kill you. I promise." His voice was soft for such a large man and Emily thought she heard a soothing tone.

She took a breath trying to relax. Maybe she did have some chance.

As if she had spoken her thought aloud, he squatted in front her and reached behind his head. Slowly he pulled the balaclava off.

Emily began to sob. She knew then she had no chance at all.

Nero waited in almost complete darkness but not alone. He was used to the former, having lost his eyes during World War II, but the latter disconcerted him as it was a novel experience. Over the decades he had only tolerated brief visitors to his sanctum three hundred feet below the National Security Agency, but never a long-term presence. The woman had been here for ten days, leaving only in the evenings to sleep in her room above.

He could hear her breathing. She had turned her light off about ten minutes ago and not said a word after reading the very thin file they had accumulated so far on the Emily Cranston situation. She was sitting behind what had been his desk for over six decades. He was lying on what appeared to an analyst's couch next to the desk, a pillow behind his head, an IV drip stuck in his left arm.

Nero wearily raised the metal wand that amplified and transformed the air coming out of the hole in his neck. "Any thoughts, Mrs. Masterson?"

"Ms.," she corrected him.

Nero sighed, the sound a metallic wheeze. "I apologize once more for my antiquated ways. Any thoughts, please, Ms. Masterson?"

"There's not enough data," she said.

Nero nodded. It was good she did not jump to conclusions. Over the course of the past ten days, Ms. Masterson had repeatedly impressed Nero and confirmed his decades of efforts to prepare her for recruitment to sit behind that very desk. It had not been an easy process and the fall-out from recent events involved in the recruiting was something they were still dealing with.

"Have you heard from Ms. Neeley?" Nero asked. That was one loose end to the affair that he wasn't satisfied with.

"I talked to her last night."

There were times when Nero knew Ms. Masterson was punishing him. This was one of them. "Did you discuss the weather? Sports? Or might it have been shoes? I understand that is a topic of much interest between women. I once listened to that show on the television—Sex and Shoes."

"Sex and the City. No. We didn't discuss shoes. We talked about you. And Gant."

"Tony Gant?"

"Yes. We never met his brother Jack. Which I'll be rectifying in a few minutes."

"And where is Ms. Neeley?"

"She was visiting in West Virginia."

"The family?" Nero knew Neeley's history.

"Gant's family."

"Yes, Jesse and the boy."

"She's—"

"Very special," Nero said. "As is the boy."

"Yes. And they almost got killed because you put them in harm's way."

Nero sighed. Masterson had not been helpful in this matter. "We could use Ms. Neeley's talents."

"I'm sure you could."

"No, *we* could," Nero pressed. "Since you retired Mister Racine, there is a need—"

Masterson's voice was harsh. "Do *not* tell me you expect Neeley to do what Racine did."

"No. I believe the days of Racine's specialty are past as it seems the days of my own. Even before we lost Racine, the true loss was that of Tony Gant. His brother Jack has picked up some of the slack. As you are the wave of the future, so is Ms. Neeley."

"She's not so sure of that," Masterson said.

"You are going to need a field agent you can trust," Nero said. "Particularly in the matter of Sanctions or else it might weigh heavily on you. Also, since Ms. Neeley is in West Virginia, she is obviously interested in Gant's legacy. His brother is certainly part of that."

"I have some questions about that," Masterson said.

"I'm sure you do," Nero said, glad to have finally drawn her interest.

"Tony and Jack were twins, right?"

"Correct."

"And they had a falling out over Jesse?"

"You could call it that. We were never really able to get to the truth of that matter as the three principals involved—Jack, Tony and Jesse, never discussed it. Jesse had taken Tony's son, Bobbie, and left Berlin years before. As a matter of fact, just before Tony had his most fortuitous meeting with Neeley. Beyond that, I know little. Perhaps you could find out more."

"Perhaps I don't want to. Jesse and Bobbie are out of the game."

"You think it's a game?" Nero asked.

"It's a figure of—" Masterson was interrupted as the intercom beeped lightly and Mrs. Smith's voice echoed out of the speaker. "They're here."

"Send them in," Nero ordered.

Mrs. Smith sported a thick gray bun resembling hair, reading glasses perched on the edge of her nose, and wore a formless sweater covering the bulk of her body. She was not a Ms. Moneypenny in any regards. She was efficient and she could keep secrets. She nodded to the three people who had just walked in. "Mister Nero will see you now."

Mrs. Smith pressed a positive access button as Bailey punched his entry code on the keypad next to the door. The door automatically swung open and Bailey, Gant and Golden entered the hallway beyond. The door swung shut as the floor sensors picked up the intrusion.

A computer's voice came forth from speakers in the ceiling. "Identify please. Name, number and code. You have ten seconds."

Bailey identified himself and gave his number and code, stopping the portals in the walls from filling the room with incapacitating gas.

A drawer slid open from the wall. "Deposit all weapons please."

Bailey deposited a large caliber pistol that had been resting in a shoulder holster, what Gant considered an old man's gun, in the drawer. Gant put the Glock, knife and belt into the tray while the other two waited.

Gant glanced at Golden. "No weapons, Doctor?"

Golden pointed toward her head. "Mine's here." She nodded toward the weapons. "Expecting trouble?"

"Always," Gant replied. "Better to expect it than be surprised by it."

"Is that a rule?" she asked.

"As a matter of fact it is," Gant said.

"You live by rules?"

Gant could see Bailey watching them, as amused as Nero's right hand man could be. "I survive by a few of them. I break others when needed."

A red light flashed and a magnetic sensor swept over the three of them. The light turned green then went red again.

Golden gave a startled sound as a strong puff of wind came out of grates below their feet. Chemical, biological and explosives sensors in the ceiling sniffed the air. The light turned green for the second time.

"Proceed, please."

The far door slid apart and they entered Nero's office. Three lights were now on above the desk oriented toward the three chairs lined up in front of his desk. Gant paused for a second, taking in the woman seated behind the desk. He'd never seen her before. He'd never seen anyone in here before other than Nero and occasionally Bailey standing in the shadows. The old man was lying on a couch to the side, looking very ill. Gant knew that Nero's condition had been deteriorating but he had not expected such a radical change behind the desk. He had always assumed that when the time came it would be Bailey who took the old man's place.

The woman was small, that was his first impression. She had thick blond hair that cascaded to her shoulders in a way that didn't seem contrived to Gant. Her eyes, what he could see of them, were dark and steady as they gazed back at him. She was young, too young in Gant's opinion, to be sitting behind Nero's desk although there were deep lines etched around her eyes, not too much different from the spider webs around Golden's eyes. Women who'd seen too much, Gant thought. *Welcome to the real world.*

"Mister Gant," Nero said, "I am sorry about your brother."

Gant believed the old man not in the slightest so he didn't acknowledge the words although he sensed both women in the room looking at him curiously, particularly the woman behind the desk.

"Is this a Sanction?" Gant asked.

"Always to the point, Mister Gant," Nero said. "We don't know yet, but we fear it might be." The blind man adjusted his head slightly, facing Doctor Golden. "Ordinarily Mister Gant would be operating solo, but I—we—" he indicated the woman at the desk—"think it's time to adjust the ways of the Cellar. So you, Doctor Golden, have been brought in to add your expertise to the problem."

"And who exactly is we?" Gant asked.

Nero raised his free hand and pointed at the woman who was in his place. "Meet Ms. Masterson. My protégé, so to speak. I've brought her in to add some perspective to my thinking and decision-making. Eventually, Mister Gant, she will be completely in charge of the Cellar."

That brought silence to the room as the implications sunk in.

"I think someone needs to explain to me exactly what is going on and what is expected of me," Golden said, her voice tight and clipped. She sat in the chair ramrod straight, her face even tighter if that were possible.

Nero rested the hand holding the voice wand on his chest. "There are those who operate beyond the bounds of what most in this country consider the law. Those whose skills and attributes are also beyond the capabilities of normal law enforcement agencies to cope with. When these people conduct a transgression, a Sanction is initiated by this office. At this moment we are gathering data to see if recent events indicate the need for a Sanction."

"And a Sanction is?" Golden pressed.

"Potential transgressors are identified by this office," Nero said. "Then a field operative such as Mister Gant is sent out. His is the final determining authority based on what he discovers, on whether the Sanction is valid and whether to implement it."

"You still haven't answered my question," Golden said.

Gant spoke up, tired of it all. "A Sanction is implemented when I kill the guilty party. After, of course, I validate their guilt."

"And how exactly do you do that?"

"Once I find them, it's usually not difficult," Gant said.

Golden considered that for a few seconds before speaking again. "And my role?"

"Good question," Gant threw in.

Nero spoke up. "Because of your background and expertise, I've brought you in to complement Mister Gant. The times are changing and it is time for the Cellar to change with them."

"What background and expertise?" Gant asked.

Bailey spoke for the first time from his position standing by the door. "Doctor Golden was the psychological screener for Special Operations Command for the past four years."

That explained her knowing Colonel Cranston, Gant thought, although it didn't explain her seeing the daughter's photo on a nightstand. "Was?"

"Doctor Golden resigned her position three months ago," Bailey said, as usual not explaining a damn thing. Gant noted that Golden's hands were gripping the arms of her chair and at Bailey's last words her knuckles had gone white.

"And what expertise does Ms. Masterson bring?" Gant asked.

Nero's head turned slightly and there was no obvious difference in the metallic voice, but nonetheless, Gant picked up the tone as the old man spoke. "I hand-picked Ms. Masterson and she underwent a rather strenuous screening process. If you question her, Mister Gant, you are questioning my judgment."

The room was silent once more for several moments. Then, surprisingly, Golden cut in. "You believe that whoever kidnapped Emily Cranston is a government employee?"

"Given the circumstances, it is probable," Nero said. "There's not enough data yet."

"You mean not enough bodies," Gant said.

Nero held up a copy of the second cache report. "Ms. Masterson believes we will receive the rest of this report shortly."

"That won't be good," Gant said. He wondered who Masterson really was and why she had been glancing at him so strangely ever since he entered. He'd known Nero was getting on in years and his health was failing, but Masterson truly seemed a strange choice to replace him.

"Rarely do we receive good news here," Nero said.

Golden nodded at the partial report. "It would make sense to send the rest of it. To make the point about Emily."

"And that point would be?" Gant asked.

Golden shrugged. "We'll find that out when we find the first cache that he wants us to find."

"He?" Masterson asked.

"My data almost insures it would be a man," Golden answered. She looked at Masterson. "You said first cache?"

Masterson nodded. "There are two cache reports. One most likely refers to wherever the target is locating Emily Cranston. The other, though, probably refers to a cache already in place. These partial reports were left with more than just a taunt in mind. I suspect we will get the rest of the first report shortly and find what Emily's fate will be."

Gant wanted to ask the old man about his brother, but he didn't want to do it in front of the others in the room. Also, he doubted Nero would tell him anything more than he'd been told by Bailey, which was little. Gant closed his eyes, blocking out the three lights shining down on him. He thought briefly of his brother's ex-wife, Jesse, but the woman behind the desk interrupted his thoughts.

"Barring new information," Masterson said, "it might be good to review Colonel Cranston's background."

"You think it's an act of revenge?" Golden asked.

"It is possible," Nero said.

The psychologist leaned forward, her voice harsh. "Did you do this for Jimmy when he was kidnapped?"

Gant was surprised at the sudden outburst from Golden.

A beeping noise cut off any reply Nero was going to make. The old man picked up his phone and listened for several moments, then put it down without a word.

"There's been a killing," he finally said. "This morning." He tilted his head toward Masterson. "All available data is being transferred by Mrs. Smith online. Please bring it up."

Hannah Masterson studied the scant data scrolling up on the screen built into the desktop. "Enterprise, Alabama. Twenty-four year old female, named Cathy Svoboda. Throat slashed at approximately zero-nine-ten. Dead at the site, which was the day care facility where she was working. Crime scene is sterile, no suspects, and the cut was smooth and clean, not a butcher job. Sterile except for one thing."

"The rest of the first cache report," Golden said.

"Yes," Masterson said. "Given to a young boy at the scene. All he can recall given his shock is that the man's face was scarred."

"In what way?" Gant asked.

"That data is not available yet," Masterson said. She held up a hand as she typed into the computer. "She was engaged. Her fiancée, Chief Warrant Office Mark Lankin, is a helicopter pilot in the reserves. When he is on active duty he flies for the Night Stalkers, the Army's classified helicopter unit."

"The timing isn't coincidence," Gant said, remembering what Golden had said about the taunting. "This girl was killed so that we'd get this report now. Today." He stood. "Do you have a copy of the rest of the report?"

Masterson nodded. "Yes. The lake in the partial is Reelfoot Lake in Kentucky."

"We're on our way," Gant turned for the door.

Nero nodded, even though Gant was already moving. "Mrs. Masterson, please start running background on Lankin and Cranston. We need to find the link."

Gant paused at the door. "It won't be in the computer." He glanced at Golden, who was still in her seat. "You coming?"

CHAPTER SIX

EMILY LOOKED ONCE more at her abductor's face and was disappointed by what she saw there. He was so ordinary. He looked like anyone else you'd find wandering the aisles of a library, picking up some milk on the way home, or walking out of a barbershop. There was nothing overtly evil about him. Nothing was even interesting about him. That was her initial impression.

A closer look at his eyes though, and she saw how he was like no one else she had ever been around. Emily was used to being noticed. Whether it was because she was young, or female, or simply because she was another human being; Emily, like most people, was conscious of other people seeing her. This man did not notice her. He was three feet away and staring at her, as he had been now for almost a half hour but he did not notice her. She realized that so far this was the most horrifying moment of this ordeal. To this man, to this person who controlled everything about her down to the moment of her death, she was of no interest. She was not even human to him. She was nothing, just a means to an end. What the end was, though, she had no idea.

Emily returned his stare. Only hers was not blank: it was filled with judgment and loathing. Then she saw the scar. It was mostly hidden by his short dark hair. But on the left side of his head there was a furrow that ran from just behind his temple to the rear of the skull. She tried to imagine what could cause such damage but drew a blank, not being aware of the vagaries of bullet trajectories once they encountered flesh and bone.

"I'm not going to kill you." He repeated it as if the statement negated all that came before it.

"Why me? What did I ever do to you? Why did you pick me?" Emily was determined not to cry one more time for this asshole.

He looked at her with genuine puzzlement. "I know you didn't do anything to me. I didn't pick you. You picked me."

"You're kidding right? How the hell did I do that?" Emily liked getting angry. It felt much better than being terrified.

"To be more exact, your father brought you to me." He had a look of sincere truthfulness on his ordinary face.

"My father?" Emily felt a cold chill settle over her. She only had the roughest idea of what her father did in the Army, but she knew he was involved in a lot of secret stuff. He'd been gone most of her life, off to some corner of the world doing things he could never talk about. "How is my father involved? How did he bring me to you?"

The man folded his arms, not answering.

"Will you let me go? I won't tell anyone about you. You'd be safe. We could pretend this never happened." Emily saw the futility immediately. For him this was already over. "How can I believe you're not going to kill me? You've kidnapped me, drugged me and marched me to this godforsaken place. Why shouldn't I think that killing me is the whole idea here?"

"Because it is not."

"Then what is the idea, damn it?"

He zipped up his pack, looked around as if he were missing something and finally stood up. "You curse a lot you know."

Emily stared up at him in blank amazement. "You're kidding, right."

"Why would I do that?" He turned and looked around at the small clearing, and then he chose a different path than the one that brought them to this place. He began to walk away.

"Wait a minute. Where are you going? Hey, look at me! Turn your fucking psycho self around and come back here. You can't leave me here. Wait! Goddamn you, wait. I'll do whatever you want. Motherfucker! You motherfucker. You can't just leave me here."

He turned his head before he stepped into the covering of the dense wood. "You really do curse a lot. Your father will understand what is happening."

Emily sat in stunned silence as he disappeared. She was momentarily shocked into silence. Then she screamed.

CHAPTER SEVEN

"WHO'S JIMMY?" Gant asked.

They were seated in the back of the Lear Jet, the muted roar of the engines filling the cabin. Bailey was seated across from them, talking on his secure satellite phone, lining up support for them in Memphis, their current destination.

"My son," Golden said.

Since this morning no one had been very forthcoming with information. Gant stared at Golden for several moments, waiting for more, then when he realized it wasn't coming he put his feet up on the table, leaned back and closed his eyes. Normally he could fall asleep within moments, a trait learned when one had to grab sleep whenever possible under harsh conditions but images of his brother intruded, keeping him on the cusp of sleep and sorrow. His right hand was absent-mindedly running along his left forearm where shrapnel from an RPG round had torn the flesh long ago. And it wasn't just his brother, there was also the image of Jesse.

"Have you notified the local authorities?" Golden's voice intruded on Gant's memories. He opened his eyes and noted that Bailey was off the phone.

"Negative," Bailey said. "We want first crack at the site. We have a helicopter waiting in Memphis to get us to the cache."

"Whoever is there could be alive," Golden said.

"You really think that?" Gant asked.

"There's always hope," Golden argued.

"Hope is not a good thing," Gant said. "It blurs reality."

Golden looked like he'd just slapped her. "Hope is all we have sometimes."

Bailey's cell phone buzzed, cutting through the sudden tension. He opened it and listened for a few moments, then closed it. "Someone's already at the cache site."

"Who?" Gant asked.

"The FBI."

"Why?"

"Someone found a body there."

"Who?" Golden asked.

"Some kid hunting with his old man," Bailey replied.

Golden shook her head. "No. Who is the body?"

"They don't know yet. FBI just got on scene."

A thunderstorm was off-shore, lightning playing above the Gulf, the thunder rolling in over the beach. Caleigh Roberts was on her first Spring Break and while the Florabama was packed, the crowd parted as she made her way to the back deck. Blond hair flowed over tanned shoulders. She wore a short blue jean skirt and a belly revealing tank top that was pink and spelled *Princess* in tiny rhinestones across her chest. She slid in among her friends from Ole Miss.

"Call daddy?" one of the frat brothers yelled.

Caleigh blushed, only highlighting her high cheekbones. She was his only daughter and it was the one requirement he'd placed on her at the same time he'd given her a Platinum Card.

The Florabama is a roadhouse straddling the Florida-Alabama border. It had started as a small clapboard liquor store that grew room by add-on room toward the shoreline then further into either state. It is surrounded by a tall corrugated fence like those around a junkyard.

A bad band was playing rock, making up for lack of talent with volume. There were three bars within sight of the deck serving shots in little plastic cups that other places put ketchup in. People were below the deck, dancing in the sand. A group of frat brothers were urging Caleigh and her girlfriends to do another shot of some sweet stuff called Tongue in Your Panties. They were all giggling wildly and Caleigh quickly forget her check-in phone call and her Dad's words.

It was only 8:30 in the PM and over a thousand people were crowded into the various rooms of the Florabama, all already in various stages of drunkenness. No one was focusing on any one thing or person, all feeling a bubbling hysteria. Caleigh was dancing and half drunk and having a very good time. She felt pretty and desirable. A special time when special things happened. Frat brothers had been flirting with her all evening but she'd grown up with them. They were just excited little puppies.

In the shadows off the deck, just outside the door into the Florabama a tall, dark-haired man leaned against the wall. He appeared to be in his late 20's, maybe early 30's, with weathered, tanned skin that gave him a sophisticated, experienced look the frat boys lacked. Caleigh had spotted him about an hour earlier. In some ways, although it was crowded, he was apart from the others. Every time she looked at him and he returned the gaze with his dark eyes, she averted her own. She continued to dance with the boys.

When she looked up once more, he was gone. She felt a moment's concern, surprised at the intensity of the feeling cutting through her drunken haze. She swept her gaze around the deck and saw him standing by the stairs to the beach, leaning against a pole, drinking a Corona and looking straight at her. As he lowered the bottle, she saw he was smiling.

He motioned for her to come over and in the crowded party no one saw her move toward him. She stopped about two feet in front of him, not quite in his personal space, but close. He mouthed something, but she couldn't hear over the band. He smiled once more and nodded toward the stairs.

Caleigh glanced over her shoulder. Her friends were among the crowd, all drunk, all young. When she turned back, he was half way down the wood stairs. She reached out for the railing, a little dizzy, and followed. She caught up to him and he tossed his Corona into a barrel, the hand continuing to move and sliding around her waist as they walked down the beach.

He stopped, facing the ocean, the surf pounding less than five feet away. There was no moon and the cloud cover was thick. He held his left arm up. "Florida." He dropped it to his side and lifted his right. "Alabama."

Caliegh laughed, a bit uncertainly.

"Areas of operation," he said.

"What?"

"Do you know what that means?"

Caliegh shook her head.

He reached forward very gently, one hand sliding up her neck into her hair. She felt herself pulled forward as if in a dream, her lips meeting his. They kissed. Again and again. She felt the surf against her ankles, her calves. It was like a dream, one she'd used to have as a young girl. He was so sweet and gentle and strong and—

She was weightless, and then the air exploded out of her lungs as her back hit the sand hard. All she could see was his dark form over her. His other hand was on her throat. There was something strange about it. It was cold, Caliegh realized. Cold and unyielding. Not warm flesh. *How could that be?*

A wave broke over her face and she blinked, trying to get the salt water out of her eyes. She was stunned, unable to move for precious seconds. His other hand was on her arm, twisting her over. She felt sand scrape against her cheek, shocking her into action. She kicked, but he was too strong, too large, and she was small. His strange hand let go of her throat and she gasped for air, sucking in a wave, coughing, trying to spit out the water, only in time for another wave to wash over her.

The hand grabbed the back of her head, finishing the turn and shoving her face into the wet sand. She felt incredible pain as sand granules cut into her wide-open eyes. Her mouth was full of sand and water, but she tried to breathe anyway. It felt as if red hot lava was pouring down her throat.

He was so mean.

Daddy. Daddy. He'd seemed so nice.

CHAPTER EIGHT

GANT LET BAILEY take point in dealing with the FBI. Bureaucracy had never been his forte and that lack had been one of the reasons he'd made the decision to move from the military to the Cellar when Bailey came calling. Even in the Special Forces, the long hand of the big green machine had made itself felt. For Gant the last straw had been the decree to shave beards off while he and his team were deployed in Afghanistan because some general back in the States had seen SF troopers—in the midst of saving the Afghani President's life from assassins—looking scruffy and called the Pentagon to complain. The concept of being a clean-shaven corpse hadn't sat well with Gant. Skewed priorities, even in the midst of combat, had shown Gant the reality of working inside such a large organization as the army. The Cellar was indeed much smaller, and Gant had generally been left to his own devices on missions, the results being the only thing that Nero cared about. This was another reason why Golden's, and to a lesser extent, Bailey's presences were a bit of a mystery to him.

Of course, there had also been the issue of his brother and the work he had done for the Cellar over the years. Even though they were twins, he had always felt one step behind his brother, following his path. It had been Tony's decision first to apply to West Point and Jack had followed. Then Tony had been the first in the Ranger Battalion, then Special Forces and on to the Cellar. And first with Jesse. And now his brother was dead. Gant felt an unusual sense of unease, which he quickly dismissed as he tried to get some sleep while he could.

It took just over an hour flight by helicopter from Memphis to reach the desolate woods of Reel Foot Lake. Darkness had fallen and Gant knew the night was going to be a long one as the chopper came in to a hastily established landing zone in a clearing and they disembarked.

According to the information he'd read, Gant knew the area was a popular hunting site and camouflaged men from the entire southeast passed through the region during the season. But hunting season was still a month off. Gant checked the slim data sheet that Bailey had printed out, forwarded from the Cellar as they got in a Blazer and were driven toward the site. According to the report, the lake had been formed in the winter of 1811-1812 when a series of earthquakes had sent the Mississippi river flowing backwards and leaving in its wake the large body of water where land had once been.

The body had been discovered just after dark, and because of cell phones had been reported quickly. The local police had called the crime into the bureau sight unseen. If the condition of the boy who discovered the body was an accurate measure then the small lake area police force figured they'd best stay out of it. The body was exactly where the now complete cache report had said something would be, a fact that Gant had no doubt Bailey was not informing the FBI or local authorities of.

Gant looked around the vicinity and saw nothing but unending loneliness harshly lit by car headlights from FBI vehicles. When hunting season ended so did the human habitation of the area. He watched the FBI men and one woman standing by the body. They had all carefully positioned their line of sight outwards, as if out of sight out of mind really meant something. Gant waited for Bailey to finish speaking to the head FBI man. Golden was next to Gant, apparently not very anxious to view the corpse. At least she wasn't asking any more questions.

The circle of FBI agents broke up as their boss came over and said a few words. They moved away with many a dark glance at Bailey, Gant and Golden. Bureaucratic pissing over turf, something that Gant usually ignored as the Cellar always had pre-eminent domain wherever it stretched its dark hand. Bailey indicated for Gant and Golden to move up. Gant slowly walked forward, taking in the feel of the location. He stopped ten feet from the body.

Golden was perfectly still next to him.

Gant catalogued the area in his mind. There was a tall pine right in the center of a small meadow. Around the base of the tree was a chain. The chain ran a few feet to the body. It was fastened to the girl's leg with a shackle. She was lying in a fetal position. The body was swollen and splotched with lividity. Gant stared a long time trying to make sense of what he saw. The ankle below the shackle was mangled and covered with dried blackened blood. A blood spattered stone lay close by. There was an arrow sticking from her upturned shoulder.

"If this is what he's done to Emily—" Golden's voice trailed off.

Bailey was squatting with his brief case open, thumbing through some folders.

"Who is she?" Gant asked.

Bailey paused, and extracted one of the files. He checked the black and white photo with what he could see of the victim's face. "Tracy Caulkins."

The name meant nothing to Gant. "And her father is?"

"Michael Caulkins. Drug Enforcement Agency. South Region commander."

Gant nodded. This was going to be a Sanction. And it was going to get worse before the end.

Emily Cranston had her knees pulled up tight to her chest and her back to the oak tree. Like most people she had never been outside in the middle of nature at night entirely alone. She'd never have believed the woods could be so noisy. Branches snapping, leaves rustling, the intermittent cries of birds and other creatures she couldn't identify.

What she feared the most, though, was hearing the sound of footsteps. She did not want him to return.

She straightened out the leg with the chain, feeling the weight of the shackle around her ankle. Her eyes darted up as something swooped across the clearing between her tree and the surrounding forest. She pulled the chained leg back in tight to her chest, wrapping her arms around her knees and rocking back and forth. A muffled cry escaped her lips and tears flowed down her cheeks.

Dawn was a long way off. And it did not promise an improvement in her situation.

CHAPTER NINE

GANT WENT OVER to interview the boy who had found her. Jackson something. The boy was back by the clearing, far from the body but close to the memory. At first glance Gant didn't think Jackson would ever really recover from his discovery. Maybe a person wasn't supposed to forget this kind of thing, it occurred to Gant as he walked over to the boy. He noted that Golden followed him, probably more to be away from the corpse than anything else. So far she hadn't been very useful and Gant still had the question of why Nero had brought her into this. He wasn't sure he bought into Nero's explanation in the office. He also found it odd that she had been living one island south of him off the coast of South Carolina. As with everything else that the Cellar was involved in, Gant did not think that happened to be a coincidence.

Gant knew change was overdue everywhere, including the Cellar, given what had happened on 9-11. Such a gross failure indicated serious flaws in the national security system and he also knew that Nero had taken the disaster very personally, even though the Cellar's mandate was to look inward at the nation's own security apparatus rather than outward.

The thing Gant liked about the Cellar was the sense of personal responsibility. When he was sent to do a Sanction, it was his complete responsibility. No passing of the buck, no blaming someone else if it went wrong.

Gant did feel bad for the boy's luck.

Checking with a local, Gant found out that the boy's name was Jackson Lerner, and he was 16 years old. Early this morning he had set off with his dad for a nice hunting trip. Why they were hunting out of season no one had brought up given the circumstances. Seeing the state of their truck, Gant had a feeling it wasn't simply for the thrill. They needed the meat.

Jackson was sitting on the ground with a man Gant presumed was his father. They both appeared a little shaky, but the boy looked like he was in pain. Gant gently eased his body to the ground, kneeling in front of the kid. The boy paid no attention.

"I'm Agent Gant." He said it to no one in particular, but Jackson raised his head.

"And I'm Doctor Golden."

The father stepped forward. "Hey. I'm Buddy Lerner and this is my son Jackson. This has been pretty rough on him. We'd been up all day and it was late, so Jackson had a hard time waking me up. He got it in his head that I was dead, too. He got pretty scared."

Gant could smell Buddy a few feet away. He guessed the boy had had a hell of a hard time waking him up. "Jackson would it be Ok if I asked you a few questions?"

Jackson continued to stare at him without really seeing anything.

Golden knelt next to Gant, a move that surprised him. "Mr. Lerner," she said, "could you help us here? We need to know what happened and he probably needs to talk about it."

"Hey Jackson, come on, you talk to this guy and the Doctor and then we can get our butts on home. Your moms about crazy with worry."

"Yeah, I want to go home." The boy's voice was a flat monotone.

Gant decided to let Golden earn her place and remained silent.

"Can you tell me how you first discovered the body?" Golden asked.

"You mean the girl?"

This was a nice boy, Gant thought and he noted that Golden flushed at his response. "Yes, the girl. How did you first find her?"

"Just after dark I climbed up in that tree." He pointed to a clump of dark trees east of them. One, a gnarled and weather- beaten, oak stood above the others. Gant noted it had a good field of fire across the field. "I got me a good spot in a blind someone must have built and waited for the moon."

Gant looked up. The moon wasn't quite full but it gave enough light to see things, but not really know what they were.

Jackson continued. "I had my binoculars and I was looking around. I spotted something shiny. I saw it a couple of times. The moonlight was hitting on something in the dark. After—you know-- I climbed down and went to check. It seemed Ok, so I got closer. Then I guess I just freaked out. I tried to get my dad, and everything just gets screwed up after that."

"It must have been terrible," Golden said. "It's a shame you had to go through that. After you woke your dad what did you do?"

Gant realized that Golden hadn't quite grasped what they had seen at the body, but he remained silent.

"We hiked back to the truck and called my mom. She called the police. We've been waiting here ever since." He started to cry. At that moment, he seemed a lot younger than 16. "I'm real sorry. I didn't know. I mean, at first I thought it was my fault. You know, until I saw her leg. I mean, I knew that wasn't me. Why would someone do that to a person?"

"Hey, Jackson." Gant reached out and patted the kid on the back. "No one here blames you. Don't you worry about that. Anyone could have made that mistake in the dark. She's been gone a while."

Comprehension flooded over Golden's face, but Gant ignored her. "You see anyone else in this area?"

"Today?"

"Any time," Gant said.

The boy shook his head. "It's a pretty dead—" he stuttered, then started over—"pretty isolated."

No shit, thought Gant shooting a glance at the father who was remaining quiet. That's why the old man had chosen it to hunt in. It had occurred to Gant on the way here that the spot might be a trap, the cache report designed to lure them in to an ambush. A four-wheel drive pulled up and he noticed that the Cellar's forensic expert was getting out. Gant reluctantly stood, towering over Buddy and Jackson.

"We know how to find you," Gant said, "so you go on home with the deputies. I heard your truck broke down."

Jackson almost smiled. "Yeah, we got to tow it home. My mom's mad about that."

"Remember, try to get over this." Gant hated himself for the patronizing statement. Maybe he was just running out of things to say. He was not impressed with Golden's professional expertise, but of course, he imagined she'd never worked in the middle of a forest with a body nearby. He made his goodbyes and walked over to join the doctor and Bailey.

"Another victim," Golden said.

"What?" Gant wasn't sure what she was talking about.

"The boy. That will be with him the rest of his life."

Gant glanced back at the boy sitting with his father. He didn't want to tell Golden that there was most likely going to be several more victims before they caught up with whoever was doing this. As Gant walked he pulled a cravat out of his pocket and wrapped it around his nose and mouth.

"What do you think?" Bailey asked the expert as soon as they were there. Bailey had a surgical mask on, as did the expert. A set of halogen lights had been rigged up and they highlighted the area.

The man who had seen everything in his 23- year career looked a little shocked. His name was Padgett and he was an MD with extra degrees in forensics and crime scene investigation and many years of practical experience seeing the gruesome situations the Cellar waded into. "She tried to smash her own foot with the stone. Tried to break the bones so she could get it through the shackle. She was too far gone from dehydration and starvation to realize it would just swell. She probably died soon after."

Bailey looked in the folder. "She was reported missing five weeks ago. Disappeared on the way home from work."

"She's been dead about three days," Padgett reported. "I'll have to do an autopsy but I'd say cause of the death was dehydration."

Gant looked around. Over four weeks chained to this tree. It had to have rained several times. He knew a person could do around four weeks without food—he'd gone three weeks one time. But water was essential. One couldn't last more than five days or so without fresh water.

Whether it was the smell of the corpse now that they were right next to it or the sudden understanding of how long the girl had been here, Golden turned and rapidly walked away to the edge of the clearing, where she knelt. The sound of her retching carried clearly. Gant could see some of the FBI men looking over, a few of them snickering evilly and making comments. Golden's reaction didn't bother Gant—in fact, it relieved him that she obviously wasn't a sociopath who could stare at death without emotion.

Padgett opened his kit and began to do some work on the body.

Golden came walking back, her gait a bit unsteady. "We've got to find Emily."

"We've got to find who did this," Gant said. He knelt down next to Padgett and felt the heavy links. "The kid probably saw the chain, probably even moving a bit as the body swelled up. Thought it was a deer--the eyes. Thought he had a big one." He looked at the arrow sticking out of the body. "They were hunting out of season."

"So?" Bailey asked.

"He took his son hunting," Gant said.

Bailey stiffened and looked at Gant. Golden had a distant look in her eyes. A breeze blew through the clearing, ruffling the feathers on the tail of the arrow.

Gant had grown up in New York. His father had never taken him hunting. His father had always worked. Always been gone. The first thing Gant had ever hunted was human. He'd never understood the concept of hunting as a sport. With Goodwine he'd done some hunting, but the Gullah ate what they caught, as had Gant. And the Gullah respected their prey. No matter how much Gant had hated whoever he was after, he'd always respected the target for the very simple reason that human prey could turn and kill him just as easily as he could do it. It was fair and equal. And in the Cellar his hunts had always ended eye to eye with the quarry. And he'd always known, looking into their eyes, that they deserved their fate. It was something that would never stand up in a court-room but on occasion Gant had crossed paths with hardened homicide detectives and they had told him the same thing: they'd known whether they had a killer by looking in the eyes.

"You have Cranston's file?" he asked Bailey. He noticed that Golden still seemed pre-occupied. Death did that to people, Gant knew. Of course he didn't know how wrong he was about what she was actually experiencing.

"Yes. And Caulkins. And I'll have Svoboda's shortly. I'll also have headquarters run deep backgrounds for links."

Gant knew what Bailey meant about deep background. In the covert world a person's file, even a classified one, only held the surface. There were dark waters that only a deep background check could begin to unveil. Gant had done things that were not recorded on any piece of paper or digitized in some computer memory. He had done things that he wished he could wipe out of his own memory.

Gant glanced at Golden. "She's right. He's taunting us. And this is just the tip of the iceberg. Have the Auxiliary report anything," he said to Bailey.

"The 'Auxiliary'?" Golden asked. "You mentioned that before."

Gant figured the question was a good sign. She was getting past the immediate horror. Give her a few more years of this and she might even be an asset. Of course she would have to last those years.

"We have a network of people who watch for unusual crimes," Bailey said, as usual not going into detail.

"This was brutal," Gant said. "And personal."

Golden frowned. "And?"

"I'm used to dealing with professionals," Gant said. "People who do a job. Not this. Who do things for a reason."

"This *was* done for a reason," Golden said. "And as you said, a very personal one. If we can figure that reason out, we can figure out who did it. That's why I'm here."

"I was wondering about that," Gant said, ignoring the flush of anger on her cheeks as he turned and walked away. He tuned out everyone. He focused on the body, allowing his senses to expand from himself, to the shackle, to the chain, to the tree, the clearing. He had to pass over to the other side, the side where all his skills and training and experience could be warped to hurt and kill.

No conscience.

No soul.

This site was not random. The cache report indicated that. Gant had put in a number of caches during his time in Special Operations. And he had recovered some too. He remembered diving in the harbor in Kiel, Germany and recovering a Nazi cache of weapons from World War II. The guns had been wrapped in oil cloth, water-proofed in plastic and still functional after over half a century. Put there near the end of the war in the hopes of supplying a Nazi guerilla force that never materialized.

A cache was designed to be hidden and only found by someone with the report. Gant looked at the arrow. But this cache had been found before they arrived. By a father and son hunting with bow and arrow out of season. Thus this cache had been a mistake. A good plan, but events had overcome it. Not by much, by only a few hours.

But still.

If Jackson and his father had shown up five days earlier, they might have been able to save the girl. Or they might have been killed by someone watching her suffer. That was something to factor into Emily's situation, although the entire point of a cache was to hide something and be able to leave and come back later and recover it, not sit and watch the site. But Gant had never heard of a human cache so this one might have developed differently.

Still, there were rules to covert operations, procedures to be followed. There was more to a cache operation than just the report. There was preparing what was to be cached. He looked at Padgett. He'd get the man's report as soon as he could autopsy the body. Then there was preparing the site, the first step of which was to put observation on the location prior to insertion of the cache.

Gant looked at the tree the boy had pointed out as his hide site for hunting. Leaving the three around the body, he walked across the field. It was an oak tree, and there were worn boards nailed in to the side to allow easy access to the lower branches. Gant clambered up. A couple of one by sixes had been hammered into position forming a rough seat about twenty feet up with an excellent view of the field and the pine tree in the center. The wood was old and beginning to rot, which indicated this had been put here years before.

Gant sat down and he instinctively knew that the man he was after had sat here also. It wasn't what someone in combat conditions would do, as the site was too obvious, but for the Kentucky woods it was good enough. But it hadn't been.

Would he and his new partner be good enough, Gant wondered? They had a week, maybe more, but they couldn't count on rain. For all they knew Emily was staked out in the desert, which could shorten the time considerably. But it would still take time to get to the desert. And he had a feeling that whoever had taken her would not want to travel far with her.

That would make the risk of being stopped too high. A day's travel, no more, Gant decided. By vehicle, since it appeared that was how she had been taken.

A week, Gant decided. For Emily. A lifetime to catch whoever was doing this.

Then he realized Golden was right: they needed to find Emily first. Catching the target was secondary. It was a novel situation for Gant.

He looked across the open field to the tree where the girl had died. He could see Golden standing there alone. Staring at the body. She looked like a ghost, an apparition.

Gant reached into his pocket and pulled out a satellite telephone. He hit the speed dial. He knew there was a good chance the old man wouldn't answer the phone this late.

He was right as he got the answering service.

When the beep came he had a question. "Mister Nero. This is Jack Gant. How did my brother die? And what happened to Jimmy, Doctor Golden's son?"

CHAPTER TEN

THE OLD MAN carried his folding chair to a spot just above the surf line and set it down so that it faced the rising sun. His skin was tanned and leathery, carved hard by the sun and ocean breeze for the past eight years. He thought those who used sunscreen were cowards and expressed as much to his wife whenever they came to the beach together, thus he mostly came alone. The morning was his time with the local papers, from Destin, Pascagoula and Panama City. It was a routine he followed every day, eating up two hours of his day. It was his daily connection to his old life and he relished it, although he would never admit it to anyone.

He read the first paper carefully, the way an accountant would read a ledger. The lines around his eyes became even more pronounced as he immediately noted the lead article on the right hand side of the front page. He read it completely, before carefully folding the paper once more and placing it down. He checked the other papers, reading their version of the same story.

Then he looked at his PDA, checking the list. He slowly scrolled through and then came to a halt when he spotted what he was half-afraid, half-hoping he would find.

He reached into his shirt pocket, peeling back the Velcro close. He pulled out a cell phone, a sleek black model with a surprisingly thick, stubby antenna as wide as a cigar and a quarter as long.

Changing programs on the PDA to his contacts list, he scrolled through the names in his address book and then dialed a local number as he saw the contact he needed. He waited while it rang, his eyes shifting down the beach to the east, where the article said the girl had been found.

"Jimmy, this is Mac," he began as a cautious voice answered. "The girl at the Florabama?"

He listened for a moment, and cut in. "Any signs of sexual assault?"

The reply was short and negative.

"Someone she knew?"

The frown deepened as he received his second negative response.

"Anything of note at the crime scene?"

As soon as he received the third negative from the sheriff he curtly thanked his source and ended the connection. Then he dialed a special 6 digit entry, accessing the phone's satellite link. There was a series of beeps as the signal was relayed through a secure MILSTAR communications satellite, frequency hopped to avoid interception, and scrambled to avoid decryption if someone did manage to intercept, before the signal finally down-linked. Two tones sounded and he spoke quickly.

"Auxiliary Two-Six-Four here. I've got a female KIA. Nineteen. Name Caliegh Roberts. No sexual assault. No known associates. The name is on the list. Drowned in a foot of water. No on site evidence. Very clean kill. Very brutal."

He cut the connection, put the phone back in the pocket and pulled the next paper out to continue reading while he waited. He'd spent twenty-five years working in the CIA. Less than two months after his retirement, a man had shown up at his house and offered him the job of being in the Auxiliary. Boredom had about driven the old man crazy within two months and he readily accepted.

The Satphone buzzed and he answered. "Yes?"

The voice on the other end was female, but not feminine. All business. "Was there anything left at the murder site? Specifically a piece of paper?"

"No one reported it. I'll check on it."

"Do that."

The man called his contacts in the sheriff's department and then the State Police. All reported back negative about any paper being left at the murder scene. He dialed his contact number and reported that.

Satisfied he had done his duty, he stood up, closing his folding chair and turned to head back to his car. But then he paused and looked once more down the beach in the direction the murder had taken place and felt a chill crawl over his skin despite the bright sun. A predator had been in the area during the night—a trained predator, the worst kind of all.

Golden walked into Sam Cranston's familiar apartment just off post of Fort Bragg in Fayetteville, North Carolina. Every piece of furniture was the same.

Same masculine decorating, but the room felt different. Maybe it was the crowd of dark-suited men who she presumed were agents, or the stink of cigarette smoke. She felt truly out of place. Then Sam saw her and waved her toward him. Golden hoped she didn't look as surprised at his appearance as she really was. Sam looked terrible. She was enough of a doctor to recognize he was in shock. He didn't smoke, as far as she remembered, but the smoke apparently came from him. He was grinding a butt into an overflowing ashtray. Golden had always wondered how nicotine had become the ubiquitous calming agent. The English made you a nice cup of tea. But in America, it was 'here have something deadly. It will make you feel better.'

She sank down onto the couch next to Sam, and put her arms around him. At first he felt stiff and unyielding, but as she held him tight, she could feel his shoulders start to loosen and then the deep spasms as he began to cry. The man she presumed Sam had been talking to before she entered the room, looked at her with dismay. An uneasy mood settled into the room—real men don't cry, she thought. But real men rarely faced having their daughter taken.

"Who are you?" As the agent said it, he pulled out his ID fast enough to let her know that he was new to the job. She had noticed that so far she had not had to show her 'NSA' card to anyone, nor had Gant offered his identification up to anyone.

Gant stood just inside the doorway of the apartment, a silent presence and she noted that once more no one asked him who he was or why he was here the same way none of the FBI people at the lake had gone up to him. They'd spent several hours in Kentucky before making the trip back to Memphis and then flying in to Pope Air Force Base in the wee hours of the morning, adjacent to Fort Bragg. During that time Gant hadn't said a word and Golden had spent the time looking at her computer screen, trying to draw up long buried theories and writing.

Golden continued to hold Sam as he cried. She looked around Sam's head and shushed the man she now knew was a Special Agent. She could tell that he wasn't pleased, but he acquiesced by turning and searching for someone to speak to. Golden returned her attention to Sam and held him until the worst had passed. He straightened and leaned over to grab a couple of tissues. She ran her fingers through his hair. Even when she had seen him right out of bed, it had never appeared so askew. "It will be all right," Golden said, the words feeling as weak as they sounded.

He looked at her. "Thanks for coming. I was surprised when they said you would be here. You know, with your son and everything else that's happened. Seeing you now, I'm glad that you did."

"I'm glad I'm here." She looked around the room and wished they had more privacy. "What are all these people doing here?" She noted that Gant had drifted closer, listening.

"Standard procedure," Sam said. "The FBI says there's a good chance this could be for ransom. Goddamn." He covered his face with hands displaying a fine tremor. "But I've got nothing, I'm not rich. I'm just an Army colonel. Why would someone do this?"

"Sam, tell me what did they say to you?"

He kept his hands over his face as if the words needed a guide to escort them out of his mouth. "She was at the beach, you know- spring break. She was there with three of her friends, and they were staying in a condo. The last night, Emily got tired and wanted to go back to the condo. Bitches. They let her go by herself. When they got back to the condo, they couldn't get in. Emily had the key. Then they noticed her car wasn't there. Luckily one of them had my number from Emily and called me. I had to raise hell to get the cops to investigate. I knew she wouldn't disappear like that. They had to drive back to school that day."

Golden did think that was extremely lucky. She could see the cops getting real worried about a twenty-one year old missing from Spring Break. "What about the witnesses?"

"There were two kids. They saw Emily in the parking lot. They said she was alone walking to her car." His voice trailed off, as he turned to look at Gant. "Who are you?"

"Jack Gant."

Golden was surprised as Sam stood, gathering himself, putting out his hand. "Geez, you were in the Ranger Battalion, weren't you, back in '93? Mogadishu?"

Gant simply nodded. "Yeah."

"Bad time."

"Yeah."

"Why are you here?" Sam asked. Then it seemed to sink in and he glanced at Golden. "Why are you here? What's going on?"

"There won't be a ransom," Gant said.

Smooth, thought Golden, real smooth and subtle. She shot a dagger look at Gant but he ignored it.

"What do you mean?" Sam demanded.

He sat in the chair opposite Sam. "Tell me what got fucked up."

Emily sat bare breasted in a small circular clearing. That was the only geographical detail she knew. She had no idea what part of the country she was in, much less the state. After the long night, her focus was on shedding this shackle on her ankle. It was steel and very heavy; it looked very much like what prisoners shuffled to court wearing. She studied the lock. It looked the same as that of a handcuff, and to that end she was in the process of ripping apart her bra. It was proving difficult, and she would stop occasionally and take a few deep breaths and think about getting free.

She had checked her underarms, and decided there was about a day's growth. She shaved every day out of some fastidious habit, which many of her friends found obsessive. If, not when, she got home, she would take great pleasure in having such a novel time clock. The problem, as she was all too aware, was that many miles could have been driven since her underarm was last smooth.

She had no idea that a bra could be so well made. It seemed impossible to rip the stitching under the cups without destroying the entire thing. Emily had started with the vague notion that the bra could remain usable. Finally, with all her strength, which was already frighteningly weakened, she tore the underside of the bra away. She gave a little cheer, as the thin curved wire dropped to her lap. She carefully straightened one side of the under wire, and crossed her captive foot over the other and gave herself some slack. She glanced around and then looked up to the sun. It wasn't visible in the small patch of sky the trees left her, but she knew it was somewhere behind her. She wasn't sure of the time of day but figured in a few hours she would know. She hoped the loon had brought her here in the early morning. That meant she had some time for the lock.

She knew that if she broke the wire she was fucked, so she promised herself she would stop when it got dark. The thought of being chained for another night made her almost nauseas. She banished the thought and focused on the lock. The wire was very thin and at first she was hesitant. Finally she decided to double the wire, and carefully weave it into a sturdier probe. For a long time she was completely immersed in the task, and thought of little except the small clicks of her makeshift key in the locking mechanism. Almost dreamily she began to think of the man who had taken her. She knew it was around three in the morning, and assuming he drove straight to this destination for somewhere in the vicinity of two days, she could be just about anywhere.

She wondered where her kidnapper was. As long as he didn't return, she realized she didn't give a damn.

She pressed on the wire and the close end jabbed into her thumb, opening up a quarter inch long cut and releasing a surprisingly large amount of blood.

Emily cursed, licked the blood off as best she could, then pressed the wound against the skirt for several minutes to stem the flow.

Then she went back to work.

* * *

"I've run a lot of operations over the years," Sam Cranston said.

Gant simply stared at him. Golden was shifting in her seat, uncomfortable. Cranston had at first ignored Gant's question. There'd been a bit of a ruckus when the senior FBI agent had come over and demanded to know who exactly Gant and Golden were and what their jurisdiction in this case was. Gant had finally been forced to show the man his ID and then recited a phone number for the man to call to confirm that he had clearance and precedence here.

The agent had made the call and been none too thrilled with whatever he'd been told. He'd ordered all his personnel from the apartment leaving the three of them sitting there, the sad eye of a now departed hurricane of activity. At least two of the three were sad—Gant had waited out the turf war with a resigned apathy.

When the room was clear he had turned back to Cranston and simply stared at him, evoking the vague answer.

"We all have," Gant said. "And I know there are missions you are never supposed to speak of. To anyone, for any reason. It seems, though, as if someone has challenged that."

"How so?" Cranston asked, as Golden's eyes flicked back and forth between the two men. Gant knew she was out of her depth but he had no time to coach her.

"Someone is testing whether your loyalty to your oath or to your family is greater," Gant said. "And that someone also has a very good idea that somebody like me would show up here and ask you what I'm asking you." Gant reached into his pocket while Cranston digested that chain of logic. Gant looked at the piece of paper. "Cathy Svoboda. She was killed this morning. Throat sliced open, very smooth job. Her fiancée is a reservist. Pilot named Mark Lankin who flew missions for Task Force 160 over the years."

Gant could see Cranston's face go white on hearing about the death, but this was no time for subtlety.

"Ever fly with him?"

"I've flown with a lot of pilots in a lot of places," Cranston said. "The name doesn't ring any bells. Jesus. Come on. They're just people in the front seat. You know that."

Gant glanced at his notes. "Tracy Caulkins. Twenty-one years old, just like your daughter. Chained to a tree in the woods in Kentucky. Died of dehydration. We got part of her cache report at the site of your daughter's kidnapping. So we know this one is definitely connected."

Cranston's face got even whiter if that was possible. "You're saying whoever did this to this Caulkins girl has my Emily?"

"It seems pretty obvious."

"And Emily is—" Cranston couldn't complete the sentence.

Golden finally contributed something besides concerned looks. "It would fit the pattern. Which means she's still alive, Sam."

"Why is someone doing this?" Cranston asked.

"Whoever is doing this knows cache reports," Gant said.

Cranston struggled to see the logic. "So he's special ops?"

"They don't teach caches at Harvard."

Cranston swallowed. "Who is Caulkins related to?"

"Her father. DEA. Southern region."

For the first time Gant picked up the slightest of flicker of recognition in Cranston's eyes. "You worked Southern Command out of Panama for a while, right?" Gant pushed. "Ever meet him?"

Cranston nodded. "Yes. We bumped into each other occasionally. But we never ran an op together."

"Not even on Task Force Six?" Gant asked, seeing that they had left Golden far behind as he referred to the military units that were seconded to the DEA to help interdict drug traffickers.

Cranston shook his head. "When I was there we avoided doing Six work as much as possible."

"Like you had a choice?" Gant let the sarcasm drip.

Cranston put his hands on either side of his head, obviously trying to think. Or block out reality, Gant thought.

"We did missions," Cranston finally admitted. "The War on Drugs. Other stuff. Panama. Colombia. Peru. The Caribbean."

Gant leaned forward. "Does anything come immediately to mind? A mission that got messed up? Someone who feels like you screwed them over in their career? Maybe someone you sent to the big house and is now out?" The reference was to Leavenworth and Gant knew someone at the Cellar was already checking the records of recently released prisoners.

Cranston's brow was furrowed, but he slowly shook his head. "I've been in the Army over twenty-five years. Special Operations for over twenty. I can't remember everyone I worked with or those I disciplined in my various commands."

Gant glanced at Golden, hoping she would contribute something, given she knew the man. She had her hand on his arm, in a way that suggested a lot more than professional comfort. Gant realized that could be an advantage and considered whether to play it. Not yet.

Gant was about to speak when his Satphone vibrated. He pulled it out, listened to the succinct report and then closed it. "Another victim we think might be related. Caleigh Roberts. Nineteen. Killed last night on the Florida-Alabama border. Drowned in less than a foot of water. Her father works for the CIA. On what, they're not being forthcoming with, but I'll find out shortly. Ever heard of him?"

Cranston shook his head. "How is Roberts connected?"

"We don't know yet other than the timing and the fact she's a family member."

Cranston looked at Golden. "Why—" he seemed at a loss for words. He swallowed. "Why are you here?"

Gant sighed and waited.

Golden still had her hand on Cranston's arm. "I'm working with Gant."

Cranston shifted to Gant. "You're not NSA."

"No." Gant relaxed slightly knowing that Cranston was finally coming back to reality.

"And you won't tell me who you work for."

"You have no need to know."

"We'll get Emily back," Golden interjected.

Hope, Gant thought.

Cranston wasn't buying it either. "That's not your mission," he said to Gant.

Gant could feel Golden's eyes burning into his skull. He started to speak, then paused. Regroup, retreat, Gant thought. Take a different approach when things are different. "No, it's not. But." He sat back. "They're aligned. My mission is whoever snatched your daughter. The faster I get to him, the better the chance we find her alive."

"Why do you think she's alive?"

"Because of the cache report. Because whoever did this has something bigger in mind and this is just the beginning."

"How do you know that?" Cranston asked.

Gant could see that Golden was also interested in his answer.

"Because, as the good doctor has noted, whoever is doing this is playing us and there are moves yet to be made." Gant stood. "You need to think. About missions you ran and people you worked with that weren't ever recorded. We'll get all the recorded ones and go through them, so don't waste time on that. Make a list." He reached in his pocket and pulled out a card that just had a number on it. "Call me when you think of anything." He looked at Golden. "Let's go."

"Where?" Golden asked.

This was why Gant liked working alone. No need to explain things. "To the most recent incident site." Better phrased than 'the most recent body', Gant thought.

CHAPTER ELEVEN

EMILY'S FINGERS BLED more, which bothered her not so much because of the pain, but because the blood made holding the wire more difficult. She had tripled the wire, which, while strengthening it, had also correspondingly shortened it, making it more difficult to work with. All morning long she had made slight adjustments to the wire, bending it so slightly, there were times she wasn't sure she had actually even done anything to it.

Taking a break, she glanced up through the leaves of the oak tree and checked the sun's position. Mid-day, give or take an hour. She carefully put the wire down on a leaf and flexed her hands, feeling the pain as the cuts in her fingers pulsed out in protest. She ran her tongue around her lips, which were already cracking.

Emily shook her head. *Do not think about water.*

Think about something else. Something useful. She tried to remember the drive. How long had she been out? She didn't think it had been more than a day. She vaguely remembered that the van had stopped somewhere en route. She'd been awake for a little while. She glanced down at her arm, at the two puncture marks. He'd drugged her again. But there had been that moment of semi-awareness between the first injection wearing off and the second one kicking in.

Something about that stop nagged at her, begging to be remembered. Emily closed her eyes, blocking out, one by one, the input from her senses, focusing inward. The way her father had taught her to focus. She flowed backward into the memory of those senses.

Had it been something she saw? No, there had only been darkness until he took the blindfold off here in the forest.

Smell? It was the most powerful of the five senses, she knew that from her physiological psychology class.

Yes. Grass. Freshly cut.

Emily felt a slight prick of excitement. He had not planned for her to awaken during the trip. But she had. So he'd made a mistake. One mistake could mean he'd made others.

She opened her eyes and picked up the wire, sliding it into the lock, gingerly working it once more, her earlier weariness replaced by a surge of energy.

There was something else from that stop. She had been slipping into a drug-induced fog, but she knew she had made a discovery during that brief window of consciousness. Something else the man didn't know. She lost herself in the thought and the lock but nothing was forthcoming.

Finally, she once more noticed the sun overhead and was happy to have at least five more hours of sunlight. She stopped picking at the lock for a moment, and studied her tree and the position of the sun.

The side of the clearing facing her seemed to be west. Unless the loon had driven beyond her little prison, and walked her back to confuse her; she would go east when she got this fucking chain off her foot. Why would he try to confuse her though? Emily doubted he planned for her to escape this tree. She had been driven from Panama City and it had been less than a day. He would not have sped, not taking the chance of getting pulled over with a blindfolded, drugged girl in the back.

Sixteen hours. Seventy miles an hour.

Emily felt some of her new-found confidence slip as she realized that added up to over eleven hundred miles. A damn big circle. The entire southeast, then north to Virginia, west into Texas. She knew that she wasn't in Florida any more: too many deciduous trees. Staring at the deep green of the newly leafed trees Emily started remembering, conjuring up the smell of green: freshly-cut grass with a mix of pungent wild onions. And then, like the gentle clicking of a metronome, she heard the wire scraping the steel and her memory fell into consciousness. The music. She had heard music then when the van had stopped. It was a canned metallic sound coming from poor-quality speakers. She could see from another memory the speakers nailed to the trees surrounding the small brick and wood building. And everywhere there is the perfectly coiffed grass around the rest area. She and her friends had driven to New Orleans many times from Auburn. The last rest stop on the Interstate before you leave the highway plays Cajun music. Once she and Lisa had stopped to pee and fell into an impromptu dance on the lawn.

She had been there. She tried to remember how long the drive from school had taken. If she factored in the additional time of leaving from Panama City that made it about four hours. If the drug wore off around the time the loon pulled onto that rest stop, then she was initially unconscious four hours. She supposed he would maintain the same travel time, so that by the time of her next and, she was sure, last shot they had traveled five hundred more miles. If he had continued west that would put her somewhere in Texas. But she didn't know of any place in Texas this well forested. If he had turned north at any time she could really be anywhere in Louisiana or Arkansas. Not Louisiana she decided looking around, unless it was the far northern part of the state. Most likely Arkansas.

The important thing was that she had some idea of her geographical location, and a direction to take if she ever got out of the shackle. She dropped all other thoughts, and focused on picking the lock. She smiled. If someone had seen her at that moment, he or she would have been stunned at the beautiful half-naked, young girl wearing a small smile of self-satisfaction. She appeared the most relaxed and confident of women.

The Sniper frowned at her smile and change in demeanor. It filled the lens of his scope and he placed the reticule right on her white teeth, his finger sliding over the trigger. It would be so easy to take away the smile and her entire essence.

But he was not that tempted. She was a piece of the plan. There were bigger and better things in store for her. She was the linchpin around which the entire plan revolved. He put the rifle down and leaned back in his camp chair set in the three-foot deep hole. He'd built the blind two hundred meters away from the oak tree, carefully camouflaging the top and leaving just a small slit in front so that he observe the target. There was a large hole in the back so that he could come and go without being spotted.

The Sniper knew what would wipe the smile off the girl's face. He reached in to his pocket and pulled out a small piece of plastic. He looked at her picture on the license. She had not been smiling when the photo was taken.

That had been smart of her, dropping it. But after chaining her to the tree, he'd checked their back trail, making sure it was covered, and found it just as she'd intended, except, of course, in the hope some would-be rescuer would have picked it up.

He took the license and ran one hard corner along the scar on the side of his head, trying to cure the itch that burned there.

It didn't help. He knew it wouldn't. There was only one thing that would cure that itch.

When the plan came together.

He slid the license back into his pocket. He would take the smile off her face tonight.

* * *

Gant watched Golden sleep. It was a short flight to Pensacola, and then there would be a drive to the coast. Golden had fallen asleep as soon as she fastened her seat belt. He was unhappy with her presence, especially after realizing her previous relationship with Colonel Cranston. Gant knew that Nero would never bow to any external pressure regarding a Sanction. But the woman behind the desk, Masterson, he knew nothing about her. Was Golden here because she was to truly be an asset or because Cranston, or someone Cranston knew who had some real power, was pulling strings? So far Golden had contributed nothing to the investigation in Gant's opinion.

"Better watch out; your head is going to burst into flames."

Gant looked into her now open eyes. "You have a bit of drool on your chin."

She didn't take the bait. "Lets just talk about it. No way are we going to be able to work together when you're acting like you got the slow girl in a three-legged race."

"What do you mean?" He tried to look surprised.

"Please do not treat me like an idiot. I know you don't want me tagging along, but that's ok. You don't know me, and you don't know my work. I understand that I haven't proven myself to you, but I don't understand this other thing: this dislike you're carrying around when you specifically don't know me."

"I don't know why I need a psychologist on this mission."

She reached into her backpack and pulled out a small laptop. "Because of what I know and what's in here."

Gant didn't like being baited into asking the obvious, so he waited.

"Speed is of the essence in tracking these perps down," Golden finally said.

"If the Cranston girl is still alive," Gant noted.

"You know she's alive," Golden shot back.

"How do I know that?"

"Because she's bait."

Score one for the shrink, Gant thought.

"The bait for what?" Gant asked.

Golden shrugged. "That, I don't know. If it were simple revenge, Emily would be dead. There has got to be a reason they're keeping her alive."

"You said *perps* and *they*."

"Are you asking how I know there's more than one or questioning my choice of terms?"

"Both."

"If you're going to ask me things you already know," Golden said, a trace of irritation crossing her face, "then we're going to waste a lot of time. You know there's got to be more than one person doing these crimes simply because of the logistics and distances involved."

Gant nodded, giving her that point.

"As far as the term perp, that comes from my background with the FBI. I was with Behavioral Sciences in Quantico for eight years before going to Fort Bragg."

Gant wished someone would have told him that. But it made her actions at the first site near the lake kind of strange. Unless she had never done field-work.

"I call them targets," Gant said.

"You would."

"You didn't do field work," Gant said it as a statement.

"You know I didn't from observing me with the body."

Gant began to wonder if they needed to talk about anything. She seemed far along the curve of his thoughts, which made uneasy. "Why did you leave the FBI?"

"I didn't. I was sent to Bragg to help Special Operations Command set up its own database. I was still assigned to the Bureau."

"A database of perps in Special Ops?"

"Profiling isn't just for bad people." Golden flipped up the lid to the laptop. "You can profile anyone. I did profiles of everyone serving in SOCOM. I also worked on profiling various positions and the type of person who would best be suited for filling that position."

Gant frowned. He'd never heard of this but it made sense. "And that's how you met Colonel Cranston?"

"Yes."

He noted she wasn't being forthcoming about that. "I still don't see how your profiling can help on this Sanction."

"I was at Special Operations Command to ostensibly evaluate personnel for assignments." Golden spread her hands. "But it's obvious someone else had something else planned since I'm here now. I suspect someone had something secondary in mind, especially given my background working with perps."

Nero, Gant thought. Always planning. Always seeding people. Sometimes waiting years for the seeds to grow and bear fruit. Which made him wonder about Masterson and how she had been seeded and cultivated. Gant waited on Golden to continue, tired of the sparring and digging.

"When I was with the FBI I was still a psychologist; I just didn't see patients any more. I was building a nation-wide database to catch serial killers by using available information. I took clues, evidence or an actual list of suspects, and tried to identify the one person whose past most closely fits the evidence of the present crime."

Gant nodded. "As you said, you're a kind of profiler."

Golden shook her head. "Not exactly. I was doing something new, something different. A profiler uses the evidence to describe the type of human being capable of the crime. My section took the profile, and tried to find the human being capable of that type of evidence. We had records beginning from the early 50's, which is about the time that information collection became common. We used anything from emergency room records to a school nurse's recording of a child's peculiar scars."

"So you think you're going to find these guys by checking out their high school truancy report?"

"That's a stupid remark. My program at the FBI faltered because the country's population was so big, and the available information on each particular person so scanty. To prove my program worked, I needed a smaller number database with more available information on each individual."

"The Army."

Golden nodded. "Yes. And not even the entire Army, but rather a specific subsection of it, Special Operations, where there are extensive records on each individual and their backgrounds and their training highly scrutinized and recorded."

"To look for serial killers?"

"No. At least that wasn't what I was told. Officially SOCOM wanted to get better at identifying the types of soldiers in its units and which ones were successful and which ones weren't so that could refine their recruitment and training process. Also, I worked with the Special Warfare Training Center, which Sam commanded, in their selection and assessment process."

Gant remembered the psychological screening process he'd gone through years ago when he'd gone into his first Special Operations unit. He mentally processed what Golden had just told him. "So you can check your database and try to find the targets that would do these things?"

"Yes. At least get us a ballpark list."

"And you planned on doing this when?"

"When you're done asking me questions." She paused. "However, I've been off the job for a year, so I need to update my database."

Gant held up a hand. "Wait. I need to understand this. I work off what I see, hard evidence. You're working off of theory. You give me a target, I'm not going to be reading him a Miranda warning. I'm going to be pointing a gun at his head with my finger on the trigger. I need more than just a best guess."

"I'm not guessing," Golden said. "I have spent most of my professional career working on the theory behind predictive indicators. Before I was recruited into the FBI I was in private practice, dealing mostly with young adults in the court system. After a few years of dealing with the broken psyches that a truly dysfunctional home can produce, I was left wondering why only a handful of men, because they are always men, become sexual sadists and murderers. At first I thought it was the depth of the abuse. Then I wondered if it was the length of the abuse. After years of investigating the backgrounds of true sexual sadists, I became of the opinion that it was the perversity of the abuse that set the stage for killing. Sometimes, I think there may be a genetic code for sadism, and that the parent introduces the stressor which produces the inevitable psychic break."

Gant took the opportunity to voice his opinion. "That's exactly the kind of crap I hate. I don't give a shit how fucked your childhood is, if you're not crazy, and these guys aren't in the legal sense of the word, your behavior is a choice. Like you said, women don't commit these crimes, yet they come from places just as fucked up. I know your work is important, but you're just giving these guys an excuse."

"OK, now I want you to tell me what you really think." Surprisingly she was smiling.

Gant realized she'd pushed him for a reaction and he'd fallen into it.

Golden leaned forward. "What my research does is to help catch these killers. I don't care if it gives them an excuse from here to China. The point is that if we can track some guy down by the cigarette burns on his feet from childhood then great.

"Of course, it's not as simple as that. But I know it can work because we did track down a killer using the database when I was at the FBI. They gave me the scene of the crime, and I gave the agents conditions that could produce such a sadistic response. And we were lucky, because the situation indicated the killer was based at Fort Sill and I was allowed access to the personnel files of everyone there."

"Tell me about it," Gant said, intrigued in spite of his misgivings.

"We had three bodies within six months all found in abandoned sheds around small farms on the outskirts of Fort Sill. The women were different races, different ages and had different builds so the conventional profilers were having trouble from the get-go. The victims had all been strangled and they also had severe postmortem injuries. They had all been violated with branches from nearby trees. Also, the branches became larger with each murder, so that the last victim was basically ripped in half to accommodate what was essentially a tree limb." She stopped talking and leaned back covering her eyes with a hand as if blocking out the picture.

"I thought you didn't do field work," Gant said.

"I did all this from Quantico. They gave me access to the photos and videos of the crime scenes."

For a moment Gant felt sorry for her. She knew too much. Had seen too many things that were beyond comprehension. He realized he had ascribed the wrong motives for her reaction at the kill scene in Tennessee. But the feeling passed quickly.

Golden finished the story. "The reinvention here was the branch. That the victims were killed by manual strangulation meant that there was strong emotion involved. The killer hated these women and killed them in a brutal but also sexualized manner. The signature of the murders, the tree branches, occurred after death.

"The victims shared no physical traits, so one must assume that they themselves were of little importance to the fantasy of this killer. The postmortem violation evolved as the killings continued. This to me was significant. I began my search in the medical records for boys or adolescents abused with branches or wood of any type. I found a medical report for a ten-year old boy born in Oklahoma. He had been hospitalized because, according to his mother, he had been climbing a tree and fell. On his way down, he hit a limb and drove a small branch up his rectum, which perforated his abdominal wall. The boy was also covered with bruises and he had old bondage scars. He was taken from his mother and placed in foster care. His mother successfully litigated for custody. He was returned to live with her. Unsupervised. After that he joined the army, but luckily for us his medical records followed him and he was arrested for the three murders. He confessed within thirty minutes."

"Shit." Gant wondered if the whole world was mad.

"No shit." Golden wasn't smiling, but she did seem to understand his thoughts.

"So when are you going to run this program?" Gant asked.

"It's been running," Golden said. "It takes a while but I really don't have enough data yet."

"You mean killings."

"I also need to update my data at Bragg."

"Why were you living on Hilton Head?" Gant asked, the unexpected question causing her to stare at him in surprise.

"After my son--" she paused. "I was offered free use of a house there."

"By who?"

"A man from Special Operations Command. Why do you ask?"

"I was living on Pritchards Island. One island up the coast. For a year and a half. Nero knew this. I don't think you were offered a house so close to me by chance."

Both fell silent as the plane banked and descended, taking them toward another scene of violence.

* * *

Emily tried to control her breathing as she increased the pressure on the wire. It had taken her four hours to get to this point. The near end pushed deeper into the open wounds on the tips of her fingers but she ignored the pain. She was on the latch, she was sure of it. And it was moving. Just a little bit more—

A guttural cry escaped her lips as the wire snapped, the bloody remnant slipping from her fingers and falling into the dirt. Emily began sobbing and this time she couldn't stop. She curled into a tight ball, arms clasped around her knees, the sudden defeat layered on top of the strain of the past twenty-four hours breaking through her dam of resolve.

From his hide position, the Sniper calmly watched the girl. Then he nodded to himself as he gathered his gear, confident she wasn't going anywhere any time soon. Most importantly, she wasn't smiling any more.

CHAPTER TWELVE

GANT LOOKED UP from the police report and watched the vacationers blissfully walking along the beach, unaware that a girl had been killed here the previous night.

"Hard to keep a crime scene intact with the tide," Golden noted. She looked at Gant. "Why are we here?"

"Unlike you, I have to be on site. I want to get a feel for the target."

"Targets."

"That bothers me," Gant said as he walked onto the beach, Golden reluctantly following. "Did you find much evidence in your data gathering of a team of killers?"

"There have occasionally been pairs of killers," Golden said. "The DC snipers. The Hillside Stranglers—Bianchi and Buono. Even cases of a small team, from two to five people."

Gant came to a halt next to piece of PVC pipe stuck upright in the sand, the only way the police had been able to mark the site of the murder. The tide was out, but according to the report, there would have been about a foot of water at this spot when the girl was killed.

Golden obviously took his silence as an indication she was to continue. "Such a team is always led by a central figure who has a very specific fantasy. This fantasy gives energy to the other members of the team and they channel themselves to serve him. Often, without this central figure, the others would probably never cross the line into criminal activity. However, they all have psychotic traits to some degree and while some claim, after they get caught, that they were unwilling accomplices, the reality is that it is very difficult to coerce someone into murder."

"That's why we have armies," Gant noted. "Sanctioned killing."

Golden nodded. "Yes. It's a delicate and controversial subject that occasionally came up during my work at Fort Bragg. Because technically speaking, often we were looking for people who could kill on command. Without remorse or hesitation, yet also follow orders."

"Someone like me," Gant said.

That silenced Golden for the moment.

Gant intruded into the silence. "You said fantasy. There's been no evidence of anything sexual with any of the victims."

"A fantasy doesn't have to be sexual," Golden said. "It's an unreal framework someone makes up in their mind to allow them to justify whatever it is they're doing."

"I assume revenge can be a framework then?"

"One of the strongest."

A car door slammed and Gant looked inland to see Padgett walking toward them. The Cellar's forensic expert had already been on scene for several hours and participated in the autopsy on the Roberts girl, right after leaving the autopsy on the girl they had found chained to the tree. He also had been in contact with the Cellar, gathering more data. He had deep bags under his eyes.

"Anything significant from the Caulkins girl?" Gant asked him.

"Dehydration was the cause of death, as I said at the scene," Padgett said. "The self-injury to the foot didn't help things. There were nuts and grass in her stomach, undigested. Toxicology was interesting. She'd been drugged with something easily available so that's not a lead. I only found trace amounts so her system had mostly flushed it, but I think that's how our target was able to transport her from the site where she was kidnapped."

"What do you have on this one?" Gant asked.

Padgett wiped his forehead with an already sopping handkerchief. "Drowned. Salt water in the lungs."

Gant glanced at the PVC pipe. Even at high tide it wouldn't have been very deep. "In one foot of water?"

"She was held down by the neck and back of the head," Padgett said. "Strange thing, though. There were marks on her neck and head, but not like any I've ever seen before." He reached into the thin file folder he was carrying and pulled out a photo.

Gant looked at the close-up of the girl's neck, ignoring the unseeing eyes that stared at him from the glossy paper. The bruises were spaced where fingers would go. Then the next photo showed the back of her skull, the hair shaved off. The same, evenly spaced marks. "What's strange about them?" He shifted, showing the picture to Golden who was close by his side. Too close. Gant caught a whiff of some fragrance, he wasn't sure what it was.

"After the photo was taken," Padgett said, "we cut and checked the flesh underneath. Either someone with extremely powerful hands or—" he shrugged—"some sort of hand-like device was used, in order to make the extreme damage we saw. There were hairline fractures in her skull."

"Prostheses?" Gant asked. Ever since the mess in Iraq, more and more troops were coming back missing pieces and parts. Body armor was effective in keeping people alive, but only went so far.

Padgett nodded. "I should have thought of that. That would explain it."

"So we're looking for a killer who is possibly missing a hand," Golden said.

"And another whose face is scarred," Gant added, remembering the report from the Svoboda killing. He tried to think of what would cause the scarring the boy at the daycare center had reported, but the details were too vague and the possible ways of getting wounded on the modern battlefield too wide. "Any sign of sexual assault?" Gant asked, even though the initial report had been negative. Golden's comment about fantasies still bothered him.

"None. But whoever held her head underwater pushed her so hard into the sand, we found abrasions on her eyes and sand in her mouth and lungs. She inhaled quite a bit of sand along with seawater."

"God," Golden whispered. "That's a lot of anger."

"Add it to your database," Gant said dryly.

"And what did you add to your database?" Golden snapped. She spread her arms. "Why did we come here?"

"It's the scene of the freshest kill," Gant said. "One-Hand was here less than twenty-four hours ago. And I don't think this spot was chosen randomly. The cache site was specifically scouted and picked."

"One-Hand?"

"We need to start getting this mission categorized," Gant said. "We've got two, possibly three targets. One-Hand and Scar-Face for certain. And there's probably another."

"Why do you think that?" Padgett asked, sliding the photo back in the folder.

"If Emily Cranston is bait," Gant said, "then someone's watching her. So let's accept there's a third and call him the Watcher." A team of three. Gant nodded to himself. He'd have to run that by the Cellar's own database of covert operations. Small enough to get in and out of places without being noticed, large enough to do damage. Off the top of his head, Gant figured it had been either a reconnaissance or sniper team. He noted that the parking lot of the Florabama was already filling up with a late afternoon crowd.

"Popular place," Golden said, following his gaze.

"Life goes on," Gant said. It was one of the reasons he lived on Pritchards Island: the contrast of coming back from a place of violence such as Iraq to the 'normalcy' of day to day living in America had always been too jarring for him.

Padgett was looking at the police report. "And One-Hand was able to do this and no one, according to the police report, remembers seeing him. Roberts just disappeared into the crowd and then ended up here. She wasn't dragged out kicking and screaming."

"So she went willingly," Golden said.

"Why would she do that?" Gant asked. "Go off with a stranger?"

Golden looked at him. "She was on Spring Break. She probably felt like she was on top of the world and could do whatever she wanted. Also the crowd probably gave her a false sense of security. We think there's safety in numbers when it's often the exact opposite."

Gant agreed with that: which was why he preferred working alone, but he didn't think this was the time to bring that up.

"Any drugs in her system?" Golden asked Padgett.

He nodded. "Marijuana. Her blood alcohol was high. One point two."

"Another reason she went off with a stranger," Golden said.

"Are we sure it was a stranger?" Gant asked. "Maybe it was somebody she knew. Her father was CIA. Could have been someone she met through her father."

"I don't think so." Golden was looking at the photos. "Although the extreme violence would indicate that might be a possibility, the condition of this body and the others makes me think they were strangers. And violence was transmuted."

"Say again?" Gant said.

Golden looked up from the file. "Quite often when the killer knows the victim, even if the actual killing is violent, subsequent to the act, there is an attempt at psychological detachment from the act. Often in the form of the body being hidden or even just covered with a blanket."

"All right," Gant allowed. "I'll go with you on that. Three killers. Who didn't know their victims. Chose them because of their fathers or fiancé in the case of Svoboda." He glanced up at the sky. "What about weather as I requested?" he asked Padgett. He could see Golden's confused look at the question but he ignored her.

Padgett pulled out another folder. "For the location where Tracy Caulkins was left, there were only two instances of rain in the past three weeks since she was reported missing until her estimated time of death. A total of an eighth of an inch."

Gant frowned. "That's not enough water to sustain her that long."

Padgett nodded. "I agree."

"There was no sign she had any container to store some at the site, right?" Gant asked.

"None was found."

"And the prediction for the southeast?" Gant asked.

"Some storm activity later this week covering most of the area."

"So Emily can drink," Golden said, finally catching on.

"Yeah," Gant said, his mind on the fact that the Caulkins girl had not had enough rain to sustain her as long as she had lived. "So the Watcher gave Caulkins water."

"'The Watcher'?" Padgett asked and Gant quickly filled him on the titles he had made up for the three targets.

Padgett nodded. "Someone had to have given Caulkins water and it most likely had to be this Watcher fellow. Anyone else would have freed her or reported it."

Gant blinked as he suddenly realized what he'd been missing. "The Florabama."

Golden turned to look at him. "Yes?"

Gant pointed straight up the shoreline. "We're standing on the Florida-Alabama border. He reached out with his other hand and placed it on the PVC pipe. "Roberts was killed literally straddling the border."

"That's not coincidence," Golden said, not quite a question, not quite a statement.

"No, it's not." Gant headed back toward the car. "I need to talk to Colonel Cranston again." He looked at her. "And you need to update your database."

Emily opened her eyes to darkness. How long ago the sun had set, she had no idea. She wished that she could have remained unconscious through the night as she tried to look around her. She could only make out a few stars through spaces in the oak tree's branches and leaves above her head. All around was utter darkness. She was lying on her back and she slowly sat up, feeling the weight of the shackle on her leg.

She tried to remember the phase of the moon. A small thing, but something that was very important now. Her stomach rumbled and she felt a surge of bile come up her throat. She fought to keep from throwing up, knowing she had no water to wash the bitterness out of her mouth if she did.

She stretched her hands out, feeling the pain in her fingertips from the wire and that reminded her of failure.

She forced her mind away from that and cocked her head, listening.

Once more it struck her that she had never realized how noisy the woods were at night. There were the sounds of numerous crickets, birds and other small creatures—a veritable chorus all around her. As a cool breeze swept across her, Emily suddenly realized she didn't have her shirt on. She quickly tugged it on. It bothered her that she had been half-naked for so long, and it bothered her even more that she had not noticed it. Just over twenty-four hours and she was already losing her veneer of civilization. She put her back to the tree and adjusted the heavy shackle around her ankle into the least painful arrangement.

She was thirsty.

She couldn't hold it in denial. Her mouth was parched, her lips cracked. Her stomach was twisted in a painful knot. How long could one last without water? She couldn't remember. She was sure she had heard it somewhere, from her father perhaps, or the Learning Channel, an arcane piece of knowledge that had not been significant enough at the time to remember. Now it was all consuming. Was it days or a week? Maybe two weeks?

Emily felt a surge of panic boil up from her stomach into her chest, causing her heart to race. Once more, the most important matter surged to the forefront of her mind: How long could she last here without water?

She tucked her knees up to her chest, wrapping her arms around them. As the sobs wracked her body, she rocked back and forth. She tried, time and time again, to regain control, but she couldn't.

Not for a long time. And it bothered her that crying meant she was losing precious water, even in the smallest amount.

The thing that stopped her was the reality slowly seeping through her emotional pain, that everything had gone quiet. No insects. No birds. No small creatures.

The forest was completely silent.

Emily lifted her head and peered about, trying to penetrate the darkness. To no avail.

Even the breeze had stopped. Perfect stillness. Except a branch snapped somewhere, not far away. Emily felt her heart freeze. She was uncertain from which direction the sound had come.

There was the rustle of something moving through the underbrush and Emily's head snapped to her left. It was behind her, on the other side of the tree. She reached down and grabbed the chain, pulling it as she tried to move counter-clockwise around the thick trunk so she could get a better angle on that direction. For about two feet the chain rotated, then it jammed on something and she couldn't move any further. She leaned sideways, trying to pierce the darkness with her eyes.

To no avail.

Emily realized she wasn't breathing, so intent was she on listening. She swallowed and took a shallow breath, but then couldn't control her lungs, gasping for oxygen in a spasm of need and panic.

Something was coming, even through her panic, she could hear it. Emily screamed, surprising herself with the surge of anger.

"Get away from me! Get away!"

There was a low growl and Emily pressed back away from it, as far as the chain would allow. "Get away!"

* * *

The Sniper was watching the wild dog through a thermal scope, the animal a bright red glow as it approached the tree. He had seen wild dogs in the area during his reconnaissance and knew they were a potential problem. All the more reason for his surveillance.

He centered the reticules on the dog's head, then changed his mind and lowered the muzzle of the rifle slightly. He exhaled, emptying his lungs, feeling the rhythm of his heart. The dog was picking up speed, charging toward the tree and the girl.

He fired, the suppressor keeping the sound of the round leaving the barrel to a low cough, the specially loaded subsonic round not breaking the sound barrier as it sped down range. The round creased across the dog's back, leaving a quarter inch furrow.

The dog yelped and spun about, galloping madly for the safety of the trees.

Emily heard the yelp and then she braced herself until she realized whatever creature was out there was going away. It crashed through the underbrush on the far side of the clearing. Emily's breathing slowly returned to normal as did the sounds of the forest. She curled into a ball, arms locked around her knees and sobbed, adding her cries to those of the creatures around her as the forest resumed its normal chorus.

Gant pulled the black Chevy blazer they had requisitioned at Pope Air Force Base up to Cranston's house. He left the engine running as he opened the door.

"What are you doing?" Golden asked.

Gant indicated the driver's seat. "You take this to Special Ops personnel. You're cleared to access all their records. Update your database."

"I want to go in with—"

"No."

"Sam is—"

"No." Gant leaned toward Golden. "You do your job and I'll do mine. There's no need for both of us to talk to Cranston. Let me get what I can here and you do your thing. Then we compare notes. We don't have time to be arguing."

Golden looked like she was going to say something, then she simply nodded. She got out of the passenger seat, walked around, and took the driver's. She slammed the door shut and drove off with a squeal of tires. Gant wasted no time reflecting on her anger, focusing his attention on the house as he strode up the short walkway. He rang the bell and the door was opened within a few seconds—Cranston had been expecting him after a phone call from Ms. Smith at the Cellar. Just as someone at Special Operations Command would be waiting for Golden when she got there. When the Cellar called, doors opened, no questions asked.

Before Cranston could say anything, Gant pushed his way in as he spoke. "We're looking for three men, maybe more. Not one. They were part of a mission involving Michael Caulkins of the DEA, you, Mark Lankin a reserve pilot in Task Force 160, and Jim Roberts of the CIA. We know two of the men we're looking for were wounded or injured somehow: one lost a hand, the other's face was scarred."

"Three men?" Cranston's brow was furrowed. "How do you know that?"

"I'm asking the questions," Gant said. He stood, waiting, as Cranston went over to the small kitchen bar. Gant saw that there was an open bottle of Scotch and a half-full glass. He could tell by the slight slur in Cranston's voice that the Colonel had been indulging. Trying to dull the pain.

"I've been thinking, remembering, trying to put things together," Cranston said. "I don't remember the pilot's name. They're just figures in the front of the chopper and God knows how many helicopters I've been on. I checked and Caulkins and Roberts were in Panama the same time I was. I was Southern Command's Special Operations liaison to—well, you know, the other organizations down there. Which meant I coordinated Task Force Six missions—counter drug operations. We did around ten or so. Several involved three man teams. Usually sniper teams—sniper, surveillance, security, standard set-up. Most of the times just observing and reporting. A couple of times taking down high profile targets in the drug trade. Different places. Colombia, El Salvador, even in Panama."

"Let's narrow it down," Gant said. "Which of the missions got fucked up?"

Cranston finished off the half glass and poured himself another. "We lost one of the teams. In Colombia. But it can't be them."

"How do you know that?"

"They were killed in a chopper crash. Accident."

"When?"

"A little over a year ago. In Colombia."

"Were the bodies recovered?"

Cranston's eyes shifted to the right. "No."

"So how do you know they died?"

"The chopper went down at sea right off the coast. No survivors."

Gant watched as Cranston gulped down half of the new glass he had just poured. He considered the fact that one of the men whose family had been targeted was a helicopter pilot. But a pilot who was still alive. That didn't add up with a chopper crashing with no survivors.

"What about Emily?" Cranston asked. "Any idea where she is?"

"No." Gant waited, but Cranston said nothing. "Other than the team you lost, any of the other missions have something happen where the team members might want to have some heavy payback against you and the other players running the ops?"

Cranston shook his head, too quickly in Gant's opinion. "No. We didn't lose anyone else. They all went fine."

Gant had had enough. He walked toward the Colonel, stopping on the other side of the bar. As Cranston brought the glass up to finish it off, Gant struck out with his right hand, snatching it out of the Colonel's hand, then throwing it into the sink, where the glass shattered.

"What the hell—"

"Your daughter's life is at stake and you're sitting here getting drunk and bullshitting me," Gant said.

Cranston rubbed his hands across his face. "I've told you all I know."

"I don't think so," Gant said. "Give me your car keys."

"Why?"

"You're going with me to SOCOM. And I'm driving."

The Sniper wore night vision goggles as he followed the blood trail. It was a difficult task, but the Sniper had been trained by native-born trackers in Borneo as part of his Special Forces schooling. He'd learned many tricks, one of the most important of which was not just to follow the sign, but to think like the quarry and project the course it would take.

The dog was in pain and bleeding. It would not suspect something was following it. Thus the Sniper knew it would be on a relatively direct path to find someplace to hide while it literally licked its wounds. Someplace it probably already knew about.

So the Sniper was able to move fast, projecting a straight line from each piece of blood spatter he found, taking into account the lay of the land, knowing the dog would instinctually try to maintain a level course in addition to a straight one.

A half-mile away from the cache site, the Sniper came to a halt and sniffed the air. There was the faintest hint of blood in the air. He got to one knee and shrugged off his backpack. He pulled out an Army issue Meal-Ready-to-Eat. He ripped open the packet containing meat and tossed it ahead of him about five feet and then waited for the scent to reach the dog.

It took over a half hour, during which the Sniper remained perfectly still. Finally he heard the dog coming forward, drawn by its instinct and desire for food. It came forward, head down, sniffing. Through the night vision goggles, the Sniper could see how starved the dog was, how its ribs protruded. He could also see the bloody furrow the bullet had dug across its neck.

The dog reached the food packet and hunger over-rode everything else. It tore into the meat. With one smooth movement, the Sniper lunged forward, knife extended. He slit the dog's throat, letting the blood spray down into the ground.

The dog was dead within ten seconds, its lifeless body sprawled in the dirt. The Sniper straddled the body and reversed the knife, serrated edge down, and went to work.

CHAPTER THIRTEEN

A RATHER UNHAPPY-LOOKING major with the insignia of the finance corps was waiting for Golden in the lobby of Special Operations Command. He escorted her through the security check-point and they got on the elevator to ride to the floor holding the personnel records.

"What's so important that it can't wait until morning?" the Major asked.

Golden looked at his name-tag. "Major Taggart. You have your orders, correct?"

Taggart glanced at her. "All I was told by my CO was to give you access to whatever you wanted."

"That's all you need to know."

"I remember you." Taggart said it not as a question but as a statement. "You used to work here."

"I did." Golden couldn't ever remember meeting Taggart before, but she knew the building was a cauldron of rumor and gossip.

"You're the profiler. From the FBI. I heard some stuff about you."

Golden said nothing as they walked down the corridor to a locked door. She had no doubt her work here had been the subject of much talk and her abrupt departure cause for even more tongues to wag. And there had probably been words spoken about her brief relationship with Sam Cranston. It hadn't been any different at the FBI: in a male-dominated profession, the actions of every woman were watched most closely.

A sign above the door read: *SOCOM G-1: Personnel.* Taggart swiped a coded card through the lock and it disengaged. He swung the door open and they entered a large room full of desks with computers on them. A nerve center of Army bureaucracy. Except in this case it was highly classified bureaucracy.

One thing that had surprised Golden when she worked in this building was the amazingly low tooth-to-tail ratio in the Army: the number of soldiers with boots on the ground actually able to engage the enemy as opposed to the number of soldiers who spent their time supporting those on the ground. There were almost four of the latter for every one of the former. She'd found that those men who volunteered for Special Operations training often were leaving regular Army units because of their intense desire to be 'where the action is'. In many cases, their wishes were not granted as they were assigned duty to a desk pushing paper or, in the modern age, electronic data through a computer.

"If you tell me what you're looking for, perhaps I can help?" Taggart offered.

Golden pulled her laptop out. "I just need to be patched in to your most current personnel database."

"We can use my desk," Taggart said. He led her over to his computer. It took only a minute to patch the laptop in to the system via a USB port.

Golden brought up her profiling predictor program. She began downloading the thousands of personnel files. "Is there a way to cross-reference people who worked together?"

Taggart nodded. "I can group-tag them according to assignments."

"Do that. Then I'll load that program." She had been thinking about what they knew about the targets—perps, she mentally chided herself, surprised she was falling into Gant-speak in her thoughts. "Also, you have access to their medical records, right?"

"Yes."

"I need a listing of anyone with a hand prostheses. Also face scarring."

Taggart sat at his computer and began typing. Golden watched the indicator on her laptop showing the progress of the download. She glanced over at Taggart. He was engrossed in his own task. As the download continued, given that she was hooked into the G-1 database, she began to type commands into her computer. Commands that had nothing to do with the task at hand.

Gant looked at the fourteen-foot high statue of 'Bronze Bruce' as he pulled up to the front of the new headquarters for Special Operations Command. "Wait in the car," he ordered Cranston.

"Hold on here—" Cranston began to protest, but a glare from Gant was enough to silence him. As insurance, Gant took the keys with him as he got out of the car. The Colonel had added nothing of note during the drive but Gant could almost feel the angst coming off the man as he thought back on his past and what might have caused the current situation. Gant still believed Cranston was lying to him about something.

Pausing in front of the statue, Gant remembered when it had been on main post, next to the old JFK Special Warfare Museum and across the street from the Special Warfare Center headquarters. Few in Special Forces felt any special affinity for the somewhat less than manly looking statue. However, Gant paused and looked at the bronze plaques bolted to the low concrete wall behind the statue and felt the stirrings of feelings long buried. On them were listed the names of those Special Operations men who had died in combat since Vietnam. It was a long list for a country that considered itself to have been primarily at peace since the end of that conflict, at least until the last couple of years. He noted that several new plaques had been bolted on since the dual invasions of Iraq and Afghanistan.

He walked to the left, going back in time and saw the names of the two Delta Force operators who'd been killed in Mogadishu trying to rescue a downed helicopter crew from Task Force 160. He wondered how many civilians even remembered that failed peace-keeping effort or the videos of the bodies being dragged through the streets. Gant remembered it most clearly, most often when he wished he wouldn't. He knew Nero believed that the war on terrorism had really thrown down the gauntlet there, when the bad guys, particularly Osama Bin Laden, believed the withdrawal meant the US was weak when it pulled out after that debacle.

He scanned the names, looking for those of other men he had known. Men who had died on missions with him or in the same area of operations. He spotted a few, the places and occasions of their death as listed in the bronze letters a blatant lie in some cases. At least the names were there though, which was more than could be said about some of the men who had disappeared or died on classified missions in places they weren't supposed to be. Men who had died in places that the US government would never acknowledge they had sent American fighting men to or on missions that could never be acknowledged as being sponsored by the United States. Men whose families had been told that they had died during training accidents. A surprising number of special operations helicopters had crashed at sea and the bodies never recovered. Which was another reason he didn't quite believe Cranston's story. If the story about that three man team was a cover-up, then they should have come up with some original cover-story rather than the tried and true chopper crash.

He scanned until he found three names dated the previous year. Died in a helicopter crash during training:

Joseph Lutz

Michael Payne

Lewis Forten

Gant noted that they were all Army and the plaque indicated they had been assigned to 7th Special Forces Group. Location of death was listed as Panama. He also noticed that on the day listed there was no corresponding loss of pilots from Task Force 160. It was possible that the chopper had been flown by a non-Special Operations crew or even been a Panamanian or Colombian army helicopter. Possible, but not likely.

Gant ran a finger inside the collar of his black t-shirt, uncomfortable out of uniform in this spot. He felt awkward, out of place. He had not expected this feeling, but standing here at Fort Bragg where he had spent quite a bit of his time in uniform, in front of the names of the dead, he knew he no longer fit. He'd lost something and he wasn't quite sure what it was.

Ghosts. Gant could feel them. He checked the rest of the wall and, as he had expected, his brother's name was not there. He knew his own name would never be up there either. Once one went into the darkness of the Cellar, they disappeared from even the shadow world of Special Operations Command. Even the CIA had the gold stars in its lobby for agents lost in the line of duty even if it didn't list all the names. The Cellar was darkness, absolute and final. Other than Nero and Bailey, Gant had rarely met other operatives of the Cellar and then only when a mission absolutely required it.

Gant had no idea how big the Cellar was or how many people were in its employ. From his experience he knew that anyone who worked for the Cellar in the field was an operative, not a support person. For support, the Cellar could always turn to other government agencies where its classification and rank could draw whatever was needed.

Gant strode up the walk, ignoring a colonel who was coming the other way and fighting back the instinct to salute. Even though it was night-time, there were a lot of lights burning in the building and the parking lot was half full. SOCOM units ran missions all around the world so it was a 24/7 operation. Gant pushed open the door to the building and stepped into the lobby. Two turnstiles filled up the way to the left of the guard desk. An elderly black man in a contract security company uniform looked at Gant, noted that he didn't have a badge clipped to his pocket as everyone else in sight did, and motioned for him to come over.

"Are you on the access roster, sir?"

"I doubt it," Gant said, giving the man his NSA ID card.

Noting the designation, the guard checked his computer. His eyes widened as the result came up. He grabbed an access badge. "You have complete clearance, sir."

Gant knew the guard was surprised at that, particularly since he wasn't wearing a uniform. He doubted few people not assigned to the building could walk through the door and be given complete, un-supervised access to the building. Gant took the badge and went through the turnstile toward the elevator.

"Tony Gant? How the hell are you? Haven't seen you in a long time."

Gant turned as a grizzled, old Sergeant Major came limping down the hallway toward him, hand outstretched. "That's my brother. I'm Jack."

The Sergeant Major nodded, shaking his hand anyway. "I remember Tony said he had a twin. I haven't seen him in years. How's he doing?"

"He's dead."

The Sergeant Major nodded once more, as if he expected that answer. "Sorry to hear that. Who was he working with? Still with Delta? He sort of disappeared."

That was a question that Gant couldn't answer. Because at the end, his brother had been working for no one. "He was retired."

The Sergeant Major frowned. "What happened?"

I don't know, Gant thought. *I don't even know how my brother really died unless I believe Bailey.* "Natural causes. Cancer."

"Shit. I knew him when we were both in Delta Force. I've been here in the puzzle palace ever since my leg got shot up in the 'Stan."

Gant shifted his feet. He'd known coming back to Bragg was going to be a tricky proposition. "I've got business upstairs."

The Sergeant Major eyed Gant's civilian clothes, highest level visitor clearance pass, but didn't ask any questions. "Sorry to hear about your brother."

"Thanks." The elevator arrived and Gant got on board. He was glad when the doors slid shut. He got off on the floor housing the G-1 section and walked down the hallway to the records center. He tried the door, but it was locked and he didn't have a code key to open it. He knocked on the door and waited. After several moments, a Major opened it. "Yes?"

"Doctor Golden here?"

The Major nodded, glanced at Gant's access badge and let him. He waited for an introduction but Gant went right past him when he saw Golden seated with her laptop. "What do you have?"

Golden looked past him to the Major. "Could you excuse us, Major Taggart?"

Taggart looked none too pleased about that, but he went out the door, shutting it behind him. Golden kept her head pointed at her computer. "Some interesting material here."

"You have some names?" Gant asked as he took a chair from across her.

"This is your military record. Quite impressive."

Gant felt the stirrings of anger, which he repressed. "That wasn't what you were supposed to be doing."

"The records end six years ago," Golden said. "I assume that is when you entered the Cellar."

"You're supposed to be—"

"Grew up in New York. Military Academy. Had a twin brother who also went to the Military Academy and served in the military and whose records also abruptly ends, several years before yours though. Just like him, you served in the Rangers and then Special Forces. And then you disappear." She looked up. "Did they show you my file?"

"No."

"Why not?"

Good question, Gant thought. "Mister Nero probably didn't feel it was necessary."

"It appeared to me that Ms. Masterson was the one in charge at the Cellar."

To that, Gant had no reply. His brother's death, the letter from his mother, Nero lying to the side of his desk and the woman behind it, this mission teaming with another non-Cellar person-- there were just too many strange things going on that he had yet to process—could not process, because the priority was the mission. And there was a clock ticking. Not just Emily Cranston cached somewhere, but other possible killings the targets might have planned.

"So what should I know about you?" Gant wearily asked.

"Nothing," she said bitterly.

"You felt it was important to know about me," Gant noted. "Shouldn't it be important for me to know about you?"

"I'm the psychologist," Golden said. "You don't need to know how your target thinks, you just need to be able to see it, right? So you can shoot it?"

"I'm your target?"

"No."

"And I do need to know how my target thinks," Gant said. He spread his hands, taking in the building. "I worked for SOCOM for years. I was trained like our targets. I did live missions like our targets did. So I think like them."

"Not quite," Golden said. "There's tens of thousands of people in Special Operations. Very few of them turn rogue. So they have something else in their psyche that you don't understand." Golden typed something into her keyboard. "I've come up with sixteen probables. I cross-checked them based on assignments and that widens the fields of possible to one hundred and six if one of those sixteen is the leader and suborned his team-mates."

"Check for Lutz, Payne, and Forten."

"Did Sam give you that?"

"Colonel Cranston said he lost a team in a helicopter crash. They were the team."

"If they're dead—" Golden began as she looked at her screen and then she fell silent for a second. "Forten is one of the sixteen."

"He's the leader."

"I don't understand. If Sam—"

"It's Colonel Cranston, Doctor Golden. I don't know what your relationship in the past was with him, but let's act professional."

Gant was surprised to see Golden's face flush and he knew he had hit her somewhere deep, but he was tired of sparring.

"If Colonel Cranston says those men died, then why do you believe they could be our targets?"

"Because helicopter crash is almost a Special Operations euphemism for getting killed somewhere you weren't supposed to be. That's something I know."

"But if they were killed—"

"Let's pretend for a moment they weren't."

Golden frowned. "How did you get those names?"

"They're on the plaque right outside this building commemorating Special Operations soldiers who died in the line of duty."

"Oh."

"Also, there's no pilot listed as killed on that date. Kind of strange to have a helicopter crash with no pilot especially when Cranston says there were no survivors." Gant hammered home his point. "Cranston's bullshitting us. Something happened to that team. Something so bad he's willing to put his daughter's life on the line to cover it up."

"Sa—Colonel Cranston wouldn't do that."

Gant stared at her. "He's already done it. I believe he thought those guys *were* dead. I think now he *wishes* they truly were. But I don't think they are. I think they survived whatever happened to them and they're back and they're pissed."

Golden's fingers flew over her keyboard. "Sergeant Joseph Lutz. Staff Sergeant Michael Payne. Sergeant First Class Lewis Forten. All assigned to Seventh Special Forces Group. All listed as killed in a helicopter crash off the coast of Panama. Their bodies were never recovered."

"Of course not," Gant said. "Because there were no bodies. You had Forten as one of your sixteen probables. Why?"

Golden looked at the screen. "Forten was given up for adoption when he was born. No record of birth mother. He bounced around from foster home to youth facility for his entire childhood. The longest he stayed in one place was two years."

"So he had a crappy childhood."

"Instability in early family is one of the indicators," Golden said. She looked up at Gant. "Are you going to listen or are you going to critique me?"

"Go on."

"He was removed from one of his foster homes when he was eight amidst allegations of abuse by the woman who was responsible for him—his surrogate mother. She was arrested two years later on charges of abusing another child. I checked on her—she's currently in prison for armed robbery."

Gant opened his mouth to say something, but he could see that Golden was anticipating him. "Yes. Bad mothers make bad sons. Men act out, women act in."

Gant frowned and Golden explained.

"It's easy to say that society places more binds on a female's ability to act out, or is it that she's simply too weak to become a predator? But what if women do become predators? What if women routinely act out their years of abuse by also becoming sexual sadists?"

Gant wasn't following, but she kept on going.

"Maybe these women simply become mothers or surrogate mothers. Now they don't have to worry about society and they are no longer the weak ones. Men go out into the world and wreak havoc, women turn inward toward their family and do the same. Here lies the difference in a fucked up adult and a murdering predator. The former has a terrible childhood indeed, but the latter has a sexual sadist for a mother. The sadist mother literally invents the abuse that the son later reinvents for his own needs. That reinvention is what I look for. It is the source."

"You're blaming mothers?" Gant was incredulous. "You're saying this woman did something that's caused Forten to act like this?"

"I'm saying that the odds are very high that a sadist who kills had a sadist for a mother. That is something my research has proven. So. Yes. Men focus their impulses outward: they kill strangers. Notice there are no serial killers who follow in their father's shoes. They would never be satisfied torturing their own children forever. They would have the strength and the means to inflict their insanity on the populace. Women, as I've said tend to abuse themselves and their children. But hey, it's just a theory. But I did come up with one of the names."

One out of sixteen, Gant thought but did not say. "We know who they are, but that doesn't help us much. What we have to figure out is what their next step is. We've been reacting. To get these guys we're going to have to act."

"To get Emily, right?"

Gant glanced over to the window, looking out at the darkness. "Emily is alive. There's got to be a reason why they're keeping her alive. And before this is over, they're going to give us an idea where she is." Gant moved behind Golden. "Let me see their files."

Golden brought them up, one by one, and Gant scanned them. When all three were done Gant had a good idea of all three men's military backgrounds and training. "All right. Here's what we're facing. Forten is the sniper and the leader. Senior man rank wise. You know about SOTI training right?"

Golden nodded. "Special Operations Target Interdiction training. A nice way of saying sniper training. I revamped their screening program."

"A screening Forten obviously got through," Gant said.

"Yes. Four years before I got here. There was a reason I revamped it."

Give her a point, Gant thought. "SOTI is sort of a fancy way of saying sniper school, but there is as much emphasis in that school on shooting things as well as people."

"I don't understand."

"You take a fifty caliber sniper rifle and shoot out a critical component in a microwave relay tower or in the engine of a jet fighter, you cripple that entire system. So we need to keep that in mind, although it's most likely Forten will be shooting people." Gant scanned down the man's list of training. "OK. Besides being a trained sniper, Forten has a couple of other special skills. He was trained as a tracker in Borneo."

"'Borneo'?"

"A big part of Special Forces training is joint training in other countries. Forten went over there and went through their tracking school, taught by ex-headhunters. So he's an expert at following and finding people. He's also a Special Forces medic. Which means he can perform minor surgery. Also knows pills and drugs."

"Like what shot to give a girl to knock her out."

"Right. Payne was the spotter for Forten. They worked together for two years. Recorded several kills in Afghanistan. Payne is a weapons man. Means he's an expert on all sorts of guns. He also is a trained scout swimmer so he can operate in the water.

"Lutz was a demo guy. So that's not good. We haven't seen anything with his signature yet, but we need to keep that in mind. He can booby-trap things, blow things up, do all sort of nasty stuff."

"Lucky us," Golden said.

Gant stood up. "Let's go talk to Sam. See if we can jog his memory."

CHAPTER FOURTEEN

GOLDEN FOLLOWED GANT out of the building. She knew he thought her theories were bullshit and her contributions so far of little value. It was a reaction she had run into many times before, both at the FBI and here at Bragg when she worked for SOCOM. She had little time to reflect on this latest issue because Gant pulled open the door to the car parked in front of a garish statue of a soldier. Gant brusquely gestured for Cranston get out. The three of them stood in the parking lot, their faces almost in shadow from the parking lot lights, with the statue looming over them as if in silent judgment. Golden decided Gant had jumped her one too many times about Sam, so she decided to remain silent and let him take the lead.

Gant snapped out the names. "Sergeant Joseph Lutz. Staff Sergeant Michael Payne. Sergeant First Class Lewis Forten."

Despite the poor light, Golden could see Sam's face go white. "They're dead."

Gant jerked a thumb over his shoulder. "That's what it says on the plaque over there and in their service records. Like you said, died in a helicopter crash. Except they didn't, did they?"

"They're dead," Cranston repeated, as if by saying it again he could make it so.

"No, they're not. They have your daughter."

Subtle, Golden thought as Cranston stepped back as if punched. He leaned against the side of his car. She resisted the impulse to reach out and comfort him. Gant was right about one thing: Time was of the essence. Even as she thought that, she realized he was right about something else: Sam *had* been holding something back. She'd sat with too many patients when she was practicing early in her career who with-held information during therapy not to recognize it now. She realized her judgment had indeed been clouded by her sympathy for Sam when they first went to his house.

"Not only do they have your daughter," Gant pressed on, "they've already killed three other girls. They slashed one girl's throat while she was working at a daycare center, right in front of the kids. The pilot's fiancée. Her name was Kathy Svoboda. And she was pregnant. So technically they've notched four kills."

Golden was startled by that last piece of information. She had not read through the autopsy.

Gant continued. "They drowned another girl in a foot of water. Jim Roberts of the CIA—his daughter, Caleigh. Eighteen years old. And they chained Michael Caulkins' daughter Tracy to a tree and let her starve to death. Cached her, just like they've cached your daughter. Coroner estimates she lasted almost three weeks there, slowly dehydrating and starving. Tracy got so desperate she tried smashing her own foot with a rock to try to get out of the shackle that held her to the tree. If we're going to find Emily before she meets the same fate, you need to tell us what happened."

Golden noticed that Gant had begun using the plural—we. He probably wasn't even aware of it, but she noted the verbal cue anyway. She focused on Sam. His head was down, his shoulders slumped. Not anything like the commanding figure she'd met here two years ago. Children could do that to you, she knew.

Sam raised his head and looked from Gant to her, searching for some sympathy. Golden steeled her face to remain passive. The way she had learned through graduate school in training and in her early practice when she'd worked with patients.

"All right," Sam finally said. "It wasn't a chopper accident. They were on a mission into Colombia just over the border from Panama. It got all fucked up. It wasn't my fault. I tried to help them. But they *did* get killed."

Gant was silent and Golden continued to follow his lead, waiting.

"It was a direct action mission," Sam finally continued. "They were a sniper team seconded out of Seventh Group. Forten was the team leader and sniper. Payne was his spotter and Lutz his security. They were infiltrated into Colombia from Panamanian airspace via HAHO—high altitude, high opening parachute," he explained with a glance at Golden— "near a village that was a key way-point in moving cocaine over the border. The villagers had contacted both the Colombian government and the DEA that they were willing to accept the substantial aid package offered if they stopped allowing the free trafficking—but part of the deal was taking out the local warlord who ran the drug net. So Forten's team went in to do that. We knew the warlord was going to strike back at the village once they no longer gave sanctuary to his couriers and we got intelligence when that was going to happen. So the team went in forty-eight hours before that. We figured if we cut off the head, the rest of the organization would fall apart."

Sam fell silent for a moment and they all could hear the hum of the parking lot lights overhead.

He picked up his story. "They were on site and everything was good. I was on the exfil chopper. We were waiting just over the border. The team reported the warlord and his men coming in to the village as scheduled. I gave them the green light to take out the warlord. Then Forten also reported seeing an American among them. Someone they thought might be a DEA agent from a badge on the man's belt.

"So per SOP I called it in to the Embassy. Found out that the DEA and the Agency had come up with something new. The DEA had gotten one of their agents to make the warlord think he was playing both sides. And they hoped to use this connection to go further up the food chain and take down a major player, someone much bigger than the warlord."

"So fuck the villagers," Gant said and Golden was surprised at the venom in his voice.

Sam wearily nodded. "Yeah. The deal was off. God-damn bureaucratic fuck up. The left hand didn't know what the right hand was doing. I radioed Forten to abort. *Ordered* him to abort." Sam shook his head. "He ignored me. Ignored a direct order. He fired, took out some of the warlord's men. Their position was compromised and over-run. The word we got back eventually via the CIA was that all three were killed."

"And you didn't even try to go in to extract them?"

Sam's face hardened. "I had my orders. We were not to cross the border. They had their orders. If Forten hadn't fired, they'd have been able to get out with no trouble. Hell, they could have walked over the damn border."

"Borders." Gant nodded. "They killed Caleigh Roberts right on the Alabama-Florida border. I don't think that was coincidence. They were making a point."

"They could have walked out if Forten hadn't fired," Cranston repeated.

Gant shook his head in obvious disgust. "Who else was involved? They've hit you, Caulkins—he was the DEA agent in the camp?"

"I don't know. Probably."

"Roberts was the CIA liaison, right?"

Sam nodded.

"Lankin was your pilot?" Gant asked.

"I suppose so," Sam said.

"Who made the decision to abort? Roberts?"

"I talked to Roberts," Sam said, "but he was relaying a command from the man who was in charge of all counter-drug operations in theater."

"And who was that?" Gant pressed.

"A State Department official named Foley. Lewis Foley."

"Fuck," Gant said. "Would have been nice to know that earlier."

"I thought they were all dead," Sam protested. "It didn't even occur to me it could be them."

"Because you took the CIA's word?"

"Yes, but we lost radio contact with them. And if they'd been captured, it stands to reason the warlord would have used them as bargaining chips. Or executed them. What the hell did happen to them?"

"Good question," Gant said. He had his Satphone out. "Anyone else who might be targeted?" he asked as he punched in a speed dial.

Sam held his hands up helplessly. "If it's them, I don't know. Foley gave the order to abort because I assume Caulkins was working the warlord. I relayed the order. I guess Lankin was flying the exfil chopper, which I was on. Why would they target him? He was just following orders."

Gant held up his hand, silencing Sam. "Seems like everyone was just following orders but no one was taking responsibility." Gant talked into the Satphone when it was answered. "I need to locate Lewis Foley. State Department. A-S-A-P. And the make-up of his immediate family."

The three stood in silence as they waited on the answer. Golden was surprised to suddenly feel very tired, as the adrenaline rush of the past thirty-some-odd hours wore off. It bothered her to see Sam broken and defeated, but even more so to realize he had been part of this whole mess and that he had lied from the very beginning. And worse, she could sense he still wasn't telling them the complete truth. And she was uncertain whether she should tell Gant that or if he already knew it as he had known it from the beginning, obviously.

Gant cocked his head listening. Then he spoke: "We need security on Foley and his immediate family ASAP. That is most likely the next target. Who do you have close by, Mister Nero?"

Gant looked surprised at the answer. "Neeley is there?" He listened for a few seconds longer then snapped the phone shut. "Let's go," he said to her.

"Wait—" Sam said

"There's no more time to stand around talking," Gant said. He paused. "Unless there's something else we should know?"

Sam shook his head. "I've told you everything. I thought they were dead. I was told they were dead."

Gant turned to Golden. "We have to get to DC to see Foley. He's the only one we know that was involved in this whose family hasn't been hit yet, so there's a good chance his is next."

* * *

Nero turned to Hannah Masterson as he put the phone down. As he expected, she spoke before he had a chance to.

"You can't commit Neeley to doing a damn thing."

"Ms. Neeley committed herself a long time ago," Nero said. "She just hasn't accepted the reality of her current situation. What is she going to do? Take up knitting?"

Masterson sat still and just stared at Nero, knowing, of course, that any non-verbal effort was wasted on him. "She has a choice."

"Really?" Nero asked. "You believe in free will?"

"Yes, I do," Masterson said.

"Good," Nero said. "So do I. But you only have a choice when you have options. What are Neeley's options?" Nero asked. When no answer was forthcoming, he pressed on. "She is what her life made her. What Anthony Gant made her. And what her own choices made her."

"And that is?"

"A tool for you to use."

"Like I'm a tool for you to use?" Masterson countered.

"We're all tools," Nero said. "Those who know that they are hold the advantage. Ms. Neeley has been putting off the inevitable. Now it's time to jar her back into reality."

"That's—" Masterson began, but Nero cut her off.

"Perhaps I was a bit harsh saying she was a tool. She's a person whose life has been shaped a certain way. Do you think she would be content sitting in the West Virginia hills keeping a home like Jesse Gant is? You spent time with her and saw her in action. And you also spent considerable tending a home and being the good wife and that didn't suit you either. The worst possible existence is living a lie."

A long silence followed that and, not for the first time or the last, Nero missed his eyes. He wondered what expressions were passing over Ms. Masterson's face. When she finally did speak, the suddenness almost startled him.

"We talked about that, Neeley and I. About how we were made into tools that men used. Whether it was her being taught the trade of killing or me being taught how to prepare a dinner for my husband's boss. But, obviously, what I was taught didn't take. And I am now a much different person than who I was. So why doesn't Neeley have the same option?"

"Neeley wasn't *taught* to be who she is initially," Nero said. "She was born that way and then had the good fortune to follow her instincts. Meeting Jean-Philippe and entering his world was not a random choice. She was drawn to it. Then Mister Gant finding her was not random. He sensed her and it was more than the bomb she was carrying. He sensed a kindred spirit. She wasn't running from things like you were. You weren't making choices, you were trying to avoid bad things. When I studied your profile so many years ago and saw what happened to you as a child and how you reacted to it, I sensed who you really were."

"So, I'm making choices now?"

"Yes." Nero paused. "And it is your choice whether or not to call Mister Bailey to go pose the choice to Ms. Neeley."

Jesse Gant and Neeley sat on the wooden porch watching the first hint of dawn creep over the mountains to the east. In the week that Neeley had been visiting, they had both fallen in the habit of rising early and bringing a steaming cup of coffee out to the deck and sitting there, watching the valley below the house slowly reveal itself. They watched the line of light creep across the lush forest.

They resembled each other, something both had noted on first meeting but not talked about. Neeley was almost six feet tall, Jesse just a shade shorter. Neeley had short, dark hair, while Jesse's was styled almost the same but red. Both were slender and in good shape. The major difference was in their faces. Neeley's skin was smooth and unblemished while Jesse's was liberally sprinkled with freckles.

Most mornings they had talked of Tony Gant, the man they had in common and had both loved. Jesse had left Tony and Neeley had been left in death by him. But the last two mornings the talk had shifted from the past and Tony, to the future and his son with Jesse: Bobbie. He was twenty-two but with the mental capacity of someone a decade younger. He was Jesse's son and Tony Gant's legacy to Neeley: on his deathbed he had asked her to take his son and she had promised that she would. It was a situation both women had danced around and finally gotten down to working out.

As promised, Neeley would continue to contribute financially to Bobbie's future although she knew the money she had taken from the drug dealers Tony had set up for her would not last indefinitely.

"Tony used to watch from there," Neeley said, as the pre-dawn light made it clear enough to see where she was pointing. "From that ridgeline. I came here with him one time. We spent two days up there. He was very proud of Bobbie."

"That didn't do Bobbie any good," Jesse noted. "Watching but not interacting."

"Gant was afraid if he contacted you or Bobbie it would bring trouble."

"Yet trouble came anyway," Jesse said. "Tony was a good guy but he lived too much in his own head. He figured if he thought something, it was real to other people. But they didn't know what he thought so it wasn't real."

"He did the best he could," Neeley said.

"I know." Jesse took a sip of her coffee, her hands wrapped around the steaming mug. "That was the Gant boys—doing their best."

"Did you know his brother Jack well?" Neeley asked.

This earned her a sharp look from Jesse. "Yes."

"He works for the Cellar, right?"

"As far as I know," Jesse said. "I haven't heard from him in years."

"I've wondered why Gant—Tony—didn't want me to go to his brother for help," Neeley said.

Jesse gave a wry smile. "He went down that road once before. He was big on not making the same mistake twice."

"His rules," Neeley noted.

"Yes, his damn rules."

"What do you mean he went down that road before?" Neeley asked, broaching a subject both had avoided.

Surprisingly, Jesse smiled wistfully. "Well they were twins, you know."

"You mean—"

Jesse shook her head. "It was nothing duplicitous. As I told you, I worked for the Cellar also for a little while. Mister Nero was desirous of having both the Gants working for him. Same face, two different places. I suppose Nero saw lots of possibilities in that. Nero is always looking for possibilities. Tony was in, but Jack was still in the Regular Army, serving in the Rangers. So Mister Nero sent me to recruit Jack."

"You're kidding?" Neeley looked shocked. "He used you like that?"

"It was who I was," Jesse said simply. "It wasn't a sexual thing. I had this aura and Nero knew its affect on men. I supposed that's why he only sent me to recruit people, not kill them."

"Shit," Neeley suddenly said.

"What's wrong—" Jesse began, but then she heard it too, echoing dimly over the forested country-side. An inbound helicopter.

Both women watched as a black Bell Jet Ranger came swooping down the valley, flying very low, military low, just above the treetops. The chopper flared over the field across the county road from Jesse's place and touched down. The side door opened and a non-descript man stepped out.

"Shit," Neeley muttered.

"Nero's dog," Jesse said as they both watched Bailey walk across the road and up the driveway toward them. She looked over at Neeley. "And he's come to fetch."

Bailey stopped at the base of the stairs leading to the deck and looked up at Jesse. "May I come up?"

Jesse stood. "Have time for a cup of coffee?"

Both women could see the struggle on Bailey's face as he considered the question. He appeared to be in a rush but his last visit here had been a difficult one. "Just one." He came up the stairs as Jesse went inside. He looked at Neeley.

"You appear well."

"No thanks to you."

"I did my duty," Bailey said in a tone that indicted the matter was not open for discussion.

Jesse came out with a mug and handed it to Bailey before taking her seat. All three could hear the sound of the helicopter's engine still running. The fact that the pilot had not shut down indicated Bailey did not plan on discussing the weather.

"Are you here for me?" Neeley asked. "Or is this a social call?"

"I am here for you," Bailey acknowledged. He glanced Jesse. "Not that it isn't a pleasure to see you again, Jesse. How is Bobbie?"

"He's doing well. No thanks to you or the Cellar."

Bailey dropped his eyes. "I apologized for that. Things got out of hand."

"You think?" Jesse said.

Bailey lifted the cup to his lips and took a cautious sip. "Mister Nero sends his regards," he said to Jesse. He shifted his gaze to Neeley. "Mister Nero sends a summons. We require your assistance in a matter of some urgency."

"We?"

"Mister Nero and Ms. Masterson."

Jesse's eyebrows lifted. "So she's doing it?"

Bailey nodded. "It is who she is. She sits behind the desk now."

"But Nero is close by," Jesse said, earning a wry smile from Bailey.

"At the side of the desk." The smile disappeared. "But I am afraid he does not have much longer."

"What's the matter of urgency?" Neeley asked.

"We can discuss that on the way," Bailey said, setting down the mug.

Neeley remained still for several moments. She glanced at Jesse and the older woman gave a slight nod. "You'll always have a place here if you want it."

"Thank you," Neeley said. She sighed and stood. Jesse also got up and went to Neeley. The two women embraced and then, without another word, Neeley went down the stairs toward the waiting helicopter, Bailey right behind her.

Neeley climbed into the chopper. Bailey sat down next to her, slamming the door shut and giving the pilot the thumbs-up. The bird lifted and sped away to the east, toward the rising sun. Neeley noted a long metal case lying on the floor at her feet and she knew what it contained. She reached up and put on a set of headphones and Bailey did the same.

"What's the mission?" she asked, tapping the metal case with her foot.

"We assume you use the same weaponry that the late Mister Gant used," Bailey said. "Accuracy International L96A1 firing NATO standard size 5.56mm by 51mm rounds. There is a freshly tooled muzzle suppressor and your rounds were loaded by our armorer and are subsonic."

Neeley knew that meant the sniper rifle in the case was essentially noiseless beyond the sound of the bolt moving which wouldn't be heard more than five feet from a firing position. "The mission?" she repeated.

"There is a man who we believe is being targeted by a rogue agent," Bailey said. "Actually, we think it's more likely the agent will be going after the man's family, and since that consists only of his wife and the two are currently in the same house, it's the same thing."

Neeley thought Bailey was phrasing things rather oddly, but then again she'd never worked with the man. Bailey pulled a manila folder out of his metal briefcase and extended a black and white photo to Neeley. A distinguished looking man in his fifties and his wife, who appeared about a decade younger than him.

"He's a State Department official," Bailey continued as Neeley committed the images of the two people to memory, visualizing them in the scope of her rifle as Gant had taught her, even though they were not the targets. It was just a technique, one that worked well. "The two are currently holed up on their summer farm in the Virginia country-side. That's where we're headed now."

"Why not just put some cops on them?"

"The State Department has a pair of security officers guarding them," Bailey said.

Neeley considered the information, putting the pieces in place. "You want the target more than you care about the safety of the couple."

Bailey's mouth twitched in what might be considered a smile as he pulled a piece of gum out of his pocket and began to peel away the wrapper. "How did you come up with that?"

"Three things," Neeley said and then she ticked them off on her long fingers. "One. It's stupid to put them out in the country where they're less safe. Bury them deep in the J. Edgar Hoover building or someplace like that and they're a lot harder target to get to. Two. They already have apparent protection so I'm going to be doing something else. Three. The sniper rifle means I'm going to be standing off at a distance not standing at their side as deterrence."

"Very good," Bailey said as he put the gum in his mouth. "And if at all possible, we would like the target to be incapacitated, not killed. We have some rather important questions to ask of him." He reached into the case and brought out another folder and spread three photographs out. Three men in military uniforms glared back at her. "The target will be one of these. Maybe two of them working in concert. But we doubt all three will be there."

"And the information you want is where the others are?"

"Correct." He pulled out another photo, this one satellite imagery. He pointed as he spoke. "The couple is in this farm-house. This is the barn. The two State Department security guys are staying outside, one doing a walking perimeter around the house and barn, the other inside this van monitoring security cameras they set up. They get relieved by another shift every twelve hours." He took out a topographic map and placed it alongside the imagery so she could get an idea of the terrain in more than the two dimensional photographic way.

Neeley evaluated the area the way Gant had taught. Which meant looking at avenues of approach to the farm-house and fields of fire. She reached out and tapped a spot on the photo about three hundred meters from the house. A small knoll covered in trees. "Here."

Bailey looked at and nodded. "Fine. We'll insert you about two klicks away on the other side of this ridge."

"The State Department security people won't know I'm there, I assume."

"Correct."

"What do I do if they compromise me? They'll think I'm an attacker."

"Don't let them compromise you," Bailey simply said. He reached down and pulled up a small knapsack. "Food, a blanket, water. Enough for twenty-four hours. And a radio. FM set to the proper frequency."

"What about exfiltration?"

"We'll come get you."

"Oh sure."

Once more Bailey almost smiled. "Mister Gant taught you well, but be assured we would not waste someone of your talents by not coming to pick you up." He reached into his briefcase and removed a small PDA. "All the information on this mission is in here. Peruse it while you wait." He brought out a small cell phone with a headset out. "Satellite direct. We're bringing in some more people later today and will contact you on how to rendezvous with them."

"Who?" Neeley asked as she took the phone.

"Two people. One of them is Jack Gant."

The first thing Emily became aware of was the smell of moisture. She slowly opened her eyes and stared at the blades of grass right in front of her face.

Her eyes focused on the tiny, glistening drops of dew on the thin green blades. She edged her head forward and her tongue slithered out, sliding along the closest blades, taking in the scant moisture.

She crawled forward on her belly, licking the grass. It was only when the shackle on her ankle jerked her to a halt did she once more become aware of her surroundings and her reality. Her face was damp, her tongue barely moistened from all her efforts. The front of her shirt was smeared with dirt and grass.

And her thirst was not slated in the slightest. Emily shook her head, more at the pathetic nature of her instinctual action than anything else. She lifted her head up and looked around, remembering the animal that had come close during the night. There was no sign of—

Emily's breathing stopped as she caught site of what was pinned to the tree she was shackled to: her driver's license. She crawled to the tree and stared at the small piece of plastic, her own image gazing back at her. A single small thumb-tack was pressed through the center of it.

There was a vertical red line on the license, which she puzzled over for a few seconds before realizing it was dried blood. And the line continued up the bark of the tree.

Emily froze, not wanting to look up, but she knew she had to. Set in the crotch of the first branch was a dog's severed head. Its lifeless eyes stared back at her. Emily tried to swallow but her throat was too dry. Her stomach heaved but there was nothing to vomit.

Emily turned her head, looking at the wall of vegetation surrounding the clearing. He was out there. She knew it. Watching her. She felt a chill pass through her body as she realized he'd come over to the tree in the middle of the night while she was sleeping and tacked the license there and put the dog's head in the tree. For her to see. She knew right away his ploy: he wanted her to despair, to give up.

Emily slowly got to her feet, feeling the strain on her muscles. She stood tall, then took several deep breaths to calm down. She folded her arms across her chest, grabbing her elbows tightly with her hands for control.

"Fuck you!" she screamed. "You will not win. Fuck you, you asshole."

In his hide site, the Sniper had adjusted the video camera set on the small tripod, making sure he caught all of Emily as she got to her feet and began screaming. He had the audio turned off, so while it was obvious she was saying something, the actual words wouldn't be recorded. Which was just as well.

He had almost an entire hour of tape recorded over the course of the last two days. His favorite was when she worked on the shackle with the wire from her bra. He'd been concerned at first, then fascinated by her meticulous efforts. He'd even felt slightly disappointed when the wire broke. But just slightly.

Her current defiance he found almost amusing. She thought herself so important. And she was nothing, a piece in the plan. He checked his watch. A plan whose next step was getting ready to unfold.

CHAPTER FIFTEEN

AIRPLANE RIDES AND murder scenes. Gant hoped they didn't find the latter when they arrived in Virginia. He was looking at the satellite imagery of the farm and the brief security summary sent by the State Department to the Cellar regarding their protection of Lewis Foley and his wife Mary. Golden was across from him, going through the personnel folders of their three targets one more time.

Gant's Satphone buzzed and he pulled it out. "Yes?"

"Mister Gant." There was no mistaking Nero's unique in-human voice. "We have an operative going in to provide coverage of the area. She'll be in place within the hour."

"She?" Gant asked as he checked his watch. They were still a good three hours out.

"Yes. We thought it time you met Ms. Neeley."

Gant's hand tightened on the phone as he recognized the name of the woman who had been his brother's lover for the past decade. He had never met her, but he had heard about her. He'd heard that she had been there when he died and according to Bailey had buried him.

"The State Department has a couple of agents on site for protection and to provide what they believe to be deterrence," Nero said.

"But Neeley isn't on site." Gant said it as a statement, not a question.

"She's in over-watch."

"All right." Gant understood what that meant and he'd done enough missions for the Cellar that he knew there was no discussing it with Nero.

"There is something else," Nero said.

"And that is?"

"Let me turn you over to Ms. Masterson."

There was a brief silence, and then the woman's human voice was on the phone replacing Nero's metallic rasp. "You left a message asking about Doctor Golden's son, Jimmy. Doctor Golden was married for eight years, divorced six years ago. Her husband was a psychiatrist also, specializing in the same field of predictive behavior. They had a son, Jimmy. She was given full custody when they divorced.

"Jimmy was living with her when she worked at Fort Bragg. He went to school one day and never came back. He was last seen in the school playground. It was immediately suspected that someone who Doctor Golden denied entry into Special Operations because of her psych evaluation might have been the culprit. However, there was also the stronger and more likely possibility it was a sexual predator and a random snatch. The police pursued the latter angle but turned up nothing. Nobody was ever found."

Gant glanced across the plane at Golden who was immersed in her computer.

Masterson answered the question that Golden had asked and that was just forming in Gant's mind before he could voice it: "The Cellar was not brought into this matter initially. The military chose to handle it themselves since it happened on post. They investigated without any success. Eventually it was brought to Mister Nero's attention, but by then the disappearance was so far removed time-wise that an operative sent to check things out reported little to work with."

But Nero got interested in Golden, Gant thought. Always the opportunist.

"The case is still open but there has been no progress in the past four months and there is no active investigator."

"Might want to reconsider that," Gant said.

"Yes, that has occurred to me" Masterson simply said. "But let's stick to the task at hand. There will be a helicopter waiting for you at the airfield. It will take you close to Neeley's over-watch position. She is at grid one-eight-five-six-one-five."

The phone went dead and Gant slowly closed it.

"What's the latest?" Golden asked as he put the phone away.

"The State Department has guards with the Foley's."

"I'm sure that's a great comfort to them," Golden said dryly.

"We'll be joining a Cellar operative in an over-watch position," Gant said as he checked the grid coordinate. "She's already on-site."

"'She'?" Golden repeated. "Seems the Cellar is very big on gender equality."

"The Cellar is big on efficiency," Gant said. He paused, considering if he should broach the subject, then decided it was best to do it before they met Neeley. "Ms. Masterson also mentioned your son."

Golden's face became a stone. "What about him?"

"She told me what happened. The Cellar wasn't informed by the military so that was why no operative investigated until Mister Nero heard about it months later."

"And?"

"Nothing was discovered." Gant pointed at her computer. "I assume you did a target search of those people you interacted with or screened at Bragg?"

Golden nodded. "Yes. I came up with twenty-six possible. But the Criminal Investigative Command only did a cursory check of those. They were convinced it was a pedophile and, like other people, weren't very impressed with my methodology. Even though I believe it was my methodology that caused this to happen."

"And you? What do you think?"

"I think it was someone I screened out of Special Operations. Someone striking at me for revenge."

"Why do you think that?"

Golden's voice was harsh. "Because nobody has been found. Whoever it is wants me to continue suffering."

Gant leaned back in his seat, suddenly very tired. Golden was still staring at him.

"After we save Emily," Gant said, "we'll check out your probable's."

Golden blinked. "Why?"

"Because you're my partner."

Golden considered that. "You said save Emily, not sanction the targets. A change in objective?"

"Both objectives are tied together," Gant said.

"Perhaps."

The Security looked through the binoculars at the roving guard, noting the way the man had his sub-machinegun casually slung over one shoulder. It was a good news-bad news situation. In several ways.

It had been anticipated that someone would be putting the pieces together of the various deaths and kidnappings. That was why the Security had immediately come back here after leaving Alabama. He'd already prepared for this possibility several weeks earlier during their mission preparation Isolation phase of this operation. However, it had not been anticipated that the response would be this quick. The call from the Sniper warning him that Foley's name had already come up had been a surprise. It meant the timeline of the entire operation needed to be accelerated.

The fact the target had run to the country farm-house was good and had been anticipated, indeed predicted. The guards were an obstacle but not a major one as they were poorly trained guards, thinking having a show of weaponry was a deterrent. So that was good. It meant that whoever had put these pieces together was severely under-estimating the threat.

The Security was in the front seat of an old mail delivery truck he had stolen six weeks earlier. He'd kept it hidden in an abandoned barn further out in the country while he made modifications to it and once the target and his wife went to ground he'd retrieved it and driven here. The windshield he was looking through was double-thick bullet-proof glass and tinted so that someone on the outside could not see in. The interior walls were lined with bullet-proof and blast resistant Kevlar blankets. The dirt bike was in the back, held in place by nylon tie down straps and facing the back doors. There were other special modifications, which had called upon his training as a Special Forces demolitions expert, all of which would come into play very soon.

The Security pulled out his one-time pad and turned to the current day. Then, using a tri-graph and the message he'd written, he combined the letters to put it in a text format that was unbreakable by anyone except the owner of the only other version of the pad. He punched the letters into his cell-phone. When the message was done he paused. Once he sent it, the clock was ticking and he had to go through with his mission. Up until now they had had the luxury of operating on their own time schedule. Now they had to move faster to stay ahead. There was always a danger in moving fast.

He reached up and felt the striated skin of his face. He remembered coming to consciousness and feeling the pain of the initial wounds from the Claymore mine. Then the ongoing agony of the varying, but non-stop tortures inflicted on them by their captors. He looked down at his ankles where he had worn the heavy iron shackle for over eight months. The skin around both ankles was now callused and rough and had remained so despite four months since the shackles had been removed. Worst of all had been the constant threat of death at any moment. There had even been mock executions to the point where any hope of living had left him.

Once you 'died' like that so many times, the only thing left powerful enough to keep you clinging on to life was hate. A hatred so deep and dark that only those who had been to a hell on Earth could understand it. It had been a hate that had bound the three of them together stronger than any love could. By accepting they were already dead they had managed to survive, and by embracing their hatred they had generated the energy and wit to escape. It had sustained them on their secretive return to the United States and the months of planning and preparation for this final mission.

The Security hit the send.

* * *

Emily had the dog's head on the ground in front of her. The smell was disgusting, the sight only slightly less so. She had it facing away so she didn't have to see the dead eyes, but that left the severed neck facing her, cut bone and tendrils of flesh exposed.

She brushed away the incessant flies and controlled her revulsion as she looked for any meat on it that she could eat. She tentatively reached out and touched the top of the skull and all she felt was bone. The dog had been starving, that was apparent even by just having the head.

"Fuck it," Emily said to herself. She picked the head up and threw it with all her might away from her.

She would not descend to that level.

Yet, the word echoed in her mind.

Neeley could barely hear the chopper behind her. She knew it was far enough away not to be heard at the farm-house or by the State Department security man. Or by whoever was in the old mail-truck that was parked in the far wood-line, hidden in the trees and shadows. She'd spotted the truck within a half-hour of settling in to her over-watch position. It was parked in the far wood-line in such a way that it couldn't be seen from the farm-house or barn area but a corner of it was visible from her higher position.

She'd contemplated going over there to check on it, but that would have required a long trek, looping around the entire area to stay under cover. And there was the possibility one of the bad guys was in the truck and could take action while she was moving. Plus, she was supposed to link up with the reinforcements coming in from the Cellar. Better to over-watch with the rifle.

There was the even stronger possibility that the truck was the State Department or some other government agency trying to build redundancy into the protection. Neeley had heard enough of Gant's stories to know that government bureaucracy was often the most dangerous enemy of all. She had called it in to the Cellar and was waiting for word back.

She'd read the information on the PDA and now understood who she was watching and why. And who the potential threats were. She was dealing with men who were professionals in the art of war and killing. They were killing innocents in their thirst for vengeance, which meant they had crossed a line into a darkness few could comprehend. Neeley realized that they had felt abandoned and betrayed on their mission into Colombia, but to her their response was beyond comprehension. Of course, what had happened to them in the time they had gone missing until now, was a big unknown. There was even the possibility they had been turned and now were working with the drug cartel.

The sound of the chopper faded and she split her attention between the farm-house, the mail truck and looking over her shoulder for her support from the Cellar. Her mind kept going back to Gant's—her Gant, Tony's—face. He'd saved her life when she was still a teenager and then in a way took her life from that day onward. And now he was still a presence because she knew she would not be here with a sniper rifle if it weren't for his past connections with the Cellar.

She heard a woman's voice raised in complaint and looked over her shoulder once more. A man and a woman were coming up the ridge, the man in the lead, a sub-machinegun at the ready, his eyes and the weapon doing sweeps back and forth in concert. He wore black fatigues and a combat vest. And the woman struggling to keep up with him and appearing none-too-happy about the traipse through the woods. Nor was she dressed for being outdoors in her long slacks and blouse.

Neeley raised an arm to indicate her position and the man spotted her right away. And then she saw his face and felt a charge run through her body. It was Tony—how Tony had looked when he was healthy. If she hadn't buried her lover herself, watched the cancer eat him down to the bone, she would have sworn it was him. But she knew it was Jack Gant, the twin brother she had never met.

Neeley scooted back slightly from her over-watch position, putting the top of the ridge between her and the target so she could greet them.

Gant lowered the sub-machinegun and stuck out his hand. "Jack Gant."

"I'm Neeley."

"I know."

The two stared at each other, their gaze only broken when the woman arrived and Neeley realized there was another presence.

Gant introduced the woman. "And this is Doctor Golden."

Neeley shook her hand. "Doctor of what?"

Gant pointed at his head. "Shrink."

"Someone down there going to need therapy?" Neeley asked.

"I'm a predictive behavior profiler," Golden said.

Neeley had no idea what that meant. She turned back to Gant, forcing herself to remember that this was not her lover of over a decade. "Foley and his wife are in the farm-house. The State Department has two men on outside perimeter duty, one walking a circle around the house and barn, the other monitoring security cameras in the van. There's something else—an old mail truck in the far tree-line. I don't know if it's part of their force, some other government agency's intrusion or the bad guys. I called it in to the Cellar to check on and haven't heard back yet."

"Let's take a look," Gant said. He motioned for Golden to take a seat. "Wait here."

Golden looked around for something to sit on and then settled for a log, on which she gingerly perched herself. Neeley moved back toward her position and as she got close to the ridge went down to her belly and began to crawl. Gant automatically did the same and they arrived at the hide site where her sniper rifle rested on its bipod and stock.

Gant noted the weapon. "Same as Tony liked using."

"He taught me how to fire it," Neeley said, feeling foolish as soon as she said it.

But Gant only nodded as he pulled out a set of binoculars and scoped out the area.

"The mail truck is there," Neeley said, pointing.

Gant nodded once more. "I see it. It was here when you arrived?"

"Yes."

"Hasn't move at all? No movement around it?"

"Nope."

Gant lowered the binoculars. "What do you think?"

Neeley liked that he hadn't come in and tried to take charge and that he was asking her opinion. "I called the truck in to the Cellar but I haven't heard back. I think we should check it out. I would have done it but—"

"You couldn't leave coverage," Gant finished for her. He glanced at his watch. "Let's give the Cellar another ten minutes to get back to us whether it's another agency. I'd hate to bust in on a truck full of SWAT guys. If the report is a negative, I'll go down there."

Neeley nodded. They lay together in silence for a few moments, their bodies within a foot of each other, both feeling off-kilter.

"You know that Tony—" Neeley began but stopped.

"Did Tony really die of natural causes?" Gant asked.

"Yes. Cancer. I buried him."

"Was he in a lot of pain?"

"Yes."

"Tony never liked being sick. He'd have preferred to go fast."

"He didn't exactly have a choice."

It was Gant's turn to feel slightly foolish for a moment. "Why did Bailey dig him up?"

"Long story," Neeley said and left it at that and was grateful when he didn't pursue it. Now was not the time or place.

"Mister Nero said you were with him at the end."

"I was."

"Thank you."

Neeley glanced over at him. "Tony wasn't responsible for the RPG attack in Mogadishu."

Gant slowly turned his head and looked back at her. "Who was?"

"A man named Racine."

"Little fucker. I remember him." Gant frowned. "But he was Cellar also."

"He wasn't in Mogadishu working for the Cellar. He was doing freelance work for a Senator named Collins."

"The one who just resigned?"

"Same."

"What happened to Racine?"

"We killed him."

"'We'? You and Tony?"

"No, Tony had already passed. Hannah Masterson and I. And Jesse."

Gant whistled and a slight smile crept across his face. "Jesse? I will have to hear this story, but not now." He checked his watch once more. "Five minutes."

CHAPTER SIXTEEN

USING A SCANNER, the Security had quickly found the frequency for the remote security cameras that had been set out. There were four, two on the main road, looking in each direction. One on the top of the barn that was doing a twenty-second long 360-degree sweep, and one facing down the long driveway leading to the farm-house. He set the jammer for the same frequency, but left it off for the moment. He got out of the truck and walked around it, making sure all the fuses were set.

The outside of the mail truck was criss-crossed with detonating cord like a Christmas tree. The Security smiled as he thought of that, fond memories of lightness and happy times trying to intrude into the darkness his life had been for the past year. The smile was gone as quickly as it had appeared as a dark curtain came down over the memories.

He was dead. Had died a year ago. All that was left was retribution.

The fuses were all set.

"I've got movement," Neeley said, as she peered through the high power scope on the rifle. "I can't make out anything other than a figure moving around the mail truck. Just got a glimpse."

Gant was already moving. "I'm going down there. See that creek bed to the right? I'll be coming that way."

"Roger that," Neeley said.

Gant slid back and got to his feet.

"What's going on?" Golden asked, totally out of the loop, as she got to her feet.

Since she wasn't armed, Gant ignored Golden and began to move fast, running through the woods, the sub-machinegun at the ready.

The Security got back in the truck and slid between the seats into the rear. He sat on the motorcycle that was strapped in there, facing the rear doors, and kick-started it. Satisfied that the engine was running smoothly, he went back to the driver's seat and started the truck.

Emily was squatting over the chain that was attached to the shackle. Despite being dehydrated, she still had the urge to urinate. She remembered reading in a science fiction short story sometime about a man who eventually cut through the bars on his cage by urinating on them in the same spot time and time again until the acid in his urine wore through the metal.

Of course it had been a science fiction story. She had no idea whether it was true or not. If she remembered rightly, it had taken the man many years to achieve his freedom. And she knew the perp was out there somewhere watching, but she figured she had nothing left to lose.

The two second trickle she let loose was barely enough to wet the chain but she felt a small sense of accomplishment. Another thousand years of this and she might actually see a result. Emily smiled bitterly to herself, her lips cracking.

That feeling abruptly disappeared as the perp came out of the tree-line stalking directly toward her, a pistol in his hand. Emily got to her feet. As he got closer he raised the gun up. Emily thought this was a bit of an over-reaction for her just peeing on the chain.

"Hey," she said, holding her hands up in front of her. "Stop!"

She saw his eyes and they scared her more than the gun. They were flat and dead. He stopped about five feet from her, the gun steady. Emily stared at it and realized there was something not quite right about the gun.

He pulled the trigger and Emily screamed.

Then she cursed as she saw the small dart sticking out of the skin of her arm. She brushed it off. "You asshole!"

The perp just stood there, staring at her like he would have stared at the tree she was chained to. Emily felt a wave of nausea and she staggered, putting her back against the tree. Her legs became wobbly and despite her attempts to remain standing, she slowly slid down until she was seated at the base of the tree.

"What are you going to do to me?" she rasped, barely able to hold on to consciousness.

Of course there was no reply. The last thing she saw before all went dark was the perp still standing there, staring at her without any emotion.

Gant hit the creek-bed and turned toward the farm-house, which was about three hundred meters away. He paused and pulled out his Satphone. The Cellar had given him the number for the State Department security detachment and he quickly punched it in.

"Jorgenson," a voice answered on the second ring.

"This is Agent Golden with the NSA," Gant said as he started to move forward again, one hand on his gun, the other holding the phone. "I'm coming toward your location via the creek-bed to the west of the house. We spotted an old mail truck in the southern tree-line and believe it to be hostile."

"What?" Jorgenson sounded rattled. "Who the hell are you?"

Neeley's voice came over the FM radio receiver in Gant's right ear. "The mail truck is moving. Heading toward the main road."

"The truck is inbound," Gant said into the Satphone. "You've got hostiles inbound," he added, trying to get some sort of reaction. "Very violent hostiles."

The Security hit the jam button shutting down the transmissions from the security cameras. He floored the truck, taking the turn onto the hard top road almost too quickly and the clacker he had set on his lap slid off. He desperately grabbed it before it hit the floor, tucking it back in place, his fingers trembling slightly.

He accelerated once more. He was a half-mile from the driveway, picking up speed.

"Truck is on the hard-top," Neeley reported. "Windshield is tinted so I've got no sight picture on the driver or any other passengers."

"The truck is on the main road heading your way," Gant relayed to Jorgenson. He had no doubt one of the targets was in the truck: who the hell tinted the windshield of a postal delivery truck?

"Shit, I've lost all video," Jorgenson reported.

"Get out of the van, ASAP," Gant ordered. "You're being attacked."

"There's something weird about the outside of the truck," Neeley reported. "Wires routed all over it."

Gant was now two hundred meters away. He could see the mail truck now, turning into the driveway at a high rate of speed. The walking guard was running toward the dirt road, weapon tight to his shoulder, aiming toward the truck. Gant also saw the door slide open on the van and Jorgenson step out, his weapon also at the ready. And Gant knew they both would be dead within the minute but weren't aware of it yet.

"Start shooting," he ordered Neeley over the FM radio.

An unnecessary order he realized as a star-shaped impact appeared on the front windshield of the truck. But the glass remained intact, which meant it wasn't a normal windshield. And not a normal truck. Gant couldn't make out the details but he could tell there was something wrong with the exterior of the vehicle as Neeley had reported.

One hundred and fifty meters.

"Move, move," Neeley whispered as she shifted the rifle from windshield to front right tire and pulled the trigger. Her exhortation wasn't for Gant, but for the two State Department guards who were standing, somewhat at attention, in the drive, watching the truck bearing down on them. She could see the mouth on one of them moving, screaming, although the sound couldn't reach this far and she realized the fool was trying to order whoever was driving the truck to stop.

Stupid.

The round hit the tire, but with no apparent effect and Neeley realized they were solid. Bullet-proof windshield and solid tires. This was going to be bad. She went back to the windshield and fired three rounds as fast as she could pull the trigger, splintering the glass but not punching through. She had put all the rounds within a six inch circle in front of where the driver's seat should be and had not penetrated, which meant the glass was stronger than normal bullet-proof material or double-layered.

There was something definitely wrong with the exterior of the truck, but before she could check it out further she saw someone open the front door of the farm-house and step onto the porch. Lewis Foley, according to the intelligence packet Bailey had given her. And next to him was his wife.

Foley had a shotgun in his hands and his wife had a pistol.

God-damn idiots, Neeley swore to herself.

She swung back to the truck and realized there were small green objects scattered all over the exterior, connected with fuses. She aimed at one and fired.

Missed.

The Security could see the two guards directly ahead, their sub-machineguns tucked into the shoulders, standing in the school-correct firing stance. The one on the left was yelling something, his mouth moving, but between the sound of the truck and the motorcycle behind him, the Security could hear nothing. Not that the man could have said anything humanly possible to stop the inevitable.

There was ping on the outside of the truck and the Security realized the sniper was now trying to hit one of the Claymores he'd rigged. He laughed out loud, because even if the sniper could hit one of the mines—a damn hard shot—it would only disable that one mine unless a miracle happened and the round hit the small fuse inside the mine.

The Security's smile grew wider as he saw the target and his wife on the porch. Better than he could have hoped. He jerked the wheel and the truck spun into a skid, stopping less than five feet from the two guards who had fired several ineffectual bursts into the truck, the bulletproof glass and Kevlar blankets draped on the inside absorbing the rounds. He was now less than forty feet from the target and his wife.

"Close enough for government work," the Security whispered to himself as he reached down and picked up the olive-drab clacker resting on his lap.

"Good-bye."

He pressed the lever on top of the clacker down.

Gant was just climbing out of the creek bed, less than fifty feet from the farm house when he heard the familiar sound of Claymore mines in sequence going off. He dove backward, landing in six inches of water as hundreds of steel ball bearings screeched by overhead.

Neeley was aware of Doctor Golden crawling up next to her as she continued to fire futilely at the truck, then shifted her aim and put a couple of rounds into the wood railing of the porch in front of Foley and his wife, trying to force them back into the house.

Then the outer sides of the van literally erupted.

"Oh my God!" Golden exclaimed.

The two guards were ripped apart, shredded like so much meat caught in a metal hailstorm. Neeley saw Foley and his wife get slammed back and slump down against the riddled front wall of the house. She didn't know if they were dead or not. It took a moment to register, but then she realized the outside of the truck had been lined with Claymore mines. At least a dozen, going off almost at once, sending their small balls of death spraying outward in a circle of death.

"Son-of-a-bitch," Neeley muttered.

"What happened?" Golden asked, still shaken at sudden bloody violence.

Neeley slammed a fresh magazine home in the rifle and centered the scope on the truck. "Come out now," she whispered.

"What is going on?" Golden demanded.

"Shut up," Neeley snapped as she got her breathing under control.

Gant crawled to the edge of the creek-bed and aimed the sub-machinegun at the truck. He could see the mangled pieces of meat that used to be the two guards. He could see the two bodies slumped on the porch of the house. One was moving, crawling.

He focused on the truck.

The Security could see the body crawling on the porch. It was him. Foley. He was creeping toward his wife who lay bloody and motionless.

"Go for it," he said. He shook his head, trying to clear the loud ringing noise that was echoing inside his skull from being at the center of the Claymore blasts.

Then he looked as best he could through the splintered glass toward the surrounding country-side. He knew there was no way he would be able to spot the sniper who'd been firing at him. He hadn't expected that.

"Change in plans," he said to himself, rubbing his scarred face and glancing over his shoulder at the still running motorcycle. If the sniper was any good, he wouldn't make it twenty feet before he got cut down.

The exhaust fumes from the bike in the enclosed space of the truck were beginning to make him light-headed as he tried to figure out what to do. *Crack a window.* He laughed out loud.

Right. And take a round right through the skull. Besides, the bulletproof windows he'd installed didn't open.

He looked at the farm-house. Foley had reached his wife and was trying to help her staunch some of the bleeding, which meant she was still alive also. "How nice. How noble," he muttered out loud. His brain was fuzzy, the carbon monoxide combined with the after-effects of the explosions combining to push away reality.

The Security had gone with the Sniper on several missions. They had trained together for years. He knew all about how a sniper worked. Given the angle of the bullets that had hit the truck, the sniper was most likely on the knoll to the north. Which meant the south side of the truck was safe. For the moment.

He shook his head, realizing he wasn't thinking straight. The armored interior of the truck was the safest place, despite the motorcycle fumes. The truck's engine was still running. The solid tires should hold. He turned the wheel and pressed the accelerator. The truck slowly rumbled forward toward the farmhouse, the right front end dipping sharply from either a ruined shock or ripped up tire. There was a bump and he realized he had driven over the body of one of the guards. He kept the truck moving.

"The truck is heading toward the house," Neeley reported.

"No shit," Gant muttered. He was moving, crawling forward, the sub-machinegun tucked in the crook of his arms. The truck was less than thirty feet away, the farm-house slightly more than that. He could see Foley cradling his wife's body in his arms but he couldn't tell if the woman were alive.

The battered mail truck rumbled to the base of the short flight of steps leading to the couple. Gant could see rounds impacting on the windshield, further shattering it and knew Neeley was keeping up the fight from her position. But as the truck came to a stop it was angled now in such a way that whoever was driving it could get out the driver's side and get close to the porch behind its cover.

Of course, that also gave Gant a covered approach on the other side of the vehicle, safe from the driver's view. Gant got to his feet and dashed to the rear of the truck.

"I see you, Gant," Neeley said. "But I can't see the porch anymore."

The truck engine stopped running, but Gant could hear another engine still going, something inside the back of the truck. Then he heard the driver's door open and he knew there was no more time.

Gant exhaled, then stepped around the side of the truck.

A man dressed in black fatigues and wearing an armored vest was walking up the steps toward the prone couple. He had a sawed-off shotgun in his hands and wore a black balaclava over his head. He came to a halt standing just short of the couple, enjoying the cover the truck provided him from Neeley. Foley was looking up at the man, a small trickle of blood flowing out of the side of his mouth. The front of Foley's shirt was splattered with blood, both his own and his wife's.

The man reached up with his free hand and began to pull the balaclava off. Gant's finger was on the trigger, but he didn't fire. He knew what was coming and what was at stake.

"Remember me?" the man shouted and Gant knew everyone's ears were ringing from the explosions.

Foley was looking up, his hands staunching the flow of blood from a wide wound on his wife's stomach. Foley shook his head. "Please."

Gant didn't hear the word as much as he could tell what it was by the way Foley's lips moved. Gant took another step closer.

Foley must have realized he hadn't been heard. "Please," he yelled. "I didn't do anything to you. I don't know who you are."

"Should have thought of that before you betrayed us," the man said, raising the shotgun up to firing position.

Gant took the opportunity to fire a quick three round burst into the man's left thigh, spinning him about. As the man went down, Gant charged forward, while firing again, putting two rounds into the man's gun arm, causing him to drop the shotgun while his other hand went to his chest. *Emily.* That was the thought foremost in Gant's mind as he kept the target alive.

Gant was stopped on the middle step, the muzzle of the sub-machinegun pointing at the target's face. Gant saw the scars that were seared into the man's skin and knew he had Kathy Svoboda's killer. And the killer of Svoboda's baby.

"Where is Emily Cranston?" Gant demanded.

The man was smiling and Gant looked down at his good hand and saw the pin for a grenade in it. Time slowed down for Gant as he then saw the live grenade still hanging on the man's vest on top of a lump of explosive charge. Gant dove off the steps, hitting the ground and rolling as the sharp crack of the grenade going off split the sky, followed immediately by a secondary explosion from the charge.

Blood and body parts splattered the ground.

Gant lay on his back for a few seconds, breathing hard.

"Are you all right?"

Gant saw Golden's face in his field of vision. She was leaning over him.

"We fucked up," Gant said.

CHAPTER SEVENTEEN

GANT SLOWLY GOT to his feet and looked over at the porch. The target was gone except for a smear of blood, the remnants of his spinal column and some chunks of meat. Surprisingly, Foley was still moving, futilely grasping at his wife with the stump of a wrist. The wife was undoubtedly dead, her throat and chest a bloody mess.

Gant shook his head, trying to clear it of the new loud ringing. The stench of death was in the air. And gunpowder and explosives. And the damn engine inside the truck was still running, the sound now a dim thrumming in the background.

He walked up the steps and knelt next to Foley. First aid would be a waste of time—the man had lost too much blood already and the wounds were too severe. Besides the severed hand, he was bleeding profusely from over a dozen places. Less than a minute Gant estimated.

"Who else was involved?" he shouted at Foley.

The State Department bureaucrat was staring at his wife's body. Shock, both physical and emotional ruled him. "I didn't do anything," he whispered, a froth of blood coating his lips. "She didn't do anything."

Then he died.

Getting to his feet, Gant added up the body count: five if he counted the target. And they were no closer to Emily. "I'm on my way down," Neeley called in over the radio. "Sitrep?"

"Everyone's dead," Gant reported.

"Golden? I lost her."

"She's here. She's all right," Gant said, although that was debatable as he watched the psychiatrist take in the gory scene. Gant was reminded of the mission he had done in Iraq the previous year and seeing the results of an improvised explosive device on a Humvee full of young National Guard troops and the surrounding innocent civilians. It was something the American public wasn't being treated to, seeing the cost of the war on 'terror'.

Looking at the carnage, he could tell that the target had indeed had more than just a grenade in the vest he'd been wearing and Gant knew he was only alive because he'd been able to get below the blast. Pure, damn luck. Gant reached into his pocket and pulled out the three photos. Despite the damage from the bomb and the scars on the face, he was able to ID the target he'd seen before it was blown to smithereens: Sergeant Lutz, the Security on the three-man team.

Gant went to the back of the truck and pulled open the door. He saw the motorcycle strapped in the rear and nodded. Good idea. Bad execution. He climbed in turned off the engine to the motorcycle and a blessed silence descended except for the ringing in his ears, which he knew from experience would last for a while.

Then he looked up and saw the piece of paper taped to the ceiling of the truck.

"Golden?" Gant called out.

"Yes?" She came around the corner of the truck, her hands bloody and Gant knew she had checked everyone for signs of life. She obviously didn't have enough experience seeing dead people. Hope, Gant thought. She'd hoped someone was still alive.

"I think we might have more of Emily's cache report." Gant stepped between the bike and the Kevlar blankets on one side, and then leaned over so he could read what was on the paper.

AREA: Talladega National Forest
FRP: Intersection Routes 219 and 183

"That forest is in Alabama," Gant said as Golden came into the back on the other side of the motorcycle and looked at the report.

Golden was pulling her cell phone out. "Do you have the number for Ms. Masterson?"

"Wait a second," Gant said.

"'Wait'?" Golden was shocked. "Emily's chained to a damn tree and you want to wait?"

Gant looked from the report to her. "It's only been three days. So if she is cached like the other girl, she's all right. Plus we don't have the azimuth and distance from the FRP to the IRP, which if I remember rightly is a stone chimney. So basically the search would have to cover the entire National Forest. I don't know how big that one is, but I bet it's big enough to take some time to search."

"Still, the Cellar can get people moving and—"

"Let's think before we act," Gant said.

Neeley appeared in the back door shaking her head. "Fucking mess," she said.

Gant agreed. "Yeah. No info from the target and no info from the Foley's. He didn't seem to have a clue why he was being attacked. Reminded me a bit of Cranston's reaction. We underestimated the target."

"But we got him," Neeley noted. She tapped the motorcycle. "This wasn't supposed to be a suicide mission. He also underestimated us."

"'A fucking mess'?" Golden repeated. "Those people are dead."

"We didn't kill them," Gant said.

"We didn't save them either," Golden snapped.

Gant and Neeley exchanged a look.

"Listen, Doctor," Neeley said, "our job wasn't to save them. They had their own security. It failed them. They should have never come out of the house. That was stupid, so they failed themselves. And he—" Neeley nodded toward the bodies on the porch—"Foley, did something in the past that contributed to this."

"Are you saying he deserved to die?" Golden demanded.

"We're all going to die, deserving of it or not," Neeley said. "His and his wife's came sooner rather than later, but they also were stupid."

"So people should die for being stupid?" Golden was adamant, her face flushed.

"What the hell is your problem?" Neeley asked. "We didn't kill them. The bad guy did. And he'd have escaped to do it again to someone else if we weren't here to stop him. It's a tough world. Suck it up."

"And the wife?" Golden pushed. "What did she do to deserve to die?"

"Hooked up with the wrong guy," Neeley said. "Happens sometimes. You pick the wrong person and bad things happen to you. And, yes, stupidity is as good a reason to die as any other. Better than most. There's people getting diagnosed with cancer every day that are going to die and they did nothing to deserve it."

Gant opened his mouth to say something, to try to calm the two women down, but he knew they were coming from such different places, both dark in their own rights, that he wasn't sure what to say.

Then Neeley saw the note. "What's that?"

Gant quickly explained, sensing Golden vibrating more and more out of place on the other side of the bike.

"So he was going to take out the Foley's and leave this partial report," Neeley summed it up.

"But why?" Gant asked.

Both women stared at him so he explained. "Why would they give us Emily's location? Not exact location, but a searchable area?"

"Because they're bull-shitting us?" Neeley suggested. "Want us to waste resources on misdirection?"

"Could be," Gant said. "Could also be an ambush."

"Or could be Emily is already dead and they're continuing the taunt," Golden threw in. "But no matter what, we should inform the Cellar and get the search started."

Gant didn't like it. "This is the first time we've gotten even slightly ahead of them. Scar-face—Sergeant Lutz-- expected the State Department guards and took them out easily enough, but he didn't expect us. At least not us being here before he hit. He expected us to show up after and see this after he was gone," he said tapping the piece of paper. "Projecting forward, they would now expect us to put all our resources into trying to find Emily's cache."

"And?" Golden demanded, the exasperation clear in her voice.

"Doing that will put us back behind them because it would follow their plan," Gant said as he pulled out his Satphone and hit the speed dial for the Cellar. He quickly relayed to Mrs. Smith the cache information, and then hung up. "They'll get locals and Feds to check out the National Park," he told Golden and Neeley. "Bailey will head there also. He's good at that sort of thing."

"And what are we going to do?" Golden snapped.

"Want to waste your time walking in the woods or do something constructive?" Gant asked.

Gant walked to the rear of the truck and hopped out. Golden followed him. The bodies—and parts-- littered about underscored the severity of the situation. Gant knew they had probably fifteen minutes or so before the police arrived. Mrs. Smith had told him that the helicopter was on its way and would land in ten. It would take them to the nearest airport where the jet would be waiting. Where to from there, was the key decision he knew he had to make.

Neeley had her sniper rifle in one hand, held loosely, her pack slung over one shoulder. She appeared calm and patient. Gant knew if his brother had chosen to spend almost a decade with her and had trained her, she could be counted on—plus she had taken out Racine. Golden looked a bit lost and definitely out of place. The learning curve on this mission was steep and she was either going to make it or fall out along the way. At this point, Gant really didn't care either way.

"Going to Alabama is a waste of our time," Gant said. He held up a hand as Golden started to protest. "The Feds and locals can get more than enough people to search. Mrs. Smith said Mister Bailey is en route there to oversee the search for the Cellar there. But I don't think finding Emily is going to be so straight-forward. They've thrown us curves all along and there's no reason to believe this will be any different.

"What I'm wondering," Gant continued, "is what their ultimate goal is? This has not been a series of random events and I think it's leading up to something. But what?" He looked at Golden. "What do you think Doctor?"

Golden seemed a bit surprised to be asked so bluntly. She opened her mouth to speak, then paused as she collected her thoughts. When she did speak, her voice was calmer. "I agree that this is part of a larger plan and not a series of random events. I also agree it's critical we figure out what the end play is." She gestured, taking in the surrounding area. "The problem is while we're figuring that out, the body count keeps getting higher and higher."

Neeley spoke up. "These guys want revenge, right?"

"Yeah," Gant answered.

"And they've been taking it on family members," Neeley continued. "Wanting to make those they feel wronged them suffer."

"Correct," Golden said.

"But the ones they're really angry at are the players, the ones that betrayed them," Neeley said. "I don't think suffering is going to be sufficient payback for our targets. I think they want their victims to suffer but ultimately they're going to want to take them out. Kill them. Pain first, then death."

Gant considered that. "So they'll circle around and come back after the principals after they've hurt them via family members? That's not too smart. We're on the case and the principals can be guarded. Better than this was done," he added, noting Golden's look of contempt.

"So they have a plan in anticipation of that," Neeley said. "One we're not seeing yet."

Gant nodded. "Definitely. And everything that has happened so far is part of it. There's a progression and we need to figure it out." He looked at Golden. "That's your job. You say you can predict behavior. Let's do some predicting."

The sound of a chopper echoed in the distance.

"If we're not going to Alabama," Neeley said, "where are we going?"

"DEA headquarters," Gant said. "I want to find out the truth behind what happened in Colombia because I have a feeling even Colonel Cranston and Foley here really didn't know the full story of what happened to that team."

* * *

Consciousness crept into Emily slowly. An awareness of a sound, an engine running, the rumble of tires on asphalt. The sniff of a scent. The feeling of something hard beneath her. But not sight. Even when she opened her eyes there was only complete darkness and she realized she was blindfolded once more.

From the sound and the feel of the metal floor beneath her, she pieced together that once more she was in the van. And it was moving. Her hands were bound behind her. The blindfold pressed in tight against her eyes. She was surprised he hadn't pinched shut her nostrils so she couldn't smell, but she realized that wasn't important to him.

Why would he move her?

It didn't make sense. Of course, Emily knew, making sense of this insanity was probably a waste of time. On the other hand, she had nothing else to do than think about her current predicament.

Something had changed. The thought came to her unbidden, flashing out of the recesses of her subconscious. She also realized that she was a means, not an end. Moving her meant that her death was not the goal of her abduction. The crazy man driving the van wanted something more out of this.

Her suffering?

But he could have left her chained to that damn tree, Emily thought. This made no sense.

She cursed to herself as the van made a sudden, high speed turn and her body tumbled against the side, the metal hard and unyielding.

She wasn't scared any more. She realized that with a strange, very calm wave of awareness.

She was angry to the point of counter-balancing the fear.

How dare this man she'd never met, who she had never done anything to, treat her like this?

Enough thinking. Emily felt around with her hands, searching. She scooted along the floor of the van. Bumping into objects. Until she found the edge of a metal stanchion. It wasn't exactly sharp, but it was the best she could find in her current state. She put her back to it and began to rub the tape binding her wrists together.

"There's something odd about this team," Golden said.

Both Gant and Neeley stopped what they were doing and looked up at her, waiting for amplification on the statement. They were in the back of the black Gulfstream, flying toward Washington. They all had copies of the case file the Cellar had accumulated so far and were reading through, trying to find what they had missed.

"And that is?" Gant asked.

"They're a team," Golden said, "but they're operating individually. I've never heard of that."

Gant frowned. "You told me that there have been numerous pairs or small groups of people who act out like this."

Golden nodded. "Yes. But they always acted in concert in the same place at the same time. Because having the other person there as a witness and participant affirms what they're doing and makes them bold. The other, weaker person--or people in this case-- may feel that participating is his only way to be accepted or cared about. He's easily manipulated through his vulnerability, low self-esteem and neediness. Team members feed each other and the whole often becomes greater than the sum of its parts."

Gant considered that. "But you're talking about your normal, run-of-the-mill killing teams. Civilians."

"There is no such thing as normal when you discuss killers," Golden said.

"OK," Gant acknowledged, "but you're wondering how these guys are operating as a team yet separately. Your theory was that one of them, most likely Forten, was the instigator and the other two, Lutz and Payne, were followers. What you're missing is that all three are way outside the bell curve. They were in Special Operations—the elite. They were trained—and trained in a way most civilians could never understand—to operate both as members of a team and individually when needed.

"Forten might have been the team leader, but I don't think he's the one instigating the other two to act. I think they're all doing this because they want to. They have to. Whatever happened to them down in Colombia was so bad it turned all three into single-minded entities of revenge. To the point where Lutz was prepared to—and did—kill himself rather than be captured."

Neeley stirred. "I just read the file today, but it seems to me that they were captured in Colombia by the drug cartel. Most likely tortured badly. I think it makes perfect sense they would prefer death over imprisonment again."

"If we project that forward," Golden said, "then ultimately they are on a suicide mission."

Gant didn't like that one bit. "That gives them a big advantage."

"How so?" Golden asked.

"They can take bigger risks than we can," Gant said. "It also means that whatever their end goal is, they don't mind dying to achieve it. You give me three guys who are willing to die and I'll take out any target in the world. Nine-eleven proved that."

"That was more than three," Golden noted.

"Four," Gant said.

"'Four'?" Golden was puzzled. "There were—"

"Nineteen hijackers," Gant finished for her. "But I think only the man in charge in each plane knew what was really going to happen. I suspect the others thought they were really doing a hijacking and would make demands, not use the planes as bombs."

That brought a long silence. Golden was the one who finally broke it. "You asked me to predict what our targets' goal is. They've been inflicting suffering on those they feel betrayed them somehow. Foley was the first primary that they killed and—"

Neeley interrupted. "I'm not sure the plan was to kill Foley. I think it might have been planned as a snatch operation on the wife and we foiled it. Grab the wife, leave the partial cache like they did with the Cranston girl."

Gant considered that, as he also processed that Golden had used the term 'targets' rather than 'perps'. "So their plan hit a speed bump. One, they didn't grab Foley's wife, so whatever role she was to play isn't there anymore. And Payne isn't there to play any more either." He shook his head. "They'd have a back-up plan. A go-to-shit plan."

Neeley agreed. "And that plan might be more bloody than their original one."

Gant nodded. "When we did our go-to-shit plan, it was always so that even if only one person survived the team's mission would be accomplished." He looked at Golden. "Once we find out what happened in Colombia, you need to re-evaluate your predictive model based on the fact that our targets are Special Operators. They're going to push the envelope of everything you've ever researched." Gant's eyes lost their focus slightly as he remembered. "I've done Sanctions before. There's a reason the Cellar exists. The normal police can't deal with this type of killer. And your normal predictive models aren't going to be able to deal with them either."

Golden nodded. "I'll do that. I'll adjust."

"We have to be prepared for the worst," Gant said.

Because Talladega was a National Forest, the FBI had no trouble taking charge of the search for Emily Cranston. They'd suborned the local forest rangers and the nearby sheriff's departments to their operation. By the time Mister Bailey arrived, the search was well under way and consisted of over three hundred men and women along with three helicopters. Of course, all they were working on was the information that some psycho had kidnapped a girl and was holding her somewhere in the Park.

Bailey entered the field command post, which was set up in the Park Ranger Headquarters. For a minute he stood in the back of the room, watching the hustle and bustle of people on a mission. He unwrapped a piece of gum and popped it in his mouth. He saw the grid lines drawn on the map of the park that was tacked to the wall and knew the FBI was playing it by the book.

Bailey shook his head and it must have been the movement that caught the attention of a distinguished looking, white-haired woman who apparently was in charge. She strode across the room, the other agents parting way for her, until she was right in front of Bailey. "You're the man I was called about from Washington?"

Bailey nodded.

"I'm Special Agent in Charge Bateman." She wasted no time indicating she didn't like the idea of oversight, even though she had no clue who the overseer was. Nero's missives to various agencies rarely went over well, although they did go over. "And you don't like something we're doing?"

"Who's the most experienced Park Ranger?" Bailey asked. "The one who knows the park the best?"

Special Agent in Charge Bateman turned and crooked a finger. A wizened little old man in a rumpled Park Ranger uniform and a battered Smoky-The-Bear hat ambled over. "Yes, sir?"

"Any old stone chimneys in the Park?" Bailey asked. He could see Bateman's frown turn to anger as she realized information had been withheld. A couple of hours wouldn't make any difference for Emily Cranston, Nero had argued, and he wanted Bailey on scene when they found the cache spot. The others could mess the scene up. Plus, there was the possibility the Sniper—Forten—was on site.

Bailey had received the report on what had happened at the farm-house and knew they had taken down one-third of the targets. There was a good chance another third was located here and could be taken out. He estimated the probability of finding Emily Cranston alive here to be rather low so he did not consider that an issue to be factored into the plan.

The old Ranger frowned in thought. "Yah. There's some old log cabins that pre-dated the establishment of the National Forest here and there throughout the Park. Most have gone to seed, rotted out. Only thing left of most of 'em is the chimney. Made them chimneys good in the old days."

"How many and where?" Bailey asked.

The Ranger walked over to the map. "There was a logging camp here. Small cluster of chimneys in the spot."

"A single chimney," Bailey said, knowing that the immediate reference point had to be exact. "And it might be near the intersections of Routes 219 and 183."

The Ranger stared at the map while he tried to remember. Meanwhile, Bateman placed herself in front of Bailey. "You've withheld information." She said it as a fact.

Bailey popped his gum. "Just learned it myself," he lied.

"Who the hell are you?" Bateman demanded.

"You have your orders," Bailey said.

"And I follow them," Bateman said, "but not blindly. Who are you? What agency are you with?"

Bailey noted that the other agents in the room had become still, trying to hear. The Ranger was still staring at the map, but even his head was cocked toward the two of them, trying to listen in. This was the part of the job that simply tired Bailey out. Turf wars and people concerned with their careers. He leaned forward, his mouth just inches from Bateman's ear and whispered.

"I'm with the Cellar."

He had to give her credit. The only obvious reaction—and it wasn't that obvious—was her face got pale. She took a slight step back and nodded ever so slightly. "All right then."

Bailey knew that she had little idea what the Cellar really was—no one outside of it did. But he also knew she'd heard the whispers and the rumors. And she appeared to be smart enough to realize that rumors sometimes never equaled the truth.

The other agents exchanged puzzled glances, wondering what had been said. The Park Ranger reached toward the map with a gnarled finger. "Here. There's a stone chimney all by its self. Not easy to find if you didn't know it was there. Mostly overgrown with vines. But it's only about a half mile from the intersection of those two roads."

Bailey looked at the map. He reached over to a nearby desk and grabbed an index card. He placed it against the distance scale on the bottom of the map, ticked off a smidge more than two-hundred meters then placed it on the map, swinging it around to an approximation of two-hundred and seventy-four degrees. He marked that spot.

"Know that place?"

The Ranger stared at it. "Small clearing. There's a big old oak tree in the middle."

"That's it," Bailey said to Bateman. "There's a good chance the target—perp—is in the area watching the girl. She's most likely chained to the tree. It could be an ambush. The perp is a trained sniper. Also has access to mines and explosives."

"Jesus," Batemen muttered. "Who the hell is this guy?"

"Might be two guys," Bailey said, adding to her dilemma. "But most likely just one." He paused. "They're former Special Operations."

Bateman nodded. Then she turned to her agents and began barking out orders. She ended with: "Let's get the girl!" Within seconds the room was clear except for Bailey, Bateman and the old Ranger.

"I've got a chopper inbound," Bateman said. "We can be there in five minutes, but I'm letting the HRT team go in first. They're already airborne and en route."

Bailey nodded. The Hostage Rescue Team was a good idea. Well-trained and as good as any domestic police force could field. Hell, they were trained by Special Operations people and had lots of real world experience.

Against civilian criminals, Bailey realized.

He followed Bateman out to the parking lot as a Bell Jet Ranger helicopter landed. They climbed in the back. As the chopper lifted, Bailey looked back at the building and saw the old Ranger standing in the doorway, staring back at him. Just before they cleared the trees around the lot, Bailey saw the old man turn away.

The chopper banked and the building was out of sight. Bailey was experiencing an unusual feeling of discomfort and he couldn't quite place the reason why.

"HRT is one minute out from the site," Bateman said to him over the intercom.

Every piece of the puzzle that was leading them to this site had been given to them, Bailey realized. The logic flow was clear: they were meant to find this spot, which meant either that they would find Emily Cranston's body or it was an ambush.

"Too easy," Bailey said.

Bateman turned to him. "What?"

"It's too easy. It's a trap."

"HRT's ready," Bateman said.

I doubt it, Bailey thought, but did not voice. He pulled another piece of gum out and opened it. "It's a trap," he repeated.

"Thirty seconds out," Bateman announced, listening in to the tactical channel. She looked at Bailey. "HRT's prepared. We've got to save the girl."

Bailey popped the gum in his mouth. He knew she had the single-minded focus. She's never been spanked, smashed, defeated, beaten by someone meaner and nastier. He had a feeling that was about to change and he knew there was nothing he could say that would get that feeling across to her.

The helicopter they were on gained altitude and Bailey could now see the two Huey choppers flying in low over the trees from the west. Men in black fatigues with body armor and helmets lined the skids, ready to jump off, weapons pointed outward. The chopper Bailey was on gained altitude so that they could now see the clearing.

Bailey noted the large oak tree in the center and the fact there was no sign of Emily Cranston. The two Hueys touched down briefly on either side of the oak tree, the HRT members jumping off and hitting the ground, and then the choppers were back up in the air to take up over-watch positions.

There was a moment of stillness. Even inside the hovering helicopter, with the turbine engines whining behind him and the blades whopping by overhead, Bailey could sense it. And he knew exactly what the feeling meant. Danger.

The HRT members got to their feet, weapons at the ready. Bailey could hear them on the tactical net. They confirmed what could be seen from the air: no sign of Emily Cranston.

But there was a chain around the tree.

One of the men moved toward the tree, made four steps, then disappeared in a flash of explosion. A couple of the others ran to his position and both also hit mines.

"Everyone freeze!" Bailey yelled over the tactical net, trying to over-ride the confused chatter that had almost overwhelmed the radio system. "Do not move."

Beside him Bateman was shocked, her eyes wide, taking in the disaster below them.

Bailey looked through binoculars at the clearing. There were three bodies, bloodied and not moving. A couple of other HRT members were down, wounded. Claymore mines, Bailey realized. Set on trip wires. The entire clearing was probably laced with them.

Bateman still seemed stunned. Bailey decided this wasn't the time to be political, not that such a consideration was ever high on his list. He turned to her. "Have your choppers drop STABO lines to those not wounded to lift them, then hover them over to the wounded and hook in. Two men on a line. Get the wounded to the Ranger station. Then evac all those in the field. Then get explosives experts out here. It's going to take a while to clear that field."

Which was the point, Bailey knew. Slow down the pursuers. It was a classic military tactic, except in this case, the true pursuers were at DEA headquarters. Bailey leaned back in the seat as Bateman yelled orders over the radio.

He turned to the side and spit his gum out of the chopper as he considered the fact that the game was getting closer to the end point.

CHAPTER EIGHTEEN

THE HELICOPTER TOUCHED down on the roof of DEA headquarters in Alexandria, Virginia and there was only one person waiting to greet Gant, Neeley and Golden as they exited. A tall man, thin to the point of emaciation, with disheveled gray hair held a hand up to his eyes to block the backwash from the blades as the chopper touched down.

Gant took point, walking up to the man. "Are you up to speed on the situation?"

The man stared at him with dead eyes. "My names Caulkins. Michael Caulkins."

An image of the girl chained to the tree in Tennessee flashed in front of Gant's eyes. He paused, not sure what to say. Golden stepped past him. "We're terribly sorry for your loss."

Caulkins looked at her with the same dead stare. "Are you?"

"Yes." Golden's voice got through to Caulkins in some way.

"Why?" he asked.

"I lost a son in a similar way, so I have an idea what you're feeling."

Score one for the doc, Gant thought. Caulkins paused, then nodded, indicating for them to follow him. They went in the roof entrance and took an elevator ride down a few floors. Caulkins led them down a carpeted hallway and into a conference room. He shut the door behind them and took the seat at the head of the long table. Gant, Neeley and Golden arrayed themselves around the table.

"What do you want?" Caulkins asked.

Gant pulled out the three personnel folders and slid them across to Caulkins. "Those are the men who killed your daughter."

134

Caulkins looked through the folders, then looked up, confused. "They're soldiers. Why did they do this?"

"They were members of 7th Special Forces Group based in Panama," Gant said. "They were running missions for Task Force Six."

Some degree of comprehension came to Caulkins face.

Gant pushed the information, slapping down photos on the desk. "These are the others they've killed." He rattled off their names and the family members. Before he got to the end, Caulkins was shaking his head.

"I know them now. Those three guys are dead. They died in a helicopter crash during exfiltration."

Gant glanced at Golden, then back at the Drug Enforcement Agent. He pulled out his digital camera, thumbed through and then showed a picture of the remnants of Sergeant Lutz's body. "One of them is dead now. Killed this morning in Virginia. He had just killed Lewis Foley of the State Department and his wife. Along with two security men.

"The other two are still out there. They've got the daughter of Colonel Cranston and we believe she's in the same predicament that you daughter was in."

"Jesus Christ," Caulkins exclaimed. "Why?"

Gant began collecting the photos. "You said you believed they died in a helicopter crash during exfiltration. Who told you that?"

"I was working the ops desk for the Southern District, Panama," Caulkins said. "The sniper team—those three guys, I only know their names, never met them-- was seconded to us by Southern Command, Spec Ops, Task Force Six."

"Colonel Cranston?" Golden asked.

Caulkins nodded. "Yes."

"Who was in overall charge?" Gant asked.

"Technically, I was," Caulkins said.

Neeley spoke for the first time. "'Technically'?"

"We had what we thought was a high level target. The team was to eliminate the target. Then they called in they had someone with a badge on the site. They thought he was DEA, but I hadn't been briefed on anyone in that AO. So I called it in to our Central Intelligence Agency liaison. He got back with me almost immediately and told me to stop the mission and exfiltrate the team. That's what I did, except the chopper crashed during exfiltration."

Gant leaned back in his chair. "Cranston told us the DEA was the agency that ordered the mission to stop and exfiltration."

Caulkins shrugged. "I relayed the order to him, so he might have assumed I was the originator of it."

"Who was the—" Gant began, but he was interrupted when his Satphone vibrated. He snapped it open, listened for a little bit, then shut it without saying a word. He looked at Golden and Neeley. "Emily Cranston wasn't at the cache site. She'd been moved. The entire area was laced with mines. Two members of the FBI's Hostage Rescue Team that went in were killed and three wounded. The site is still not secure."

"You were right," Golden said.

Gant ignored the acknowledgement. He stared at Caulkins. "Who was the Agency liaison? Jim Roberts?"

Caulkins nodded. "Yes."

"And you don't know who the man with the badge in the village was?"

"No."

"He wasn't DEA?" Gant pressed.

"As far I knew, he wasn't."

"This is bullshit," Neeley said.

Everyone turned to her in surprise. Neeley looked at Caulkins. "I'm sorry about your daughter, but everyone has a different story about what happened to these three guys. The only thing everyone agrees on is they thought the guys died in a chopper crash and we know for sure that wasn't true. Since one of them was killing people this morning and the other two are on the loose."

"Believe me," Caulkins said, "I want to know the truth too. I've checked as much as I can here and as far as I can tell the DEA did not have an agent in that village. And the decision to abort the mission came from the CIA—I only relayed it."

"Why did the CIA want you to abort?"

"I don't really know."

Gant stood. "Is there anything else you can think of that might help us figure out what these guys are up to?"

Caulkins nodded. "There is something—it was only a rumor and I didn't think much of it at the time, but in light of what I've since learned, there might be more to it."

Gant waited.

"There was talk among my field agents about the CIA running some sort of black op in Colombia. Lots of money exchanging hands."

"With who?" Gant asked.

"The cartels of course," Caulkins said.

"Why?" Gant was getting tired of digging into darkness.

"I don't know and I'm not likely ever to find out," Caulkins said. "And neither are you."

"We'll see about that," Gant said.

They walked out of the room and headed for the waiting helicopter. Gant turned to Neeley. "After the chopper drops us at Langley it will take you to the airfield. There will be a jet waiting for you to fly you to Alabama and the cache site."

"Emily Cranston's not there," Neeley said. "What do you want me to do?"

"Get a feel for the site. For the person who did this."

Neeley reluctantly nodded.

The first conscious thought Emily Cranston had was that she was no longer moving. The next was that she was lying on something hard. She was on her back and she realized that she no longer had the blindfold on.

Still, she didn't open her eyes. She wasn't sure she wanted to see where she was now. The air was different. Warmer. Drier.

She could sense she was not in an enclosed space. At least not as enclosed as the van had been.

And the damn shackle was still on her ankle.

Emily opened her eyes and blinked. A clear blue sky was above her, framed by a perfect circle of wood. Emily blinked once more, turning her head. She was surrounded by a wooden wall, perfectly round, eight feet high. She was chained to a bolt set in the very center of the wood floor, the open space about twelve feet in diameter.

Not as tight as the van but still enclosed. So much for her senses.

"What the fuck?" Emily muttered as she struggled to get to her feet.

The wood was old. Bleached by the sun. There was a trace of sand on the floor.

Emily stomped her foot and was surprised to hear an echo. The floor wasn't solid. She got on her knees and wrapped her hand around the metal bolt that the chain to her shackles was locked to. She pulled as hard as she could but it didn't budge in the slightest.

She continued to try for several minutes until she was panting. Finally she gave up for the moment and sat down, running a swollen tongue over her parched lips. It had been over two days since she'd had anything to drink other than the scant drops of dew. She was grateful that she had been drinking water in the night-club rather than alcohol.

Thinking that made her realize how long ago that seemed. To be part of the real world, the normal world. Where her largest concern had been not getting asked to dance. When she had worried about the extra weight that was now coming off faster than any diet in the latest fad. Emily would have laughed if her parched throat would have allowed—now she was grateful she'd had that weight on.

Emily looked up at the wooden ring above her head, then at the planks making up the circular wall. She'd never seen anything like this. Had the crazy man built this just to stash her? It didn't make sense, given that he had simply chained her to a tree at the last place.

She got to her feet and stomped down, listening to the slight echo. That meant there was empty space beneath her. A cellar? But then what had happened to the roof? Had there ever been a roof? And there were no doors. Emily walked to the end of the chain and was just able to touch the wall. The wood was old. Each plank was about eight inches wide. She slapped her hand against one and it felt very solid. She slowly walked the circumference of her new prison, checking each plank, one by one, hoping perhaps that one would be rotted or weak.

No such luck.

Emily returned to the center and sat down next to the bolt that held her in place. She had thought the tree was bad, but at least there had been things to look at and the feeling of space. Emily felt closed in, more imprisoned than she had before. She had no idea where she was, what was on the other side of the wooden wall.

"Help!" she screamed at the top of her lungs. She repeated the cry several times, but there was only silence, not even an echo of her scream. Which made her miss the sounds of the forest even though those sounds had turned threatening at night. All she had was a uniform wooden wall and the blue sky overhead.

Emily lay on her back and stared up at that sky and felt as if her heart were going to sink through her back, into the floor and keep going down into the earth itself.

It had taken the explosives experts three hours to remove the rest of the mines from the clearing. They were all not only rigged to trip-wires, they have been booby-trapped. Bailey recognized the handiwork and the pattern: it was the way Special Forces demolitions men were trained to prepare an ambush on a potential helicopter landing zone. It had just been pure luck that neither of the insertion choppers had hit a trip wire with a skid. If that had happened there would have been a very high body count and a destroyed chopper—stuff that would have been hard to keep out of the news.

Still, two men were dead and three wounded. Emily wasn't here, nor was the target. Mister Nero would not be happy. Nor would he be particularly unhappy, Bailey knew. Bailey paused as he walked toward the oak tree as he suddenly remembered it was Ms. Masterson who sat behind the desk now, not Nero. Since joining the Cellar over thirty years ago, Bailey had known no other boss than Nero. In fact, to Bailey, Nero *was* the Cellar. Ms. Masterson's placement behind the desk was the most disconcerting thing Bailey had ever experienced and he had seen many strange things in the employ of the Cellar.

Bailey had instructed Special Agent in Charge Bateman to keep her people at the perimeter after the area had been cleared. He wanted to see the site alone and without interference. She had not been pleased—with that or with two dead agents. Lots of paperwork, lots of explaining, lots of sadness over loss of life. Bailey wasn't into any of the above so he didn't concern himself.

Bateman had demanded more information, indicating a very strong desire to be 'in' on the mission of tracking down the target. Bailey had ignored her requests and told her to do as ordered. He would have thought she would have seen with what had just happened that this was something the FBI could not deal with. The HRT team was the best they had—what did she think they could do for an encore?

He surveyed the area, keeping in mind the site where they had found the Caulkins girl. Gant had found the surveillance position that had been used by one of the targets. Not only in advance of the cache being put in, but based on recent information, also manned while Caulkins slowly dehydrated and starved.

Bailey moved to his right, toward a clump of bushes and a large log. He clambered over the log and saw the carefully constructed surveillance position. It was, as he expected, sterile. Bailey stood where the target had been watching Emily Cranston chained to that tree.

It took a hard man to do that, Bailey knew. He'd served with and fought against many hard men. The closest person to the type of these targets was a man named Racine who the Cellar had used on missions for many years. When the job was particularly nasty, and especially if it involved women, Racine was the man Nero had turned to, even though both he and Bailey had detested the sociopath.

There were dangers to using such men, Bailey reflected as he looked at the oak tree. Unknown to Nero and Bailey, Racine had been doing un-sanctioned freelance work for a United States Senator. Work that had hurt the United States during the debacle in Mogadishu over a decade before. And Racine had eventually become more of a liability over the years, one that was terminated quite efficiently by Ms. Neeley and Ms. Masterson, sort of their final exam before joining the Cellar. And while the US Army and the US government had probably been more than happy with Sergeants Lutz, Forten and Payne and the work they had done over the years in the country's service, they too were now liabilities. Liabilities with the best training in inflicting death and destruction in the world.

Bailey stepped back over the log and walked toward the tree. He side-stepped a splotch of still wet blood. When he got within ten feet of the tree, he halted once more. There was something white nailed to the tree, about eye-level.

A piece of paper.

Bailey nodded. The next step in the trail.

The compound was set on an island in the middle of a lake in Northern Maine. The island wasn't large, barely four acres, but it was thickly covered with trees, which mostly hid the six buildings. The perimeter of the island was patrolled by guards, two in a small boat that circled the island in a random pattern and a shift of four on the land itself, set in small watch towers positioned to cover the entire shoreline.

The inhabitants of the compound lived in a limbo between prison and protection. It was debatable whether the guards where there to protect them or keep them from leaving. It was also debatable how many of the two dozen inhabitants had any desire to leave given their life expectancy would probably be hours, at best days, if they were spotted by the wrong people out in the real world. The wrong people being those they had betrayed in order to save their own hides.

The compound was under the control of the CIA although the guards were contracted from private security firms, mostly ex-Special Operations Forces types. It was considered plush duty, beating work in Iraq or Afghanistan, where most of them had spent several tours of duty. The CIA used these contractors not only because its own ranks were stretched thin, but for deniability in case the compound was ever exposed in the media. In the same manner the CIA had gotten the Army to take the fall for Abu Gharif in Iraq.

This was because the compound was quite illegal as none of the twenty-four people being held there had ever been charged with a crime and had been secretly brought into the country. The compound did not 'officially' exist on paper. It was funded by the multi-billion dollar Black Budget that saw little government over-sight. The same budget that funded the Cellar.

Spotter was on the top of a mountain on the shoreline three quarters of a mile from the island. He and the Sniper had checked out the area extensively during their mission preparation. They'd spent three months getting ready before snatching the first girl, carefully preparing their primary plan and the numerous contingencies. Things were moving fast now. The lack of an after-action report from the Security in Virginia meant he was most likely dead.

This did not bother Spotter. Indeed, it had been anticipated that they would lose at least one of their number by now. The plan would still go forward. And death was preferable to what they had experienced in

Colombia. And even more so for what they had experienced when they came back to the States.

He had a large spotting scope set up on a tripod in front of his field chair and had been using it to survey the island for the past twenty-four hours after arriving here from the Gulf Coast. The guards were good, rotating their patrol so that there was no distinguishable or predictable pattern to it. Also, one of the guards was on a small knoll on the north end of the island, the highest point on it, armed with a sniper rifle with which he could cover the entire island.

Frankly, though, Spotter didn't care about the guards. He was more concerned with the people being held there. One in particular. This was the man who the scope was trained on as he sat at a small table, reading a book.

Spotter knew the man's face intimately.

The small radio earplug in Spotter's ear crackled with a brief break of squelch and he pulled his eye back from the scope and looked in the other direction, downhill. Within a minute the Sniper appeared, striding up the slope, a backpack over his shoulder and his black metal case containing his rifle in one hand.

The Sniper nodded as he came up next to Spotter, putting the case down and taking the backpack off. "Any change?"

"No." Spotter vacated the seat. "He's in the scope."

The Sniper took the chair and put his eye to the spotting scope. He remained still for a long time, then pulled back. "You pin down where he sleeps?"

"Third building, second window. He's the only one in the room."

"Good."

"Do you know what happened in Virginia?" Spotter asked.

The Sniper shook his head. "No after-action report, so I assume he's dead. I wasn't able to pick up much information. They're not making it public, that's for certain."

"And the girl?"

"She's in position."

"The video?"

"En route with further instructions." The Sniper leaned over and opened up the metal case, extracting the rifle. A thermal scope was mounted on top and a bulky suppressor graced the end of the barrel. He removed the spotting scope from the tripod and replaced it with the rifle.

"We should make him suffer first," Spotter suddenly said, earning him a surprised look from the Sniper.

"We agreed. That's not the plan. Too dangerous."

"He'll never know it was us," Spotter argued. "He'll die not knowing."

"We'll know," the Sniper said. "That's the important thing. And he's only a bonus hit." He tightened down the bolt holding the rifle in place. "Come sun-down, he dies."

CHAPTER NINETEEN

THE CIA HATED the Cellar. At least, those with high enough clearances to know of the Cellar's existence hated it specifically. The rest of the employees of the sprawling intelligence organization only heard whispers of the Cellar and few had ever encountered one of its handful of operatives. And such encounters were never welcomed. The CIA liked to think of itself as the biggest, baddest man on the block and the concept, even if whispered, that there was someone, not as big, but meaner, out there did not sit well. That someone from another organization could slap down anyone in the CIA riled its members.

This, of course, was part of the overall problem that the Cellar was trying to overcome. The rivalries, the egos involved, between people and organizations that were supposed to work together in defense of the country.

Gant knew all this as he walked into the lobby of the new CIA headquarters in Langley. There were people he knew who served in Able Danger, a highly classified and compartmentalized part of Special Operations Command, that had identified a cell of the nine-eleven hijackers over a year before the event and wanted to relay the information to the FBI but had been denied permission to pass it on. Gant knew that Nero was chafing at the bit to expand the role of the Cellar from chasing down rogue operatives to breaking down the walls between the bureaucracies.

It was not something Gant felt positive about because he had a feeling that attempting to do that would have the reverse effect: suck the Cellar into the world of bureaucracy. He shoved these thoughts from his mind as he walked through the lobby and focused on the current situation.

They had parted company with Neeley at the airfield—she was on her way to the cache site to meet Bailey who had found a partial cache report. Once more the partial was worthless by itself listing only and Immediate Reference Point (IRP) of a road crossing railroad tracks and an Azimuth and Direction (A/D) of one hundred and sixty degrees and four hundred and twelve meters to the cache.

Given there were tens of thousands of rail-lines crisscrossing the country, this information was of little aid. It was another taunt according to Golden. Gant had not found that observation very insightful.

Golden was still with him, but so far she had been of limited use. If he took away all her contributions to the mission so far, nothing would be different in his opinion other than a couple of the people they had interviewed might feel a bit worse for the process. She had come up with the names of the three targets, but only as part of a possible group of sixteen. Gant had gotten the three names much more easily and quickly.

So Gant was ignoring her, focusing his attention on the mission. Two men had died today at the cache site—two innocent men who had only been doing their jobs. Two more innocent men had died this morning at the farm. So he was not in the best of moods when one of the many suits moving through the lobby came toward him and stuck out his hand.

"Mister Gant?"

Gant ignored the hand. "Yes."

"Deputy Director Roberts is waiting for you."

Gant simply nodded and the agent, after a moment of confusion, lowered his hand and turned on his heel, leading them toward an elevator. As they walked Gant glanced to his right at the memorial wall. He'd seen it before. Eighty-three stars adorned the wall, one for each CIA officer who'd been killed in the line of duty. Gant knew that even today, thirty-five of the names represented there had never been made public, still classified, even in death.

Memorials to the dead, he mused, thinking back to the wall at Bragg, as they got into the elevator. Bureaucracies seemed to go for those. While they were touted as testaments and honor to those who they represented, Gant believed they were designed more with the living, who would see them, in mind. Everyone wanted to be immortal, at least in thought.

The Cellar had no such memorial. In fact, Gant had no idea how many people were in the employ of the Cellar. He worked for Nero and he had always worked alone prior to this mission. Bailey had always been his mission briefer. When he needed logistical support, he used the power of the Cellar to commandeer it from whatever various government agency he needed to.

The elevator came to a halt and the nameless flunky led them down a carpeted corridor to a door, which he rapped on lightly, then opened, beckoning them in. Gant slid by the man, Golden following and the door was shut behind them.

The room was dimly lit, the shades closed, only a small light in the corner pointing up illuminating it. A figure was seated in the chair behind the desk but that was all Gant could make out. He had memories of meeting Nero in his dimly lit underground chamber.

"Deputy Director Roberts?" Gant asked.

"Yes." The voice was low, almost a whisper.

Another father in pain, Gant thought. He couldn't see Roberts' face as the man was deep in the shadow of his chair.

"My name is Gant. I'm from the—"

"The Cellar," Roberts interrupted. "I've been waiting for someone to show up from that place."

"If you've been waiting," Gant said, "then you know who they are."

"I've been getting reports," Roberts said. "Lutz, Paine and Forten. We thought they were dead."

Gant walked forward and sat down in one of the two seats in front of the desk. Golden took the other. He hoped that as a shrink, she would appreciate the importance of silence and waiting, letting the other person do the talking. So far, she seemed to.

Roberts reached forward and turned on a desk lamp. Gant wasn't surprised by the man's appearance. His face was long and drawn with deep, dark pockets under his eyes.

"My wife—ex-wife—is making all the funeral arrangements. I'm not invited." He sighed deeply. "She doesn't know, but she does know. She knows this had something to do with the job. I loved that about her when we were first married. That she knew things without me having to tell her. You know. Because I couldn't tell her much at all about what I was doing. Now I hate it."

Roberts reached out and picked up a letter opener, a miniature Samurai sword that he began to play with, flipping it through his fingers. "Yesterday I wondered if this was some sort of, I don't know, mis-direction mission. A test. To see how I handled things. I've seen some strange shit in my time here at the Agency. But when my ex called me, I knew it was real. She was with the body in Alabama. I knew she'd never go along with anything about Caleigh. I knew then she was indeed dead."

Gant glanced over at Golden. She looked thoughtful and concerned and he realized she was slipping back into her therapist mode. He turned back to Roberts. The man wasn't looking at either of them. His eyes were on the flashing metal blade of the letter opener as he moved it about under the light.

"She'll never forgive me." He laughed, a dry, forced noise. "Not that it matters with Caleigh dead. I guess Caleigh will never forgive me either."

Gant stirred. The waiting thing was all right, but it was time to get on task. Roberts looked up. "Which one of them killed her?"

"We don't know," Gant lied. "One of them is dead now. Lutz."

Roberts looked surprised, lifting ever so slightly out of his despair. "I didn't hear that."

"He died this morning," Gant said, "trying to attack Lewis Foley of the State Department and his wife. Unfortunately, Foley and his wife were killed in the attack. As were two State Department security people. And two FBI HRT team members were killed today trying to find another girl who was kidnapped by these guys."

Roberts slumped back in his seat, dropping the letter opener to the desktop. "Fuck."

"Yeah," Gant said. "So tell me what happened so we can get the other two."

Roberts lowered his head, putting his hands on either side, rubbing his scalp. When he spoke it was so hard to hear him that both Gant and Golden had to lean forward in their chairs.

"It was relatively straightforward. Columbia. Drug trafficking. The DEA got the village elders in a major transport hub for the Cartel to turn. Promised them lots of cash, lots of aid. And protection from the local warlord. That was the key. So the team was sent in as protection. They were to take out the local warlord who was moving the drugs. We had a tip when he would be showing up to punish the villagers."

"And?" Gant pushed, earning a hard glance from Golden.

"It was a stupid and naïve plan," Roberts said.

"Of course it was," Gant agreed. "Taking out the warlord would only delay the inevitable. But you didn't care about that. What did you care about?"

"We had a deep cover agent," Roberts said. "It's like—" he paused as he tried to think—"like a damn wedding cake." He used his hands as he described. "Layers. Big on the bottom, lots of bottom feeders. Getting narrower as you go up. The warlord was like layer three up. But the agent, he was getting close to the, you know, the little statue of the couple on top. The key players. There are two people who run it all down there and we'd been after both of them for a very long time. And our agent was close to one of them.

"Took him three years. Three years deep under cover. Working from Miami down south, through the food chain of traffickers. Selling his fucking soul to go up the bad guy feeding chain. Selling his God-damn soul."

Roberts was breathing hard and Gant looked over once more at Golden. She was perfectly still, watching. He turned back as Roberts continued.

"He was my older brother. Served in the Marines. We went through the Agency course together. I got promoted faster than him. He didn't care. He wanted to be in the field. I wanted to be in charge.

"He left everything behind. His life. His wife divorced him after a year of only seeing him once and took the kid. He stayed on the job. He went under deeper than anyone we ever had. He was like one of those fucking people in a National Geographic show breathing God-damn special liquid mixture in their lungs so they could go deeper into the ocean depths than anyone else ever went before.

"There were times he was out of contact for so long, we figured he'd been discovered and killed. He went three months once without making contact. He couldn't take the chance, he told me when he finally made a meet. And he had to do things, bad things, to prove his cover."

"Like go to a village in the company of a warlord?" Gant asked, confused about why an undercover agent would be carrying a badge.

Roberts shook his head. "No." He sighed. "That was me."

Emily lifted her head, cocking it to one side to try to listen better. There was a distant sound, one she couldn't quite make out yet. It was late afternoon to judge by the shadow that had climbed up the eastern side of the wood.

Distant thunder? But it was steady and getting closer.

Emily got to her feet and went toward the side of the enclosure that seemed to be closest to the approaching rumble. The entire wood structure began to vibrate.

Earthquake? Emily had never experienced one. But it seemed to steady and non-stop. And it was moving, coming closer, getting louder. There was another sound now, underlying the rumble, almost like metal on metal. Getting nearer at a rapid pace. It was indeed metal on metal she suddenly realized.

The blast of the train's whistle caused her to jump, it was so close and unexpected.

"Help!" Emily screamed. "Help me!"

Utter frustration blanketed her as the train rumbled by, very close by the sound, yet she knew her yells were drowned out by the roar of the train's engine and the rattle of its wheels on the metal tracks.

Emily pounded her fists on the wooden panel as the train went by. People were so close, yet they might as well have been a hundred miles away. The train must have been a long one because it sounded like it was right next to her for over five minutes, then finally the sound began to recede. Emily listened, ears straining, until finally silence ruled once more.

Emily shook her head as she walked back to the center and sat down. She couldn't let it get to her. She had a feeling the bad man had specifically picked this location so that she could hear the train come by so close—suddenly she realized what she was enclosed in. A water tower from the old days, when trains needed water for their steam engines.

Emily took several deep breaths. If she could get out of this, she could be rescued. She was close to people. At least there were people when a train passed. She looked at the bolt, the chain, the shackle and the lock. As before, the weakest part was the lock. And she still had one under-wire left. Emily stretched her hands out, feeling the pain from the still un-healed cuts she'd inflicted on herself with her last attempt.

She didn't care. She had to do something.

There was another bright side to her current location, she realized as she pulled the remains of her bra off and began working the other wire free. She wasn't being watched.

"What happened?" Gant asked.

Roberts ran a hand across his forehead, the fingers shaking ever so slightly. "Mike—my brother—had a line on one of the two top Cartel leaders in Colombia. He'd been going after him for three years, like I told you. I mean, these guys are like ghosts. They let others stand out in front and take the public heat and the hits. These guys are the real power and to get to meet one of them, well, it's damn near impossible if you hadn't been in their inner circle for decades. And Mike had a meeting scheduled with one of them. You have no idea what he had to do in order to get that meeting set up."

"Actually, I probably do," Gant said. "He had to prove himself and the only way to do that is with blood."

Roberts looked startled, then nodded. His eyes shifted back and forth and Gant knew what he was about to hear would haunt Roberts until the day he died, but Gant didn't care. Whatever had been done had most likely gone wrong and now a lot of other people were paying the price.

"We knew going in it was going to get dirty. We had to weigh things. It was already nasty on the street level with the drugs and the money getting channeled to terrorists. Most people don't know it, but there is a definite link between drug money and terrorists."

Gant noted the tone of justification that was creeping into Roberts' voice. The man was going to spend many sleepless nights trying to convince himself of what he was trying to convince them of right now. Gant also knew that there had been definite links between the US government and drug money when it had been expedient. Money was money was the feeling at times.

"For the greater good," Gant said. He kept his tone level. In reality, he didn't condemn Roberts. He knew Nero had often made very hard decisions, always for the greater good of the country. And Gant had been on some missions where the price paid had been very high, beyond what was acceptable in the 'normal' world. He had long ago left the normal world behind. For the first time, Gant realized with a degree of surprise, he was almost happy that the targets had kidnapped Emily Cranston. It made the ethics of the current Sanction very cut and dry.

"Yes," Roberts said, anxious for any sign of empathy. "We actually held a meeting. Myself, the Director of Operations and the Chief of Direct Action. To decide how much we were willing to give up to get Mike in place."

"So how many lives did you decide it was worth?" Gant asked. He could see Golden taking this in, her eyes wide. Time for her to grow up, Gant thought.

"We knew it would take at least one," Roberts said. "We were willing to go as high as three."

Golden couldn't remain silent. "What is wrong with you people?"

"It's the way the real world works," Roberts said. "You want another nine-eleven?" He didn't wait for an answer. Now that it was out on the table, he seemed anxious to be done with talking about it. "It wasn't going to be random and we agreed that whoever we gave up was going to be dirty. Someone who was already betraying us. So Mike gave up a dirty DEA agent to the Cartel."

"The one who had brokered the deal with the village," Gant said, starting to see the pieces falling into place.

"Yes. Except we didn't know about that deal. We just knew this guy was working an op against the Cartel, mid-level, but he was also taking bribe money. He was giving up who the Cartel told him to give up. Essentially getting rid of their competitors.

"We were working very high-level. So we were taken by surprise when we finally got wind of what was planned. Mike had already tipped off the Cartel about the agent. Mike and a couple of Cartel guys picked him up. Besides, it was a stupid plan, as you pointed out."

Roberts licked his lips and his eyes were downcast. "They took him to a place—a place where the Cartel extracted information from people. And punished those who got in their way. They tortured him. That's when they found out about the deal. But even the agent didn't know that the team had been scheduled to go in and take out the warlord. That was being generated by the higher-ups in the DEA in Panama City. Who, of course, didn't know about our op."

Roberts voice went up slightly. "We couldn't tell them. It was too dangerous. So the left hand didn't know what the right hand was doing. The

Cartel decided to punish the village. And they wanted it to be known that the DEA could not be trusted. So they wanted someone to go in there with a badge, standing with the warlord. Mike said he could take care of that. And he sent a message to me. Along with the kidnapped DEA agent's badge. So I went."

"What happened to the agent?" Golden asked.

Stupid question, Gant thought but didn't voice.

"He disappeared and we assume they killed him. Which would have actually been merciful after the damage they probably had done to him during torture. I've seen what they do to people. Same as they sent a message by what they did in that village."

"Which was?" Golden pushed.

Roberts eyes got distant as he remembered. "They killed pretty much everyone. Let a couple of old women go free so they could spread the story that the DEA was not to be trusted."

"How many people killed?" Golden demanded.

"Fifty. Sixty. I didn't count."

Golden sat back as if she had been punched in the sternum. Gant ignored her.

"And the Special Forces team?" Gant asked.

"When they spotted me they called it in to Task Force Six which bounced the query to the Embassy. The duty officer knew I was down there. He didn't know why or what for, but he called me on my satellite phone. I ordered the mission to be aborted. If those God-damn guys had just followed orders, everything would have been all right."

"Except for the dead DEA agent and villagers," Golden said.

"It's a war," Roberts said. "Sometimes there are casualties."

"So Caleigh was a casualty of war?" Golden asked.

Gant could see the question strike home as Roberts flinched.

"Why are they going after family members and not the people directly responsible?" Gant asked.

Roberts shook his head. "I don't know."

"To cause emotional pain," Golden said. She was staring hard at Roberts. "It's working, right?"

"It's working," Roberts admitted.

Gant tried working through all the pieces. "Did your brother get the Cartel leader?"

Roberts let out a deep breath. "No."

"So it was all a waste," Golden said.

"Is your brother still under cover?" Gant asked.

"No. The whole thing fell apart. He got pulled out and is working here at Langley now."

"And the warlord?" Gant asked.

Roberts looked startled. "What about him?"

"What happened to him?"

Roberts hesitated and Gant felt a surge of anger. "Just God-damn tell me," he snapped, surprising Golden with his anger.

"I tried to use him as another angle of attack on the Cartel leader," Roberts said. "It didn't work so we pulled him out into protective custody."

Gant rubbed a hand against his temple. What a cluster-fuck. "So he's safe. Where?"

"We have a secure compound where we keep people like him."

Gant slapped the top of the desk. "Where?"

"Maine." Roberts frowned. "Why?"

"Our targets are Special Forces. Don't you think they're going to finish their original mission?"

CHAPTER TWENTY

IT WAS HER fourth night of captivity. It took Emily several minutes to figure out the exact number. One night in the van being taken to the forest. Two nights in the forest. And her first night here. She no longer felt hungry. There were no more rumbles of protest from her stomach. She didn't understand why that was and did not take it as a positive development. Even her mental gymnastics to view her growing weight loss in a positive light had faded to nothing. Skinny and dead wasn't a good combination.

Thirst was another matter, a constant that was steadily growing worse. Her mouth was beyond parched. Her skin felt dry and tight. Her hands and feet were swollen. But the largest tell on her level of dehydration was the lack of tears. She realized she had not produced tears when she cried in many hours. The crying jags would come on her unexpectedly and were becoming more and more frequent.

Another train had come by just after the sunset and she had been able to see the glow of the train's lights over the lip of the cistern. She couldn't help the surge of frustration as she futilely screamed for help as the train rattled by.

The silence that descended after the train passed was absolute, once more making her miss the noise of the forest although not the animals. She realized from both the lack of sound and the lack of humidity that she had to be in an almost desert environment, which meant she had most likely been moved west from her previous location.

Emily lay on her back, staring up at the stars. She had made no progress on the lock using the wire from her bra. Remembering her earlier failure she had been loath to put much pressure on the wire, but she also knew that to turn the tumbler would take a strong effort, a Catch-22 gamble that she was not ready to take. She had the wire in her left hand, a piece of security and there was a part of her that felt if it broke, she would break.

The wire was to be a last resort now, when she reached a critical point. People had to be looking for her. Perhaps a helicopter or plane would fly overhead and someone would spot her. Perhaps she was being held for ransom, although she knew her father was not a rich man, and it would be paid and then she would be rescued.

There was a constellation almost directly overhead but Emily had never studied the stars so she had no idea which one it was. She imagined her father would know and then be able to pinpoint where she was on the ground from the alignment of the stars but that skill, along with others he had possessed, she had never had much of a desire to learn.

She realized she had not thought of her father or mother much at all since she'd been kidnapped. Their divorce had created a chasm between all three of them that had not begun to heal. She knew they would be frantic about her being missing. A small, selfish part of her relished the thought that they would finally be focused on her and not their own situation.

Not that it did her any good.

Something fluttered by overhead, startling her out of her emotional musings. She cocked her head, trying to hear the beat of wings again. And it came, closer and then something landed on the lip of the cistern.

A large bird. A black figure against the dark sky. Emily wearily got to her feet to see it more clearly. If she could catch it, then she could drink its blood. Eat whatever meat was on its bones. It could—

Emily froze as she realized it was a buzzard.

And it was waiting for her meat.

Gant was glad to be on his own. On the way to the airfield Golden had suggested she do more research on the two surviving targets while Gant went to Maine to try to figure out exactly what they were up to. It was a plan, albeit a half-ass one in Gant's opinion. As the jet carrying her raced west, Gant was on board an Air Force Combat Talon that he had specifically requested be put on standby for his use after the debacle in Virginia. Gant was dressed in black combat fatigues and the rear half of the aircraft was full of gear on several pallets that he had put in as a standing packing list for the aircraft, allowing him to be prepared for numerous contingencies. The front quarter of the aircraft cargo bay was separated from the rest by a thick black curtain and was lined with computer and imaging consoles, manned by Air Force specialists.

The Talon was the Special Operations version of the venerable C-130 Hercules cargo plane. It was equipped with terrain-following, and more importantly, terrain-avoidance radars, which allowed it to fly at operational speeds as low as two hundred and fifty feet above ground level in adverse weather conditions.

Sitting in the back of the specially equipped cargo plane, he used one of the secure satellite communications consoles and dialed Nero's special satellite secure number. Even though it was nine in the evening, he felt reasonably confident he would get the old man.

He was surprised when a woman answered on the second ring. "This is Ms. Masterson. What can I do for you, Mister Gant?"

"Is Mister Nero there?" Gant asked, realizing his mistake right away.

"Mister Nero is indisposed at the moment," Masterson said.

A silence played out, then her voice came back, sharper. "I assume you called for a reason. I received your situation report an hour ago. You're on a flight to Maine and Doctor Golden is on her way to interview Sergeant Forten's adoptive mother. One of his adoptive mothers that is, the one she felt was critical in the formation of what he is now. At least according to her predictive behavior model. Is there something else I need to know? Or that you need to know?"

Gant held back his sigh. "Do you have any suggestions as to a course of action?"

"That was hard, wasn't it, Mister Gant? This is the first time since you've started on this Sanction that you've asked my opinion."

"You have all the data," Gant said.

"It's about more than data."

Gant forced himself to relax his grip on the phone. "There's a pattern to what they're doing. I don't quite see it yet, but I'm guessing they're taking out the warlord next, then they'll start going after the primary players whose families they've already hurt."

"You're guessing?"

"Based on my experience, yes."

"I concur with your guess," Masterson said. "The initiating event was the kidnapping of Tracy Caulkins over three weeks ago. By itself, that raised no alarms. They chained her to that tree in Tennessee and kept her alive, barely alive, while they waited to do their next step and she grew weaker and weaker.

"The next step, of course, was the kidnapping of Emily Cranston and the leaving of the two partial caches," Masterson continued. "They must have known that would start the clock ticking. Not the kidnapping, but the cache reports. A very clear indicator of who the perpetrators were and their background. And they also must have known the connection between Cranston and Caulkins would be made relatively quickly. So they moved faster. They took out Kathy Svoboda and Caleigh Roberts within twenty-four hours. By doing that, they let us know this wasn't the work of one individual. These were not random acts done in a random order."

Gant was following her reasoning, which was in line with what he had already figured out. What she said next though, he had not thought of. "They left the rest of Caulkins cache report with Svoboda's body. That was to misdirect us while they moved forward. In essence, we were moving backwards. Three weeks back. A smart ploy, but one you must have sensed."

Gant couldn't tell if she was being serious or if she was pointing out his failure.

"It was your initiative," Masterson said, "that got you to the farm in Virginia in time to interdict Lutz. They must have considered that a possibility, but not one with a high probability. So score one for the good guys."

"But they still got Foley and his wife," Gant said, still trying to figure out what Masterson was really saying.

"And we got Lutz. They were collateral damage."

Gant thought Masterson should have a long talk with Roberts about collateral damage. "So what about Emily Cranston?"

"She's still alive," Masterson said. "She has a role to play beyond that of simply tormenting the good colonel."

"What role?"

"Well, she already played a role in the ambush that killed two of the FBI's Hostage Rescue Team members. That ambush was meant for you. Those who operate in the covert world, such as our targets, must have heard whispers of the Cellar, so they wanted to use that cache ambush as a counter-action against us. But again, we out-maneuvered them. Since they gave us a partial on her new location, I foresee her having another role to play. So there will soon be an event where we get the rest of the cache report."

"Taking out the warlord in Maine?"

"I think that is the next action but I don't think they will leave the rest of the report there," Masterson said. "It doesn't fit what they've done before. I just talked to Doctor Golden reference this matter and she believes they will act in pattern."

Gant silently cursed. She'd just talked to Golden. First, before talking to him. Just great. "What pattern?"

"According to Golden they will recreate the original mission with regard to the warlord."

"Sniper."

"Correct. I concur with her belief in this matter."

Gant glanced down at the pile of gear on the pallet at his feet, already deciding what he needed and what could remain on the plane. He gestured toward one the pallets, getting the load-master's attention. He indicated for the man to begin rigging what he needed with a parachute. Then he considered whether he should radio ahead to the CIA compound and warn the guards.

"Who else is left for them to leave the rest of Emily's new cache report with?" Gant asked even as he decided against the warning until he was sure of his guess. The guards' priority would be protecting the compound and its inhabitants, not taking down the attackers. A reaction in the guard force could scare off the targets.

"A good question," Masterson said. "And frankly, I don't know. I believe there's a piece to this entire thing we haven't yet seen."

"Maybe more than one piece," Gant said.

"Quite possibly. They have had quite a bit of time to plan this."

"Not much else to do when you're imprisoned and being tortured for months on end," Gant said.

"Correct." Masterson's voice was dry, unemotional. "And we have only had three days to react. I think you've done quite well."

Gant was surprised. Nero had never praised or complimented him in all the years and over all the missions he had run. He didn't know what to say.

"And my friend Neeley?" Masterson asked.

Friend? "What about her?"

"Has she been helpful?"

"Yes."

"And Doctor Golden?"

"Uh—"

"You feel she has not been of assistance?"

"She's trying," Gant allowed.

"It is a steep learning curve to suddenly be thrust into this world," Masterson said and Gant read something into that statement.

"I don't have time to be a teacher and—"

"Who taught you? Who was your mentor in the covert world?"

Gant felt a weight on his chest. "My brother, Tony."

"And he taught Neeley. And Neeley taught me. It's your turn to teach. I have great expectations of Doctor Golden."

The phone went dead.

The Sniper looked through the thermal scope. He was strangely depressed. The target was clear in the sight. Lying on his bed in the pre-fab building, reading a magazine.

It should not be this simple.

Not after all that had happened. The pain and terror of those ten months spent in the prison in Colombia. Perhaps the Spotter had a point. Perhaps something closer, more personal and slower would be better. The Sniper could remember every single devious and painful physical and psychological torture that had been inflicted on his body and mind over that time period. He had no doubt he could replicate the worst of them.

But that wasn't the plan. Always best to stick with the plan, the Sniper thought. Not sticking with the plan was what had started all this a year ago.

For a moment the Sniper paused, even shaking his head, as if that could make things clearer. Orders. Betrayal.

Colombia. The mission. Take out the warlord. Who he was now looking at through his scope. Why hadn't he done that?

The Sniper removed his off-hand from the gun and rubbed it along the side of his head, tracing the scar. He could feel pain, throbbing deep, right into his brain, searing through skin and bone into his very essence. Just like the probes and blades of the interrogator had.

The questions that made no sense. That there was no correct response to.

He'd told everything he knew to stop the pain and it hadn't stopped it. And the pain of that betrayal of the Code that he had sworn to uphold had cut as deep as the knife.

Why hadn't they come for him and his team?

The Sniper centered the reticules on the target's head. He had already adjusted for the elevation difference and the slight breeze. With a little luck the body wouldn't be found until early morning when all the detainees had roll call. By then the Sniper and Spotter would be long gone, moving on to the next phase of operations.

Why had they been abandoned?

The Sniper felt the rhythm of his breathing and of his heartbeat.

He shut down the murmuring in his brain.

Then he heard the inbound aircraft.

Gant was behind one of the imaging specialists, staring down at the thermal display the man was working. He had used the Talon two years previously in the same manner, to hunt for a target on the ground using heat signature and it had worked quite well. He had checked the satellite imagery faxed to the plane of the area around the CIA secret compound and traced out the most likely spots for a sniper to set up.

The pilot had the plane flying as slow as possible, just above stall speed, as he began to follow the path Gant had traced. The thermal hot spots flashed by quickly, barely giving Gant time to try to identify them. Deer were easy. There were numerous specks of heat—squirrels, rabbits, etc.

Needle in a forest, Gant thought as the pilot put the plane in a lazy, slow bank. Gant could almost sense the plane slipping, losing altitude but he trusted the pilots as he kept his focus on the screen, his hands gripping the back of the imager's seat.

"We've got a query from the compound," the pilot announced the intercom. "We're violating restricted airspace."

"Click me in," Gant ordered, keeping his eyes on the screen.

The headset crackled for a second and then Gant heard what the pilots had been receiving: "Unidentified aircraft, this is the United States government. You are flying over restricted airspace. Break off on a heading of nine-zero degrees immediately or face dire consequences."

Who the hell came up with this crap? Gant wondered. He let go of the imager's seat and hit the transmit. "This *is* the United States government, security clearance Alpha One One Six. I am over-flying your position in an Air Force C-130 to search for possible intruders."

There was a long silence and Gant could well imagine the confusion in the small headquarters for the compound.

"Identify yourself," the voice finally came back with.

"I gave you my clearance," Gant said. "Check with your higher for my authorization."

Gant frowned as he spotted two glowing objects flash by on the screen. Two human forms, lying prone on the ground. He contacted the pilot and indicated for him to circle round.

"What are the intruders after?" the voice from the compound inquired.

Gant considered whether he should answer that question—tell them the intruders were a sniper team and who they were there to kill. He decided against it. "Do you have a reaction capability off the island?"

"We have two vehicles at the landing."

"Get your reaction force ready. I'll be on the ground shortly."

The Sniper was looking up as the familiar sound of the four turbo-prop engines of a C-130 cargo plane grew closer. It was a sound anyone who had ever served in an airborne unit could easily recognize. Finally, he saw the silhouette of the plane fly directly overhead, less than five hundred feet above them. And he recognized the jutting radar pod and Fulton Extraction whiskers on the front of the plane, indicating it was a Special Operations Combat Talon. This was not a random C-130 flight. He glanced over at the Spotter who had a set of night vision goggles glued to his eyes.

"What do you have?" he asked.

The Spotter lowered the goggles as the plane began to bank. The Sniper already knew they had been spotted and the plane was circling back for another look.

"Blacked out MC-130 Talon with no identification markings," the Spotter said as he lowered the goggles. "And it's coming back for another look," he added unnecessarily.

First Virginia and now this, the Sniper thought. Whoever was after them was fast, very fast. Faster than they had worst-cased. He briefly wondered if the ambush at the empty cache site in Alabama had achieved anything.

Déjà vu. If he'd had a sense of humor, the Sniper might have appreciated the irony of his current situation as it indeed mirrored what had happened in Colombia when they'd tried to take out the same target. However, whatever reservoir of humor he'd gone into that mission with had been quickly drained under the brutal hand of the torturer.

"We should exfiltrate," the Spotter said.

The Sniper nodded but he had already put his eye back on the thermal sight and was zeroing in on the target. Nothing was going to stop him from fulfilling the mission this time.

Gant tightened down the straps on his parachute harness one last time and looked across at the load-master holding on to the static line cable attached to the pallet holding the off-road motorcycle. Both men took a subconscious step back as the back ramp cracked open, revealing the night sky and allowing the swirling wind to blast them. Gant had spotted a clear cut opening less than a quarter mile from the two heat signatures and that was where he had directed the pilot to drop him.

It wasn't a very big opening, perhaps a half-mile long by a quarter mile wide, so Gant had also ordered the pilot to take the Talon down low, below safety restrictions, to less than four hundred feet above ground level. Gant edged forward, to the very lip of the back ramp, his eyes focused on the red light glowing up in the darkness of the interior tail of the plane.

"The ramp is open," the Spotter reported, tracking the in-bound Talon through the night vision goggles. "We're going to have company."

The Sniper ignored him, his entire essence focused on the target. Lights were going on in the compound, which meant whoever was in the plane had alerted the guards. There wasn't any more time.

The Sniper squeezed the trigger.

The sub-sonic round raced down the barrel, through the sound suppressor and through the night sky. It punched through the thin plywood wall of the building and hit the target in the side of the head, taking most of his skull with it as it continued across the room and buried itself in the rough wood floor.

The Sniper was on his feet, breaking the rifle down.

The light turned green and Gant stepped off into the darkness as the load-master shoved the pallet. Barely two seconds after leaving the aircraft, Gant's chute snapped open, jarring him.

He barely had time to glance down, note the ground was coming up fast, get his body into landing position: feet and knees together, knees slight bent, elbows rotated in front of his face as his hands pulled on the risers to try to slow his descent.

Gant slammed into the ground, the impact up the right side of his body until he came to a halt, breathing hard. He took that split second to savor being alive, then he quickly got to his feet and unbuckled his harness. He put on night vision goggles and scanned the area for the pallet. He spotted the other parachute about forty feet away and he made his way toward it, his MP-5 sub-machinegun at the ready.

The small plug in his ear came alive with the information that the warlord had been shot. For Gant that was good news, confirming that the two thermal images he had spotted were indeed his targets. He nodded as he reached the padded pallet with the motorcycle strapped on top of it. The targets were close.

CHAPTER TWENTY-ONE

IN THE CELLAR, the radio traffic from Maine was being relayed by the Combat Talon through secure Milstar satellites to the small speakers set in the room's ceiling. Nero was back from his treatments. He used to take them in the office, but now that it was Ms. Masterson's domain, he had agreed to take them in the small room in back of the office that was his inner sanctum. The doctor and nurse had just left, the door swinging securely shut behind them and he had returned to the front room.

Nero was coughing as he lay on the couch, his lungs laboring to draw air in. Hannah Masterson was perfectly still in her chair, listening as the Talon reported that Gant was away cleanly and the aircraft was taking up a racetrack over the targets in order to relay their thermal position to Gant.

"Very good work," Nero said when he finally got the coughing spate under control.

"Nothing has been achieved yet," Masterson said.

"Where is Neeley?" Nero asked.

"Gant sent her to Alabama to look at the latest cache site."

"Now that was a mistake," Nero said. "Bailey was there."

"Yes, it was a mistake," Masterson agreed. "He still has too much of the Lone Ranger in him. It was a subconscious reaction toward Ms. Neeley. He has the same problem with Doctor Golden. I discussed it with him just a little while ago."

"And how did Mister Gant react to the discussion?"

"If he survives this contact, we'll find out."

* * *

Gant kick-started the dirt bike and revved the engine. He wasn't going to sneak up on the targets riding the noisy machine, but he didn't need to sneak nor did he need to track. The eye in the sky and orbiting satellites would do the tracking for him. He turned on the small GPS display set on top of the center of the handlebars. It was up-linked to the aircraft and satellites circling overhead. The back-lit screen came alive, took a few seconds to access both the orbiting GPS satellites to fix his position, and synch into the transmission from the Talon, which was tracking the people on the ground using its thermals.

A small flashing dot appeared in the very center. Gant's own position. He twisted the throttle, keeping the clutch in neutral, anxious to get going. Two tiny red dots appeared—the targets. A line across the bottom displayed the barely visibly direction and azimuth to the targets: *Bearing 160 degrees. Range 3,740 meters.*

As he watched, the two dots crept across the screen slowly, moving southwest. Gant looked up. Through the night vision goggles, he could see a dirt road along the edge of the clearing, a lighter line against the dark black background of the thick forest. He raced toward it, and then turned south.

"Immediately inform me if the targets stop moving," Gant ordered, the throat mike transmitting the message to the orbiting Talon. The last thing he wanted to do was race up on a sniper who was ready to shoot. And he couldn't keep watching the GPS and drive at the same time.

"Roger that."

"Status of reaction force from the encampment?" Gant asked.

"Two boats are shore-bound from the island. We are in contact with them and will coordinate to prevent fratricide. We'll put them on your GPS as soon as they are on the ground and live on their own vehicle GPS."

"Link me to them on this frequency," Gant ordered.

"Roger that. You are call sign Alpha One. They will be Bravo Two. Over."

There was a crackle of static, then the voice was back. "Bravo Two, you've got Alpha One on the net. Over."

"Who the hell are you?" a new voice demanded, the lack of proper radio etiquette indicating the degree of confusion.

"This is Alpha One," Gant said. "I radioed you from the air and am now on the ground on motorcycle in search of two targets. They are trained Special Operations soldiers, one a sniper. So approach with great caution. Over."

"No shit. They just shot one of our detainees through the head inside his room. What the fuck is going on?" There was a short pause. "Over."

"The two targets are our mission," Gants said. "We would like one taken alive, the other can be eliminated. Over."

There was a longer pause. "You mean killed? Over."

"Roger that."

"Fuck. Will comply. But why take one alive?"

"Do it," Gant snapped.

Gant goosed the motorcycle and crested a slight bump in the road. The trail descended into a narrow lane in the forest, the lighter line of the dirt trail turning darker. He did not like the look of that. "Talon, azimuth and distance to targets?"

"One five two degrees. Two thousand, three hundred and six meters. They are still on the move on foot. Over."

Gant accelerated down into the thick Maine forest. The trail wasn't taking him directly toward them but it was closing the gap.

"This is Bravo Two. We are on land and mounting our vehicles. We have one Humvee and one Ford F-150 pickup. We are heading toward the targets. Sounds like they're heading for the main logging road that heads for the hard-top state road. We are up-linking with Talon now on GPS. Over."

Gant pushed his speed, knowing that the targets had to have a vehicle parked near the logging road. If this were a normal police procedure, it would be the time to call the State Troopers and the local Sheriffs. Have road-blocks set up. But if this were normal Gant wouldn't be here and the Cellar wouldn't be involved. And if he made that call, there would be many local people grieving in the morning over the loss of their loved ones. Also, he doubted that the locals could take one of the two alive—the incident in Virginia had proven that the targets were more than willing to give up their lives.

This was the Cellar's job. His job. He'd have one shot at it.

"We're mounted," the CIA reaction force team leader announced. "We're heading for the logging road. Over."

"Can you interdict?" Gant asked.

"We'll know that when we get there. Depends how quick they get to their vehicles. Why did they do this? Who are these guys?"

"They're rogue," Gant said. "They've killed innocent people. And they'll kill you if you're not careful. Over."

Gant took a turn slightly too fast and he felt the dirt bike's tires almost slide out from under him. He corrected and then accelerated. He wondered how pilots could fly helicopters with night vision goggles as he was having a hell of a time simply driving the motorcycle. The small screen inside the goggles tended to distort depth perception.

"Targets have reached the road," the imager announced. "Just got the heat signature of an engine starting. They are now mounted. One five zero zero meters from your location. Wait one."

Gant slowed down. The logging road he was on curved to the right and he could only see down it about two hundred meters.

"Targets are in a van. It's moving west on the main logging road. Over."

Gant checked his GPS. He was about four hundred meters from the main logging road. He could see that there was only one red dot now—the targets' vehicle. "You're sure both of them got in the vehicle?" he asked, still leery of the sniper.

"Roger that. Take a left when you reach the road."

There were other symbols on the screen now. Two small blue dots—the reaction force from the compound. They were on the main logging road about two kilometers behind the red dot. Gant accelerated down the dirt road, between the tall pine trees lining either side, knowing he would reach the main trail just about the same time as the reaction force crossed by. He slowed slightly, wanting to avoid a collision with either the Humvee or pickup.

He alternated between quick glances down at the GPS and paying attention to the road. The intersection was coming up and he slowed further so he could take the turn onto the main logging trail. The slow became an abrupt halt as a Humvee roared by right in front of him, followed closely by a pick-up truck. Both vehicles were blacked out and Gant assumed the drivers were wearing night vision goggles.

Gant gave the motorcycle gas. As he turned left he noted that the only difference between this road and what he had been on was that it was slightly wider, but still composed of rutted dirt.

"I'm right behind you," he called out into the radio.

Seeing that the road appeared as a relatively straight line on the GPS, Gant accelerated to keep up with the other vehicles. He had the motorcycle's headlight off and the brake light disconnected so he raced through the darkness as a swift, black shadow. He saw no tell-tale red lights ahead and assumed the targets had done the same.

Gant took a chance and glanced down at the GPS to get an idea of spacing. The targets were about a kilometer ahead of him, the reaction force splitting the difference.

Inside the van, the Sniper slid between the seats as the Spotter drove and went into the back. He threw open a panel they had cut in the roof and looked up into the night sky. Even over the rumble of the van's engine he could hear the C-130 overhead and he had a very good idea what it was doing. He slid on a pair of night vision goggles and peered down the road behind the van.

He spotted a familiar bulky form about five hundred meters back. No mistaking the silhouette of a Humvee. He looked past it and caught a glimpse of a second vehicle.

The Sniper reached down into his vest and pulled out a small transmitter. He flipped up the protective cover and pressed the red button with one hand while he ripped off the night vision goggles with the other.

A ball of flame leapt into the dark sky, followed seconds later by the rumble of the twin explosions taking out the reaction force's vehicles and the men inside.

Gant slammed his right foot down on the rear brake as he squeezed the right front brake lever. He turned the handlebars at the same time, skidding to a halt as hot metal flew past him. He was blinded, the explosions over-loading his goggles. Once halted he ripped them off and stared at the burning vehicles holding the goggles in one hand while the computer inside tried to compensate for the overload.

The Humvee had run into the drainage ditch on the right side of the road and was in flames. The pick-up truck had been thrown on its side by the force of the blast and slid to a halt in the middle of the road.

Gant cursed to himself, realizing he should have considered the strong possibility that the reaction force vehicles would have been booby-trapped. It was what he would have done if he'd had the time to prepare for this mission. He ignored the confused inquiries from the Talon as he put the goggles back on.

Gant accelerated, whipping around the pick-up truck and past the Humvee. He kept his focus on the target's vehicle which was now in sight, about seven hundred meters ahead. He could see someone's head poking up out of the top of the van and debated whether to slam on the brakes and take a quick shot, but it was too far for the sub-machinegun. He needed to get closer.

"How many were in the reaction force?" Nero asked.

"Seven," Masterson answered.

"And now it is Mister Gant who is out-numbered," Nero said.

"Perhaps we should—"

"No locals," Nero said.

* * *

165

The Sniper slid his night vision goggles back on and looked back at the burning vehicles, bright flares on the screen. All according to plan. Except for the Talon. That had been unexpected.

He glanced over his shoulder, checking their position. The Spotter was slowing the van, also aware of their position. They had rehearsed this several times, twice at night using goggles, one of over a dozen variations of escape and evasion plans they had come up with. So far, this one was working quite well.

The Sniper looked back to the burning vehicles and blinked. A blur raced past the burning Humvee. A motorcycle.

The Sniper grabbed a metal container hanging on a hook and opened the lid. Then he tossed it up into the air over the rear of the van, the can tumbling and releasing its contents.

Gant saw the man poking out of the van throw something into the air. He had scant seconds to make a decision. He immediately braked. The motorcycle skidded and he almost lost control, then came to a halt. He let the bike fall over, ignoring it, as he snapped up the sub-machinegun and aimed at the van, finger caressing the trigger.

And that's when his night vision goggles flared, blanking out everything with an overwhelming pulse of bright light.

Gant ripped them off and stared toward the van, blinking, trying to regain his vision. There was no longer a need for night vision goggles as the sky above the van was streaked with arcing, red-hot flares. At least thirty or forty, Gant estimated as he watched them reach their apex, then arc over. That was when he realized something was different about these flares, as they had no parachutes to bring them lazily back to earth.

He looked below. The van was parked on the edge of the road near a bridge over a racing river. Gant began running forward, the stock of the gun still tight into his shoulder. The flares were hitting the dry timber and undergrowth, igniting fires. Something stuck to the bottom of his boot and Gant looked down: a caltrop, a three pronged device designed to rip into tires was stuck in the sole. He carefully pulled it out and looked about: the trail was littered with them. That was what the man had tossed out of the van just before firing the flares.

"We've lost thermals," the Talon reported. "We no longer have the targets under observation. Last position was in the van. We're circling, trying to see if we can pick them up outside of the fire."

More out of frustration than anything else, Gant fired a quick burst from the MP-5, stitching a row of bullet holes in the back panel of the van. He knew both men were gone, but he made his way carefully to the van. The side door was open. Gant stuck his head in, looking for any sign there might be a piece of a cache report but there was nothing. The two targets had not planned to leave the van but they had been prepared to lose it.

His shoulders were hunched, half-expecting the van to explode. Gant quickly got out of the van and looked around. The woods were burning wherever a flare had come down, in some cases the pockets of flame were merging, threatening a major fire. The targets could have gone in any direction. The flares and subsequent fire meant they had been prepared to thwart thermal tracking from the air.

What else would I have done? Gant thought.

He spoke into the throat mike. "Talon, you need to call the local firefighters to get this thing under control. Where does this river go?"

"Wait one."

Gant looked at the cool water rushing by underneath the bridge and he knew his targets had jumped into it, going with the flow. The water would mask their image so that thermals wouldn't pick them up when they got outside the ring of fire.

"The river empties into a lake about two kilometers downstream. Pretty big lake, about ten kilometers long by six wide. One side of it runs along the main state road."

Gant nodded to himself. The targets could come ashore anywhere. They most likely had a vehicle cached close to the road and would merge with the traffic. Gant considered calling the state authorities to place a road-block and discarded the idea as quickly. The targets would be prepared for that also.

"Alpha One, this is Talon. I have a secure communication line open and someone requesting to speak to you. Call sign Cellar One."

Nero's call sign. Gant sighed and walked down the road to a place where he was clear of the fire. "Go ahead, Cellar One."

"Mister Gant."

Gant flinched as he recognized the voice. Masterson. "Yes?"

"It appears our targets have gotten away and we are no closer to Emily Cranston's location. I don't suppose you found the rest of the cache report?"

"I did a cursory search of the van and didn't spot it. If they wanted us to find it, they would have left it in the open as they did the others. We won't find anything of importance in the van because they left it and didn't destroy it."

"And the targets succeeded in completing the mission they started in Colombia a year ago."

Gant didn't answer because it wasn't a question.

"And Neeley is wandering around looking at a cold site in Alabama while you're in the middle of a fire. Literally. At least in Virginia, working as part of a team, you got one of the targets. Here all we have are eight bodies."

Gant reached the dirt bike. He sighed, then nodded to himself. "I fucked up."

"The world is changing, Mister Gant," Masterson said. "That's why I'm here. You've never faced a team of rogues before. When it was individuals, you could go your own way and deal with the Sanctions. You need to be part of the team, Mister Gant. Use your team. Or else I will put Neeley in charge."

The satellite connection went dead.

CHAPTER TWENTY-TWO

NEELEY SHUT OFF her satellite phone and pondered the position Hannah Masterson had just put her in. She had remained quiet during the conference call, not comfortable with secretly listening in, but doing so at Hannah's request. She had also not been thrilled with Gant's order to come here to the cache site. And even Bailey had expressed surprise upon seeing her arrive as he was preparing to leave. A bullshit mission for a bullshit reason.

Neeley walked around the open space near the tree, occasionally checking the pictures, notes and drawing she'd been given on arrival, while Bailey followed her. She finally came to the oak tree and stared at it in the harsh light of the klieg spotlights set up all around.

"How old was she?" she asked Bailey who was a shapeless form a few feet away.

"Nineteen."

Neeley considered that. "When I was nineteen I was with Jean-Philippe in Berlin."

"I know," Bailey replied.

"She was partying with her girlfriends when she was kidnapped," Neeley said, remembering the file, one of dozens she'd quickly read.

Bailey remained silent.

To be nineteen and that carefree. Neeley was having a hard time comprehending it. Jean-Philippe had been a terrorist, involved in the black market in Berlin. Their friends—their acquaintances—had all been shadowy figures in a gray world. It should have come as no surprise to her when he betrayed her. Handed her a bomb to carry on board a commercial airliner. But it had been. And that had been when she met Tony Gant, the current Gant's twin brother. He'd taken the bomb, taken her, and her life had never been the same again.

Then she realized something about the current situation: Emily Cranston hadn't had her Gant. Her person to step in when the evil of the world invaded. She was out there all alone. Neeley shivered, trying to hide the reaction from Bailey, who stood there like a statue.

"They cached her again," Neeley said.

"Of course."

"But in a worse place."

"Why do you think that?" Bailey asked as calmly as if they were discussing the weather.

"Because they're bad people," Neeley said. "And bad always goes to worse."

Bailey nodded. "True." He cleared his throat. "But how could it be worse?"

Neeley considered that. She pointed at the tree. "Here she was in the middle of the woods. Alone. Isolated. No hope."

"Ah," Bailey said. "They put her in a place with false hope."

"Yes. And not isolated. Closer to people. So close she could hear them or at least know they were close. But yet in a place where she couldn't contact them."

"Quite intriguing," Bailey said.

Neeley turned and faced him. "Not intriguing. It's her life."

Bailey blinked, a strong sign of emotion for him.

"She's being tortured in a game she never was a player in except by birth. She never made a conscious act that brought her to this."

"What difference does it make?" Bailey asked in a level voice. "It does not change the parameters of the mission."

"It does," Neeley snapped. "Our targets know she isn't a player. They're using her—and they killed the others—to cause pain to the players. But in the end, our targets are going to want to take out the players. The question is, how does caching Emily Cranston help them achieve that goal?"

"It keeps us running in circles while they have another plan?" Bailey suggested.

Neeley nodded. "Most likely. Misdirection. And it's probably a plan that's already in play."

"We have security on the primary players," Bailey said.

"In four different places," Neeley noted. "In their homes, where the targets know they will be. Where the targets can already have planned their attack. Maybe we should bring them together in one, more secure place. Someplace these guys couldn't have thought of."

Bailey considered that. "Not a bad idea. I suggest you run it by Mister Gant."

Neeley shook her head. "I think I'll run it by Doctor Golden first, then the two of us will talk to Gant."

Doctor Golden stared at the old woman in the pale blue jumpsuit, trying hard to keep her feeling of utter disgust off her face. Golden remembered now that one of the major reasons she'd gotten out of private practice—besides the financial implosion of the clinic she had run with her husband during their divorce—was her growing lack of patience with those who were mentally ill and inflicted their sickness on others with no remorse.

Lois Egan stared back at Golden. Her hair was pure white, short and matted, long overdue for a date with a comb. Her face was tight, the skin tight to the skull. But it was the eyes that betrayed the inner demon: they danced and skittered about, rarely focusing, but when they did, there was a darkness in them that Golden had seen before. Golden noticed that all of Egan's fingernails were chewed down as far as possible.

They sat on opposite sides of a gray table in a gray room. Golden figured that the studies on the psychological effects of varying colors on the prisoner psyche had not trickled down to the particular institution. A burly female guard stood behind Egan, baton drawn. The in-briefing officer had told Golden that Egan had three incidents of violence on her prison record in the past eight years. And the reason Egan was serving ten to fifteen was armed robbery. No one had been pleased to arrange this meeting well before dawn, but such was the weight of the Cellar that the prison staff had complied.

Egan apparently did not like silence, because she spoke first. "What do you want?"

It was interesting to Golden that that was Egan's first question rather than wanting to know who she was. "Some answers."

"Then ask some God-damn questions instead of just sitting there." Egan leaned forward. "But first, got some smokes?"

Golden had always thought that a movie cliché, but on the way to the meeting room her escort had handed her two packs and corrected that misperception. So Golden pulled both packs out and slid one across the table and kept the other in front of her. Egan snatched the pack in front of her and eyed the one across the table. Her eyes darted up, bore into Golden's for a hateful second and then danced about, not locking onto anything.

"Your son," Golden said.

171

"Don't got no God-damn son."

"Adoptive son."

"Which one? Had three."

"In three different states. You lied on the adoption forms. And all three were eventually taken from you. You used them to get welfare and adoption money. When the database sharing between states got better and you couldn't extort money via flesh, you used a gun. Probably a more direct and less dangerous technique in the long run."

A frown furrowed Egan's forehead. "What the fuck are you talking about?"

"Lewis Forten."

Egan snorted. "That little shit? What's he done? That's why you're here?"

"You abused him."

Egan's head turned and she glanced at the guard, who showed not the slightest interest. "Fuck you. That's bullshit. Is that what he told you? He's a man now. Can't he be a man? What's he whining about me, blaming me for something he did? Bullshit."

Golden said nothing.

"Christ," Egan finally said, "I had him only for two years maybe. That was a long time ago. Other people had him. Why you here talking to me?"

"What did you do to him?" Golden asked in a level voice.

"I didn't do nothing."

"I'm not here to get you in any more trouble," Golden said. "And I haven't spoken to Lewis. I'm trying to find him. Before he kills anyone else."

Egan's eyes stopped shifting for almost five seconds. "He killed someone?"

"Quite a few people," Golden said. "And if you give me information that helps us find him, it will reflect—look—very good for you."

"How good? What can you do for me?"

"Tell me about Lewis."

"Fuck." Egan had the pack of cigarettes in her hand and was stripping off the wrapper. Golden glanced at the guard who was standing next to a prominent *No Smoking* sign. The discussion about killing had caught the guard's attention and the guard nodded, ever so slightly, in regard to Golden's lifted eyebrow.

"Go ahead and smoke," Golden said.

"Who the fuck are you?" Egan asked as she ripped open the pack and slid a cigarette out, lighting it in one smooth move.

"I'm a psychologist. A profiler. And I'm assigned to Lewis's case."

"What exactly has he done?"

"Killed. Right now the toll is in the double digits."

"Fuck."

"Indeed."

"You can get my time cut here?"

So much for empathy, Golden thought. Of course if Egan had been capable of empathy neither of them would be sitting here. Masterson had not specifically told her she could get a reduction of Egan's sentence, but the woman in charge of the Cellar had also told her to use any means necessary to get information. Golden figured Egan deserved as much empathy as she showed.

"Yes."

"How much time?"

"That's not up to me."

Egan inhaled deeply, happily. "What the fuck can I tell you about that little dip-shit that will make a difference?"

"I don't know yet since you haven't told me anything."

"Fuck." Egan drew in another lungful, exhaled, stared at the burning tip of the cigarette. Golden could almost feel the other woman's mind trying to dredge up memories, the effort seemed so great.

"He was a little shit. Bad. I knew he'd turn out to be no good. That's why I tried to discipline him. Control him. He needed control." Egan nodded. "That's what I did. I did him right."

"How?"

Egan leaned back in her chair, still savoring the smoke. "He got kicked out of school, did you know that?"

Golden had that in her file. In fact, it was the thing that had been the first alert in her profile database. She remained silent, letting Egan play out her feeling of power and righteousness.

"Little shit kept getting into fights. And got his butt kicked more often than not because he didn't care who he fought. Bigger, older, tougher, didn't matter to him. Dumb shit. I tried to tell him. Teach him, but I didn't have no man around. He needed a man around."

Yes, he did and that wasn't his fault that there wasn't, Golden thought, but once more didn't voice.

"Damn school got tired of the fights. Kicked his ass out. What was I supposed to do with him?"

Golden thought of the last time she saw Jimmy. Backpack slung over his shoulder, dressed warmly, waiting for the school bus. Smiling. The hole inside her chest yawned wider, threatening to draw her in.

"He didn't like being in the house," Egan said. "He was always off. In the woods. The creek. The housing development on the edge of town where the riff-raff lived. Hanging with those other bum kids, I suppose. Cops brought him back a couple, three times."

Five, Golden thought. More indicators that had flagged the file.

"Fucking kids," Egan said.

Golden pressed the balls of her feet down on the floor, a technique one of her advisers in college had taught her.

"He was a damn thief. Always picking up this and that without paying. Got caught, the dumb shit. I mean, if you're going to do it, do it right. He got smart with a cop one time and got his damn skull smacked open. Cost me a couple hundred bucks at the clinic to get him stitched up."

Golden forced herself to nod, as if in sympathy. She felt disconnected, as if she weren't even here.

"Burned down the chicken coop," Egan said and Golden forced herself to focus in. Egan held up the matchbook. "He always stole my matches, my lighters. I don't know what he did with them except that one time he burned down the damn coop."

This information hadn't been in the report on Forten but it fit perfectly as fire-starting was one of the significant indicators of future dysfunction.

"Bed-wetting?" Golden asked.

Egan's eyes flickered. "How the fuck did you know? Hell, yeah. More crap to deal with. He was a teenager. Why was he doing that? You know what a pain in the ass that is? Had to teach him how to wash his sheets."

No time for 'raising the sociopath 101' Golden thought.

Getting no answer, Egan continued. "Then the cats. Jesus H. Christ." Egan pulled another cigarette out.

Golden stirred. "The cats?"

"He killed them. No matter what I did, he killed them. And when I didn't bring another home, he lured them in."

"How did he kill them?"

Egan shrugged. "Cut them. Smashed their skulls with a rock. Does it matter?"

"How many cats did he kill?"

"Six. Seven. Those are the ones I found. Christ knows how many I didn't. One time he stole a little kitten and then when the mother came looking, killed both. A couple of times he cut them open in the bath-tub."

Golden frowned. Blood had not seemed to be a motif in the killings so far except for the girl in Alabama whose throat had been sliced. And they didn't think Forten had done that from the intelligence they had.

"How did you punish him?" Golden asked.

Egan's eyes danced about. "You know."

"No, I don't."

"Who do you work for?" Egan demanded.

"How did you punish him?"

Another cigarette, the flash of the lighter. "Spankings."

"With your hand?" Golden didn't buy her spanking a fifteen year old boy.

"Sometimes a belt."

"What else?"

Egan laughed. "Fuck it. I'm in prison. I strung the little shit up."

Golden blinked. "What?"

"I tied his hands behind his back, had the rope over a pulley in the basement and strung him up. There. Happy? Didn't make no difference. He'd just hang there and scream and cry and beg and tell me he'd never do it again and then he'd go do it again."

Severe trauma as punishment. All the pieces were there. But not much more of use. "Is there a place where he would hide?" Golden asked.

Egan shrugged. "The woods. He liked the woods. But he always came back."

"Any special place in the woods?"

"How the hell would I know? It's not like I followed him."

Golden tried to think but she was so tired. She tried to remember the last good night of sleep she'd had. She thought of Emily Cranston and forced herself to focus. "Is there any place Lewis ever spoke of wanting to go to?"

"What, like Disneyland?" Egan snickered.

Golden kept her voice flat. "We need to find him, and the more help you give us, the more help we'll give you."

Egan's forehead furrowed as she tried to think. "I don't know. It's been such a long time. No place I can remember. You know—" she said suddenly—"there was something else he did. With a dog. He staked it out in the woods. Attached its leash to a tree. Left it there. I don't know how long, but I knew something was wrong when I could smell the stink. Ain't nothing like the smell of dead things. I went out there and found it. He swore it wasn't him. But I know it was. Sick little fuck."

Think like Gant. The thought came to Golden unbidden. What would he want to know? But beyond that thought, nothing came to her. Golden slid the other pack of cigarettes across to Egan and stood. "If I think of anything more, I'll send the questions to you."

Egan nodded. "Yeah, sure."

Golden headed to the door but Egan's question stopped her:

"I was right, wasn't I?"

Golden turned. "About what?"

"The way I treated him. He deserved it. He was bad."

Golden fought the desire to step up to Egan and slap that smug look off her face. She knew it was hopeless, that she could never get the other woman to see how backwards she had everything. She went out the door.

* * *

175

It was very hard for Emily to open her eyes. She lay curled in a tight ball, her arms looped around her knees, pulling them to her chest. She knew the sun was rising: she could feel the temperature slowly rising.

Three more trains had come by during the night. For the first one she'd yelled as loudly as she could but for the second and third, she just lay there having visions of people sitting in air-conditioned dining cars, sipping on glasses of sparkling, cool water.

There was no point in opening her eyes, Emily reasoned. Nothing would be different. And that vulture might still be there, waiting. One thing she had noted was not a single aircraft flying by overhead, not even the faint contrail of a jetliner at thirty-six thousand feet. Not that she had anything to signal an aircraft with. A signal mirror had not been among the necessary items for a night of bar-hopping with the girls. She imagined one of her friends would have had a compact, which would be quite useful right now, but other than her license, she'd had nothing.

Her head hurt. A constant throbbing pain, that she imagined had to be caused by dehydration. This was her fourth day without water. And she wasn't sure she was going to make it through to sun-down.

Reluctantly, Emily unclasped her hands, then loosened her arms. She stretched her legs out and immediately cried out in pain as her left calf tightened into a ball of agony as the muscle cramped. Emily thrashed about out on the wooden floor, the chain attached to the shackle rattling un-noticed as she tried to un-cramp the muscle. She rolled, jamming the ball of her foot against the bolt and pressing, trying to relieve the pain and stretch the muscle back out. She wrapped both hands around the calf and it felt like a solid rock, so knotted were the muscle fibers.

"Please, please, please," Emily hissed as she tried to work the cramp out. After a minute of exquisite pain, the muscle slowly began to loosen. Emily lay there panting, actually almost feeling good, basking in the relief from pain, her thirst and hunger pushed aside for the moment.

She happened to look up and blinked.

Then she smiled with pure joy for the first time in quite a while.

CHAPTER TWENTY-THREE

GANT LOOKED UP as Neeley and Golden walked into Mrs. Smith's reception area. He had been cooling his heels for over a half-hour waiting for their arrival. The time could have been better spent taking a shower and getting some food, but Mrs. Smith had told him that he was to remain here until they arrived. As they came in, he stood and turned toward the Cellar's secretary.

"Wait a second," Golden said, catching him by surprise.

Gant was tired. He wore the same smoke-saturated black fatigues from his chase in the Maine woods. He had a two-day growth of stubble on his chin and he couldn't recall the last time he'd had a meal. He slowly turned to face the two women and right away knew from the looks on their faces and their body language that they had allied.

"What?" Gant asked, making no effort to mask his irritation.

"We need to coordinate," Golden said. "Before we talk to Masterson or Nero."

"Coordinate what?" Gant asked.

"Our plan," Golden said.

Gant raised his eyebrows. "The two of you have a plan? I'm all ears. I haven't even heard what both of you found out, so I'm pretty much clueless about what to do next."

Golden stood straighter. "I posted the summary of my interview with Forten's foster mother."

"I'm sure you did," Gant said, "But I haven't had time to read it." He shifted his gaze to Neeley. "As I haven't had time to read your report on the cache site. So if you want to talk, how about both cutting to chase and telling me what you think?"

Behind them, Mrs. Smith cleared her throat. "Mister Nero and Ms. Masterson are waiting."

Gant laughed, so tired of it all. "I was waiting here for a while too." He looked at Mrs. Smith. "How about ordering us a pizza or something?"

Mrs. Smith didn't bat an eye. She picked up the phone and dialed the cafeteria up in the main building. Gant went over to one of the chairs aligned around the coffee table and slumped down in it. "What's the plan?"

"First," Neeley said, staring him straight in the eyes, "it was a bullshit mission sending me to the cache site. Bailey was there and filed a report. I could have helped you in Maine."

Gant took a deep breath, then slowly exhaled and nodded. "All right. I accept that."

Neeley and Golden took seats flanking him. Gant waited. Golden was the next to speak. "We think the ultimate goal of our targets is to kill those men they feel are responsible for what happened to them. They've already killed Foley. That leaves Caulkins, Cranston, Roberts and Lankin. Four men in four different places. Places where our targets knows they will be, even though they do have guards. We suggest we bring them together in one place, a location that our targets will not have planned for."

Gant considered that. As he was thinking, Neeley spoke up. "If the targets can't find the four, they can't kill them."

"Maybe they don't want to kill them," Gant said. "Maybe the targets want those men to suffer the rest of their lives."

"Then why did they take out Foley?" Neeley asked.

Gant shrugged. "I think we messed up whatever they had planned for Foley or his wife. You've seen these men," he said to Golden. "They're suffering. Death might well be a relief for them."

Golden shook her head. "They're suffering but I don't think that's going to be enough for our targets. They went to Maine to finish off the warlord. I think they're going to finish off these men."

"Where do you suggest moving them?" Gant asked.

"Fort Bragg," Neeley said. "The Delta Force compound. It's about as secure a place as you can find."

It was Gant's turn to shake his head. "Bragg is where our targets trained. They know that place and they know people there. Not a good idea."

Mrs. Smith cleared her throat. "Mister Nero and Ms. Masterson are waiting for you."

Gant stood. "Let's ask Ms. Masterson what she thinks since she's now the brains of this operation."

The three made their way through the security checks into the Cellar's inner sanctum. Masterson was behind the desk, Nero on the couch to the side. An IV was hooked up to the old man and he didn't raise his head as they came in.

"I understand you have a proposal," Masterson said.

Gant wasn't surprised—he had no doubt the outer office was under constant surveillance and Nero and Masterson had heard every word.

Golden stepped forward. "We think we should consolidate the four men our targets are after. Put them in a secure place."

"And that would achieve?" Masterson asked.

"Hopefully it might save their lives," Golden said.

Masterson looked to Neeley. "You agree?"

Neeley nodded.

Then Masterson turned her attention to Gant. "And you?"

"Hiding those people isn't going to get us any closer to the targets. Or Emily Cranston."

Masterson considered for a few moments. "But it might indeed save their lives. We'll do it. And I agree that Fort Bragg is not a good idea. I suggest we bring them here to Fort Meade. We have a safe house out in the range area that we can have secured."

Gant stared at the woman behind the desk, trying to get a read on her. He thought she was agreeing much too quickly to this plan, but didn't say anything.

Masterson switched her attention once more, this time back to Golden. "I read your report on the interview with Egan. We can see where Forten's penchant for chaining living things out in the woods began. But do you have anything that can help us predict what he'll do next?"

"Not from the interview," Golden said. "We'll get the rest of Emily's cache report. The question is where and when."

"If we wait until they give it to us," Gant said, "it will be too late for her."

Nero's metallic voice cut across the room. "A question, if I may?"

Everyone turned to him. Nero's head was turned to the side, solidly resting on a pillow. His voice machine was resting on the pillow in front of his throat. "These men have targeted the families of those they feel betrayed them. Do any of them have families of their own?"

Gant wanted to kick himself for missing such an obvious avenue of approach. Masterson's fingers flew over her keyboard as Golden opened up her briefcase and pulled out the personnel folders of the three targets. "Lutz was single. As was Forten. But Payne had a wife."

"I've got the address," Masterson said. "Fayetteville, just outside Fort Bragg. According to my data, Payne's wife claimed his death benefits and remarried less than six months after he was reported killed in the supposed helicopter accident."

Gant felt a cold knot in his stomach. "I'd get the locals on it but it's probably too late."

Golden looked at him. "What do you mean it's—" she paused as she realized what he meant. "You think they're dead?"

"Most likely dead and the bodies well hidden," Gant said. "Probably the first order of business the targets did when they got back to the States. They wouldn't want to leave bodies around because that would have brought focus too soon."

Masterson was typing as she spoke. "I'll have the local police check out her last known location."

"What else have we missed?" Nero asked, the artificial voice without inflection but Gant felt an implied rebuke.

"According to the CIA," Gant said, "our targets were captured by the drug cartel in Columbia. Held for eight months. Tortured. I've got two questions: why didn't we make an attempt to get them back? And two, how did they escape?"

"I've checked into that," Masterson said. "No attempt was made to get the men back because they were officially reported killed in an accident by Southern Command."

"By Colonel Cranston, right?" Gant asked.

"Correct. So no one was looking for them because no one knew they were alive," Masterson said.

"So Cranston did fuck them over," Gant said, earning a sharp look from Golden. He ignored her. "But why did the Cartel keep them alive? And why didn't the Cartel try to make a deal? Use the three as leverage against the United States or at the very least a political statement?" When there was no answer, Gant pushed his second question. "And how did they escape?"

"The DEA agent," Golden suddenly said.

"What?" Gant was confused by the sudden switch.

"The CIA guy—Roberts. He said they gave up a DEA agent in order to get his brother who was undercover closer to the head of one of the Cartels, right?"

Gant nodded. "Yes."

"Who was this agent?" Golden asked.

Masterson looked down at the computer screen set into the desk-top and typed on the slim keyboard. "I'm checking. Why do you want to know?"

"Because," Gant said before Golden could explain, "Roberts told us the DEA agent was presumed dead. Just like our targets. And he was a prisoner of the same Cartel group our targets were held by."

"So he might not be dead," Nero said. He shifted his head between Gant and Golden, the raw skin where his eyes had once been, almost seeming to see them. It was as if he were measuring the two of them in some manner.

Gant could also tell that Golden was staring at him but he couldn't determine her mood—whether she was angry at him for stepping on her line of reasoning or happy that he had quickly seen where she was going. She was back in therapist mode, hiding her emotions.

"Robert Finley," Masterson said, reading her screen. "He'd been with the DEA for eight years. Reported as killed in the line of duty last year, body never recovered."

"Any tags on his file?" Gant asked.

"'Tags'?" Golden repeated.

"Roberts told us Finley was dirty," Gant reminded her. "A tag is a classified note on the file indicating what that might be."

"None," Golden said.

Gant frowned. "That doesn't add up with what Roberts told us."

Neeley spoke up. "Maybe they kept it in house."

"Roberts is CIA," Gant said. "Finley was DEA. If the CIA suspected Finley was dirty, there would be a tag in the Cellar's records."

"Perhaps Mister Roberts was not telling the truth," Nero said.

Another piece of the puzzle clicked into place for Gant. "So everyone was fucking everyone down there. Roberts and the CIA gave up Finley, who was just doing his job. Then they gave up the team, which was just doing its job because of a bureaucratic screw-up. The bottom line is I think we're back up to three targets, not down to two. I think Finley is still alive."

Emily listened to the rumble impatiently, wishing it would grow closer, much like the trains that rattled by. Thunder. A sound many feared but to Emily sounded as sweet as anything she'd ever heard. The dark sky above her flickered with distant lightning and Emily began to count each time she saw it. The time lag between the light and the thunder gave her an idea how close the storm was.

She's spotted the wisps of storm clouds earlier—the cause of her smile. She'd lain on her back, watching the sky darkness as the clouds thickened.

There was a flash close by, followed less than two seconds later by thunder. Without conscious thought, Emily's tongue slid out of her parched mouth and across her cracked lips. She could taste the moisture carried by the wind. Her entire body was vibrating, even her skin sensing the dampness in the air.

The first drop hit her in the middle of her forehead.

From inside the helicopter Gant saw the stooped over figure waiting for them, silhouetted by the bright landing lights on top of CIA headquarters. Gant slid open the side door of the Blackhawk helicopter but didn't get out. He glanced across the cargo bay at his new partner. Neeley wore a long black leather coat. She had a sniper rifle secured to the inside of it with Velcro stays. He knew she had body armor on underneath the black turtleneck she wore. Golden sat next to her, silent, her taut face reflected in the glow from the screen of her laptop computer. Gant had no idea what she was doing.

Roberts climbed into the chopper and Gant leaned around him, sliding the door shut. It was loud in the back of the helicopter as it lifted off and Gant extended a set of headphones with boom mike to Roberts, similar to what he, Golden and Neeley were wearing.

"We're on a private channel," Gant informed Roberts as soon as he had his set on. "Pilots can't hear us."

Roberts nodded. "I got the message. I don't see the point of hiding me some place."

On the flight here, Golden had told Gant to expect this—a death wish. "I don't much see the point either." He could smell the alcohol coming off of Roberts. He hadn't just been sitting in his office working this late at night.

That stopped conversation for a little while as the Blackhawk flew through the night sky, the pilots dark figures in front with night vision goggles covering their faces, making them almost seem to be part of the machine rather than masters of the machine. Gant saw Neeley lean back, her long legs encased in dark pants, black leather boots sliding along the metal floor then up on to the canvas seat right next to Roberts, invading his space.

"Where are we going?" Roberts finally asked, glancing from Neeley back to Gant.

"Fort Meade," Gant answered. "A secure site on post."

"Just me?" Roberts asked.

Gant knew the man wasn't stupid. "No. The others whose families were targeted will be there also."

Roberts nodded and slumped back in the canvas seat, whatever little energy he had draining out of him. Gant found that an odd reaction for someone whose life they were saving.

"You lied to us." Neeley said it in a low voice, her body not moving in the slightest.

Roberts twitched. "I didn't—"

Neeley's boots slammed down on the floor with a thud they could hear even through the headsets. "'And ye shall know the truth and the truth shall make you free.' John, verse eight, line thirty-two. It's inscribed right there in your own CIA museum. Kind of a joke don't you think consider your stock and trade is lying."

"I told you what you asked," Roberts said.

"So it was our fault," Neeley said. "We just didn't ask the right questions? Is that it?" She didn't wait for an answer. "Bullshit. Some of the things you told us were flat out lies or at best, withholding of the truth."

"Such as?" Roberts shot back.

Gant had his hand on the butt of his Glock. He didn't think Roberts would get violent but one never knew. He glanced at Golden and her attention was no longer on her laptop. She was watching Roberts very carefully.

"The DEA agent who you gave up to the Cartel," Neeley said. "Who you *betrayed*. He wasn't dirty, was he?"

"They're all dirty down there," Roberts said. "Everyone knows that. Too much money not to be."

"So you were dirty?" Gant snapped.

"What?" Roberts was confused, whether by the question or the switch in interrogators, Gant didn't know, nor did he care.

"You worked Central and South America. The nexus of the drug trafficking world. You're a government employee. GS-whatever the fuck level you are. Not like you're making that much more money than Finley did. So by your logic you have to be dirty too."

He could see Roberts' head snap up at the name. "I wasn't dirty."

Neeley leaned forward. "You don't call setting up a United States government agent to be tortured and killed by drug dealers being dirty?"

"He was taking money—"

Neeley didn't back off. "So you had him tortured and killed by some of the worst scum to walk the face of the planet? That puts you on such a moral pedestal. And what proof did you have that he was dirty? We haven't been able to find anything—no tags on his classified files-- and the Cellar knows everything that goes between agencies. If the CIA suspected a DEA agent of being dirty, there'd be a tag. Or else you—and those who you worked with—violated the most basic principle of covert operations. So you're full of shit."

Gant tapped Roberts on the shoulder startling him. "Finley's not dead, is he?"

Roberts eyes grew wide. "Yes, he is. The Cartel got him."

"But there was no body, right?" Gant asked. "You just assumed he was dead. Just like Cranston assumed the three Special Forces guys were dead. Well, as we know now, they aren't, so maybe Finley isn't either."

Roberts rubbed a hand across his forehead and closed his eyes. Gant could see it was shaking. Roberts was in much worse shape than he'd realized. Gant knew the loss of his daughter was terrible, but Roberts was-- Gant stopped and considered the sequence of events. Only two kidnappings and caches.

He turned to Neeley and held up three fingers, indicating for her to switch intercom channels. He could see Golden trying to figure out what he meant so he held up the switch on his wire in a place where Roberts couldn't see it. As soon as both women switched channels, he spoke.

"Roberts and Cranston. They have something in common in the pattern. Both daughters cached. Roberts' daughter had been out there so long she'd died. Cranston's daughter is dying. On the others, it had been a straight kill."

Neeley nodded. "Yes. So?"

"These guys haven't done anything randomly or without reason," Gant said. "So why the two girls cached?"

Golden spoke up. "To make their fathers suffer."

"They outright killed Caulkins daughter," Gant noted. "Drowned her on the beach. Why didn't they cache her? Does he get a different level of suffering?"

Gant waited, wanting to see what Neeley and Golden came up with. He realized he was looking for confirmation, a very strange sensation given he'd always worked alone.

"Leverage," Neeley finally said.

Gant felt the thrill of the hunt begin to surge. "Yes. And leverage for what?"

"There's only one reason for leverage," Neeley said. "To get someone to do something."

They all turned and looked at Roberts, who know was slumped forward, his elbows on his knees, his head in his hands.

"And he didn't do what they asked him to," Gant said.

"Jesus," Neeley whispered as the implications sank in. Gant could see that Golden was still trying to figure it out. She'd learn, Gant thought. What had happened to her son had hurt her so deeply, he realized, that while it made her aware of the horror of what mankind was capable of it had also dulled her abilities.

While Neeley was reflecting on the horror that Roberts had allowed to be inflicted on his daughter, Gant was distracted by Golden's voice on the intercom.

"I've pulled Finley's file. Quite interesting."

Gant simply stared at her, waiting for her to give him the information.

"I was wrong," Golden finally said. "I said that Forten was the leader, but that the other two men displayed amazing initiative while separated from home. You," she said, nodding at Gant, "ascribed that to them being highly trained special operations soldiers. But we didn't know about Finley then."

"How does he change things?" Gant asked.

"Finley is the leader. He's the one who's been coordinating all of it," Golden said.

"We've picked up no indication of that," Gant said.

"Finley's childhood is very similar to Forten's—I'm sure they bonded over that. The advantage Forten had though, was that he was moved around. Finley stayed with his mother for sixteen years before running away, forging a birth certificate and joining the Marines. He excelled in the Corps." She looked up from her computer. "He was a trained sniper. Recorded seven confirmed kills in the first Gulf War and a dozen unconfirmed."

Just what we need, another sniper, Gant thought.

"He left the Corps and joined the DEA. His service record is exemplary except there are several notes that he had a tendency to use extreme force and bend the rules."

"I'm surprised the Cellar didn't recruit him," Gant said.

"There are a couple of abnormalities in his records," Golden said. "His mother disappeared three years ago. Simply vanished. Finley was supposed to be undercover in Colombia at the time."

Neeley stirred. "'Supposed to be'?"

"He was unaccounted for during the week of her disappearance," Golden said. "But her body was never found and no record of him entering the country was ever discovered."

"But he didn't like his mother," Gant said it as a statement, not a question.

"Right," Golden said.

Gant thought about it. "So he gets betrayed by the CIA. Snarked up by the Cartel. The team gets betrayed. Snatched by the same cartel. Probably adjoining cells. A lot of bonding over the pain. Finley had worked the Cartel and he offers them a deal. Release the four, get them back in the States, and they'll wreak murder and mayhem."

"That's the way it most likely developed," Golden acknowledged.

Gant held up two fingers, indicating they should switch back to the frequency Roberts was on.

"Which one contacted you after Caleigh was kidnapped?" Gant asked. "Finley or Forten?"

Roberts slowly brought his head up from his hands. His eyes were hollow, dead. He simply stared at Gant without responding, although his lack of protest was confirmation.

"Which one contacted you?" Gant pressed. "Finley or Forten?"

"Finley."

Gant glanced at Neeley. He was disgusted with Roberts but he felt another surge of excitement as he realized all the parameters of this mission had just shifted. "What did he want?"

"He wanted me to kill three men."

"Cranston and the others?" Neeley asked.

Roberts shook his head. "The three men who were with me when we decided that giving Finley up to the Cartel was an acceptable price. CIA men. Two of them higher in rank than me. The Director of Operations and the Chief of Direct Actions."

"And the third?" Gant asked.

"My brother."

Neeley shifted angrily. "A little more detail might be helpful. When did he contact you? How?"

"I received a videotape via FedEx two days after she disappeared," Roberts said. He sighed deeply. "It was of Caleigh. Chained to a tree. There was a partial cache report in the package also. The same as the one you guys received later. The note with it said if I did what they asked they'd send the rest of the cache report."

"And you refused?" Even with all he'd seen over the years, Gant found this hard to believe.

Roberts stared at him. "Kill three people for one life? And I was supposed to believe that someone who would chain a young girl to a tree in the middle of the woods would keep his word? You know better than that. They would never have let her live."

Gant knew there was no arguing the point with Roberts. He'd made some sort of pact with an inner devil and it was killing him. "What did you do?"

"I went to the Director of Operations and the Chief of Direct Actions. They did everything they could to try to find her using in-house resources. My brother went out into the field to try to find what he could."

Gant knew Roberts was referring to the Direct Action section of the CIA—the one that did the dirty work. "But they had trouble working in the States?"

"Yes. And we couldn't bring the FBI in."

Gant glanced over at Golden. She didn't look as shocked as she had at other things.

"But you knew it was Finley?" Gant asked.

Roberts nodded. "Had to be. He was the one who would want those men killed."

"So Finley knew he was set up in Colombia?"

Roberts nodded. "Yes."

"How?"

"I've asked myself that same question," Roberts said, "and the only answer I could come up with is that the Cartel told him. Which answers the next question of how he got away. They let him go. Just like they let Lutz, Payne and Forten go. Which also explains how they got back into the United States illegally. The Cartel turned them and sent them back here for vengeance, which was fine with the Cartel. Cost them nothing to get several senior US agents killed."

With this new information Gant was already trying to project ahead, thinking like the bad guys. "So using your daughter didn't work. The question is will it work on Cranston?"

"Fuck," Neeley muttered, pulling out her Satphone.

"Hold on," Gant said.

"Cranston's already at the safe house," Neeley argued.

"Cranston won't do anything until he's there." Gant indicated Roberts. "Right?" He asked Roberts.

The CIA agent nodded. "He'll be under orders to take all of us out. He'll wait."

Gant glanced over at Golden. Once more she was shocked, taken out of her element into a realm where death and violence was the norm.

"What did they promise you if you do as they asked?" Gant stared hard at the man. "How were they going to release your daughter?"

"They sent me the same partial cache report. They promised to send the rest of it to whomever I designated if I did as they demanded."

"Which you thought was a lie?" Neeley asked.

"Why would they do that?" Roberts responded in turn. "These guys don't give a shit about anyone."

Golden spoke up. "Do you?"

Roberts glared at her. "I dealt with the reality of the situation."

"And now?" Golden pressed.

"I'm a dead man," Roberts said.

"Oh, fuck you," Gant said. "I don't give a damn whether you live or die. What I do care about is the young girl who is chained up somewhere. If I thought our targets would give up the rest of the cache report if Cranston kills you assholes I'd hand him the gun. But you're right. I don't think even if Cranston does what they want, that they'll give up the rest of the cache report."

"Unless they want something else," Neeley said.

Gant turned to her. "Such as?"

"The three CIA men that our friend here was supposed to take out. Finley would still want that."

Gant nodded. "We could make a deal. But we have no way of communicating with the targets."

"Cranston does," Roberts said.

Everyone turned to him and waited.

"When they sent me the video of Caleigh," Roberts said, "there was one of those disposable cell phones in the package. I was supposed to call them and tell them where and when I would do it. I think they wanted to watch to confirm."

"What did you do with the phone?" Gant asked.

"We tried to call them to see if we could get an idea where they were. There was one number programmed into it. A cell number. Disposable, sold somewhere in Florida. We called, someone answered but didn't speak. They stayed on the line for ten seconds, and then hung up. We weren't able to track down the answering phone."

Gant looked at Golden. "You know Colonel Cranston well, right?"

"Somewhat," Golden said evasively.

"Would he kill those men to get Emily back?"

Golden was silent, then nodded. "Yes."

Gant turned to Neeley. "I think it's time we bring your partner, Ms. Masterson, in on this. We're going to need some leverage of our own."

Neeley nodded and turned on her Satphone. Gant grabbed a remote plug and slid it into the side of her phone so that he and Golden could listen in. He ignored Roberts. As far as he was concerned, the man was right: he was dead already. And Gant had a feeling quite a few more people were going to be joining Roberts shortly.

CHAPTER TWENTY-FOUR

GANT LET GOLDEN do the summarizing of what they had just learned from Roberts and just figured out. Masterson had answered the call, but confirmed that Nero was listening in, which made Gant feel slightly better. This entire mission was turning into what his buddies back in the army would call a cluster-fuck.

It took Golden about five minutes to get the man and woman who ran the Cellar up to speed. During that time, Gant checked his GPS and noted that they were only twenty minutes out from Fort Meade.

There was a moment of silence when Golden was done, the only sound in the headsets the slight crackling noise made by the satellite feed going through several Milstar satellites and being scrambled, frequency hopped and then unscrambled.

"There is a piece missing," Masterson finally said.

"Finley," Golden said.

"No," Masterson replied. "These men came to the United States on a mission. If it ends with Cranston killing the others, including Roberts, at the safe house, then they still will not have completed their mission."

"The three other CIA men," Gant said.

"Very good, Mister Gant," Masterson said. "And Finley has yet to surface. Our three special operators have been targeting those who betrayed them. Finley's focus is the four who betrayed him. He tried to get them through Roberts by caching his daughter and it failed. What would be his next move?"

Neeley spoke up. "We were wrong. Doctor Golden and I. Bringing the potential victims together played right into their hands. It's what they wanted us to do"

"Correct," Masterson said.

"But you let us do it?" Neeley protested, half a question, half a statement.

Gant was beginning to see the big picture and it wasn't a pleasant one. But he kept his mouth shut. They were ten minutes out from Fort Meade according to his GPS.

"What exactly is the goal here?" Golden asked. She was staring at Gant, as if accusing him of something and he knew she thought he'd been in on this from start, not knowing he'd just figured it out himself.

"There was a reason Finley's file didn't have a tag," Masterson said. "There never was one. But there should have been a flag on the DO, CDA, Roberts and his brother's file."

Gant, Neeley and Golden all turned and stared at Roberts in the dim light in the back of the chopper. He saw the looks and his head sunk down on his chest, his eyes closed.

"So *they* were the dirty ones," Golden said, as if by saying it, she could comprehend it.

"Correct," Neeley said.

"How long have you known this?" Gant asked.

"Mister Nero and I had our suspicions from the beginning," Masterson said. "The entire cache angle seemed odd for a pure revenge mission."

Gant didn't feel too bad. He had figured out the cache anomaly on his own. "So Roberts, his brother, the DO and CDA never made an official search for Roberts' daughter?"

"Correct," Masterson said. "That was the key thing that got Mister Nero and I to truly suspect that we might be looking at this entirely the wrong way."

Everyone on the radio was startled when Roberts suddenly spoke. Gant realized he must have switched frequencies on the intercom while they were discussing all this. "We did it to try to accomplish our mission."

"Bullshit," Gant snapped.

"No, really," Roberts was almost begging to be believed. "When we realized we needed to really get the head of the Cartel to trust my brother, we knew we had to up the stakes."

Nero's metallic voice cut through his protests. "As Mister Gant just succinctly put it, bullshit, Mister Roberts. Because there is no explaining the five million dollars you and your brother have in an account in the Caymans. And the similar accounts the DO and CDA have."

"You gave up your daughter for money?" Golden was even more incredulous than she had been.

"It all went wrong," Roberts cried out. "We thought we could play both sides. Take the head of the Cartel's money, find low level information and people, in order to get him to trust us, then turn on him and take him out when we were close enough."

"But none of this was authorized," Nero said. A statement, not a question.

Gant had his hand on the butt of his Glock, belatedly realizing they had failed to search Roberts before allowing him on the chopper. Out of the corner of his eye he could see Neeley had her hand inside her leather coat, also on alert.

Roberts head began shaking, back and forth very slowly, as if by the very act he could deny all that was being said and had happened. Suddenly he spun to his right and Gant drew his pistol. Gant was bringing it to bear as Roberts jerked open the handle on the cargo door and threw himself out of the helicopter into the night sky.

Gant slowly holstered his weapon, Neeley doing the same. He leaned across and slid the door shut.

"Mister Nero," he said over the radio. "Ms. Masterson. Roberts just sanctioned himself. What now?"

"It's time," the Sniper said as he turned the van onto a dirt road.

The Spotter didn't respond, sitting in the passenger seat, his clothes still wet from the river. They'd been driving for two hours straight since getting in their back-up vehicle. They were heading south through Maine. The two men had not talked much, the close call weighing on their minds. Or at least on the Sniper's mind. He glanced over at his partner, uncertain what the man was thinking or feeling.

The van's headlights illuminated a lakeside cabin. Beyond the cabin, a hundred foot dock stretched out over the water and a small floatplane was moored at the end. Just another piece in the elaborate plan they had spent months putting together.

Inside the cabin was another part of the plan and the Sniper was slightly concerned about the Spotter's reaction to what had to be done now. They had delayed this as long as possible, the Spotter arguing that it was the prudent thing, but the Sniper had his doubts about his partner's sincerity. The Sniper missed his Security man, a person he knew he could count on. In Colombia, it had been the Spotter who had broken first under the torture. Of course, they had all broken eventually.

The Sniper brought the van to a halt right in front of the cabin. He opened the door and got out. He waited as the Spotter hesitated, then finally exited the vehicle. The Sniper led the way to the door of the cabin and pushed it open.

"Honey, we're home," he called out with a smile. He noted that the Spotter didn't appreciate his sense of humor.

"Why don't we just go?" the Spotter asked, stopping the Sniper in his tracks, midway across the main room.

"That's not the plan," the Sniper said. He pointed back to the door. "Wait for me in the plane if you don't want to be part of this." He waited, then the Spotter nodded.

"Let's do it."

The Sniper walked across the main room and threw open a door. A foul smell wafted out of the bedroom. The Spotter's wife was tied to the bed, arms together over her head, ankles bound together with a rope. Since they'd left her here she had fouled herself, contributing to the smell. But the main source of the stink was the body slumped in a chair at the foot of the bed.

The Spotter had had no problem putting a bullet through the head of the man his wife had married less than six months after he'd been declared dead. Who his wife had taken into his bed while he was being tortured and threatened with death every day.

The Sniper walked to the head of the bed and looked down at the woman. There was a gag tied tightly around her head and she stared up with wild eyes. Forty-eight hours tied here with no food or water, the body of her new husband sharing the room—the Sniper has no sympathy for her. It was nothing compared to what they had suffered in Colombia.

"You should have waited for him," the Sniper said.

The woman nodded furiously. The Sniper laughed. "Too late." His hand was reaching for his pistol when his cell phone rang. He pulled it out and flipped it open. "Yes?"

He listened for almost a minute. Then just said "Roger that" and snapped the phone shut. He glanced at the door where the Spotter stood. "The next phase is in movement." He gestured at the woman. "Do you want to do the honors?"

The woman was moaning, trying to speak through the gag. Her arms and legs were drumming on the bed, a desperate and futile attempt to do something, anything.

"Remember the pain?" The Sniper asked the Spotter. "Do you remember that stinking place where they kept us? Remember how you told us the only thing that kept you going was wanting to come home—to this? To a woman who betrayed you?"

"She thought I was dead," the Spotter murmured.

"She should have had faith in you." The Sniper knew this would not go the way he wanted. He drew his pistol and aimed. The Spotter still had not moved. The woman was crying. The Sniper fired once, the round hitting her right between the eyes, cutting off the crying and stopping her struggles.

"Let's go," he said, holstering the pistol.

* * *

Emily sat in half an inch of water. She leaned over and took a careful sip. She'd forced herself not to gorge, not to over-indulge like she had when the evil man had given her the water bottle. She had all night. The water wasn't going anywhere. The storm had been short and fierce, pelting her with large drops and she'd reveled in it.

She felt strong, refreshed. And clean. She knew the water she sat in was not the purest and there was a faint hint of sand in it from the bottom of the cistern, but she had never tasted anything so wonderful.

Re-energized, Emily peered in the dark at the shackle around her ankle.

Now was the time.

The thought came to her unbidden, but as loudly as if someone had shouted it in her ear. It didn't make sense practically—with the water in the cistern she was in the best condition she'd been in since being kidnapped.

But it was time.

The rain was a respite, a relief, but a false one. For the dryness would come again. And the thirst. And she would grow weaker and weaker until she wouldn't have the strength to free herself.

It was time.

Emily took the wire she had so carefully doubled and then doubled again. She slid it into the keyhole for the shackle. She ignored the pain from the un-healed cuts from her last attempt. She went to work on her last chance for freedom.

CHAPTER TWENTY-FIVE

"WE'RE ONE MINUTE out from the safe house," Gant announced. "What's the plan?"

Neeley was kneeling on the floor of the cargo bay, pulling an MP-5 submachinegun out of her kit bag. She checked a magazine of rounds, then slammed it home into the weapon, pulling the cocking lever back. Gant already had his sub-machinegun out and ready across his knees. Neeley pulled a pistol out of the bag and offered it to Golden. The doctor looked at it for a few seconds, then reached out and took it.

"You let Cranston do what he plans to do," Masterson said.

"What?" Gant exclaimed.

"Tell him Roberts jumped," Masterson said. "He'll believe Doctor Golden. Once he knows that, there's nothing to hold him back from taking out Caulkins and Lankin."

"What's to keep him from taking us out?" Neeley asked.

"Because you'll tell him the Cellar has approved the sanctions of Caulkins and Lankin," Masterson said.

"And then?"

"And then tell him the Cellar has also approved the sanctions of the CIA's Director of Operations, Chief of Direct Action and Roberts' brother. We're closing this entire mess out."

Gant had been expecting that. "And then?"

"Have Cranston call on the cell phone the targets provided him and tell them that he'll deliver those three to wherever Emily is currently cached. You will accompany him. I have operatives out picking those three up right now and consolidating them. I'll have their precise location to you shortly. Is this clear?"

"Yes," Gant said.

"Neeley?" Masterson asked.

"Clear."

"Doctor Golden?"

Gant glanced at her. She finally nodded. "Clear. But what about Colonel Cranston?"

"He will be the last one to go down," Masterson said.

The radio went dead just as the chopper flared for landing.

Gant stood, sub-machinegun at the ready. He slid a pair of night vision goggles over his eyes and turned them on. Neeley and Golden stood behind him, their own weapons in their hands, also wearing goggles. Gant opened the cargo bay door and walked out into the small open field in front of the one story bunker-style building. There were no lights on in the building and the front door was wide open.

"No guards," Gant noted. Behind them, the sound of the helicopter's blades and engine began to wind down.

"Gant," Neeley said in a very calm voice. "Don't move."

"What?"

"Your chest," she said.

Gant looked down and saw a small red dot right over his heart. Even though he had a vest on, he had no doubt that the shooter had a sniper rifle with a 'hot' round that would punch right through.

"Colonel Cranston?" Gant called out.

"Everyone just stay right where you are," Cranston's voice echoed out of the darkness from somewhere just ahead of them. "I've got a fifty caliber Barrett centered right on your chest, Gant. I don't care what body armor you're wearing, it will go through it and you and keep going for another mile."

"Caulkins and Lankin?" Gant yelled, even though he knew the answer.

"Dead."

"The guards?"

"Sleeping. I spiked their food. I'm not killing any more innocents. Nor allowing any more innocents to die. Where's Roberts? Hiding in the helicopter?"

"He's dead," Gant said. From the voice, he figured that Cranston was on the roof of the bunker. Out of the corner of his eyes, he could tell that Neeley and Golden were remaining perfectly still.

"Bullshit," Cranston called out. "You're protecting him."

"I'm from the Cellar," Gant said. "Why would I protect someone who betrayed his job and his country? He jumped out of the chopper on the way here, not less than two minutes ago."

The red dot on Gant's chest didn't waver. "Susan?" Cranston called out. "Is this true?"

"Yes, Sam. We learned the truth about what he and the others at the CIA did."

"Those fuckers," Cranston cursed. "They used me."

"And you used the Special Forces team," Gant said, taking a step forward.

"I said freeze," Cranston snapped. "I *will* kill you."

"Why?" Gant asked, taking another step. He noticed that Neeley had her sub-machinegun up, stock tight to her shoulder, remaining still, but that Golden was matching his steps forward. "I'm an innocent. Do you know where Emily is? Have you called them yet?"

"How-- I was waiting for Roberts," Cranston said.

"To leverage him to give up the other three in the CIA?" Gant asked.

"Yes."

"Wouldn't have worked," Gant said as he took another step. "You saw the photos. Unlike you, Roberts gave up his own daughter rather than give in. You think you could have leveraged him now?"

"But Emily—" Cranston faltered.

Gant took another step closer, Golden at his side. "We'll get Emily," he said.

"How?"

Gant suddenly saw Cranston as the man stood up from behind a small berm to the right of the shelter's door. He held the heavy sniper rifle in his arms, then slowly lowered it, dropping it. Golden ran forward and threw her arms around her former lover whether to control him or comfort him, Gant wasn't sure.

Gant pointed at the couple, indicating for Neeley to keep an eye on them while he moved around them and into the shelter. It was as Cranston had said. Caulkins and Lankin were dead, a single round to the back of their head, slumped in their bunks. They probably never knew what hit them. The six guards were out cold on the floor but still breathing.

Gant went back outside. "Do you have the cell phone they sent you?"

Cranston nodded. He reached into his pocket and pulled out a small flip phone. "But what can I say to them?"

"Tell them you'll bring them the CIA's Director of Operations, Chief of Direct Action and Roberts brother. But you'll only deliver to wherever they have Emily. And we'll want proof of life before we make a swap."

* * *

The Sniper put the floatplane into a steady descent. He could make out the river through the night vision goggles and knew he had to hit at exactly the right spot to have enough straight water to bring the plane to a halt without hitting a bank. He reached down and flipped the plane's wing lights on and then off just as quickly.

Less than three seconds later, the bright blip of an infrared strobe-light, invisible to the naked eye, but glaring in the night vision goggles. He focused on that point, trusting it and the instruments.

Emily lifted her head out of the quarter inch of water she had been lapping at and cocked her head. A noise. Not a train. Getting closer.

An airplane. Propeller driven. She slowly got to her feet, right hand firmly holding what remained of the folded underwire. Her hands were bleeding again, but the wire had held. She felt like she was close, very close, to turning the tumbler.

She slowly turned her head, tracking the aircraft. It was low, according to the sound, and passing from her right to left.

It was the first unusual thing that had happened since she'd been here.

And she had a bad feeling about it.

She squatted down over the lock and went back to work with a new sense of urgency.

The Sniper touched down on the river just adjacent to the strobe light flashing on the bank. As soon as the plane's pontoons hit water, the light went out. The Sniper concentrated on slowing the craft, counting to himself, knowing how much straight river he had ahead. With three seconds to spare he had the airplane at a halt. He reversed thrust on one engine, giving a little power to the other and turned the plane around. Slowly, he cruised the plane back the way he had come.

The IR strobe came on once more and the Sniper spotted it immediately. It was no longer on the bank, but rather held by a man seated in a small rubber boat on the river. The Sniper slowed further and then cut the engine.

"Throw out the anchor," he ordered the Spotter who had yet to say a word since they left Maine.

* * *

Emily was twisting the wire, ignoring the pain shooting through her fingers and the blood that coated them when the sound of the plane engine suddenly cut off. She didn't pause.

The Sniper stood on the pontoon of the floatplane and tossed the duffel bag of gear to the man standing in the rubber boat. He reached back and grabbed another bag from the Spotter and tossed it over. Then he carefully stepped from the plane to the boat, the Spotter following.

The man who had taken the gear sat back down in the rear and goosed the small electric motor, driving them toward shore. He ran the bow of the boat up on a pebbly shoal, grounding. He stood up and stepped out.

"Status?" The Sniper finally asked, breaking the silence.

Drug Enforcement Agent John Finley turned and faced the two Special Forces men. "Sergeants Forten and Payne. It was regrettable that we lost Sergeant Lutz."

"He accomplished his mission," Forten said. "A casualty of war."

Finley nodded. "And have you accomplished yours?"

Forten glanced at Payne. "Cranston took out Caulkin and Lankin."

"Good for you." The sarcasm was evident in Finley's voice. "And I assume you cleaned up the mess with Sergeant Payne's wife and new husband?"

"Yes," Forten said as Payne glared at the DEA man.

Finley moved toward shore. "And Cranston? We can close out his daughter now?"

"No." Forten said sharply, causing Finley to pause.

"'No'?" Finley repeated. "What good is she to us now? Of course, if you want to let her suffer, that's fine with me."

"Cranston isn't dead," Forten said.

"Why not?" Finley demanded.

"He called us to confirm Caulkin, Roberts and Lankin's deaths. And to make us an offer."

Finley stood very still. "And that offer was?"

"The Director of Operations, the Chief of Direct Action and Philip Roberts for his daughter."

Finley leaned slightly toward Forten. "And how is he going to do that?"

"He's bringing them here."

* * *

The near end of the wire cut deep into Emily's thumb, causing her to hiss in pain but she didn't stop. She kept the pressure up, uncertain whether she was on the tumbler or not. Tears began to flow as the pain increased, but she still didn't stop.

The pain grew so great, Emily thought she would pass out. Then there was a click and the wire slid out of her thumb into the quarter inch of water on the floor of the cistern. Emily gasped for breath, trying to combat the pain, her mind not yet processing what the click had meant. She didn't dare believe.

Emily put her thumb in her mouth, almost savoring the taste of the blood. She stared at the shackle. Nothing appeared different. With her free hand she reached down and grabbed it.

Nothing.

She removed the thumb from her mouth and used it on the other side of the shackle and pulled.

Nothing.

Emily felt the tears well up in her eyes once more. One last time she pulled and with a slight screech of metal giving way it opened.

Emily stared at her freed ankle in disbelief.

CHAPTER TWENTY-SIX

THE BLACKHAWK HELICOPTER landed on the top of CIA headquarters in the midst of a massive Mexican stand-off. Mister Bailey stood to the side of the landing pad holding a gun on three men. Surrounding him were a dozen CIA agents dressed in black with automatic weapons.

"This is going to be fun," Gant muttered as the wheels settled down and he opened the side door. He stepped out, Neeley at his side, both of them weapons at the ready.

"Good evening, Mister Gant," Bailey called out over the noise of the chopper, seemingly unconcerned about the ring of weapons pointed at him. The three men were flex cuffed, hands behind their back, and looked decidedly unhappy at the current situation.

Bailey continued. "I tried to explain to our comrades in the Central Intelligence Agency that I am acting under the Cellar's pre-eminent mandate. They don't seem to be accepting that. We are awaiting the arrival of the Director himself."

Gant stared at the three senior bureaucrats. In the harsh glare of the landing lights, their faces were pale, their normal bravado shaken. He'd ordered Cranston to stay in the chopper—no need to add him to the mixture.

The sound of the chopper lessened as the pilot went to idle. Gant checked his watch. According to the rest of the cache report they had received during Cranston's phone call to the targets, Emily was located in north Texas. From here they were to go to the airfield and board a fast plane to get close, then board another chopper.

"This is bullshit!" One of the men cried out.

Gant walked past Bailey who was placidly chewing his gum but very alertly keeping his weapon trained on the three. "Who the fuck are you?" Gant asked.

The man drew himself up in his finely tailored suit. "I'm Hugh Stanton, Central Intelligence Agency, Director of Operations."

Gant shrugged. "You heard of Finley? Forten? Payne? Lutz?"

Stanton took a step back. Gant looked at the other two men. "Who's Paul Roberts?"

"I am." He was tall, tanned, with shoulder length hair and Gant could tell right away he had not left his undercover days behind. Some never could.

"Your brother is dead," Gant said.

"You fuckers," Roberts snarled.

"He killed himself," Gant said. "Threw himself out of the chopper when the truth was finally given the light of day."

A muscle twitched on the side of Roberts' face. Bailey popped his gum. "Calm down." The hand holding the pistol was rock-steady.

Everyone turned as the door to roof access slammed open and a man in a finely cut suit came walking out. Gant recognized the Director of the CIA from his photos and the man looked none too pleased at the current situation.

"Who's in charge here?" the Director demanded.

"The Cellar," Bailey said calmly. "These three men have been seconded to the Cellar for the duration of the mission."

"What mission?" the Director was confused.

"You don't have a need to know," Bailey said. He popped his gum once more. Then he spit it out, the sodden mass landing at the Director's feet. "You may call Mister Nero if you have any questions. Do you have any questions?"

The Director's face flushed beet red. "When will they be back?"

"Ah, that's the question, isn't it?" Bailey said. He wagged the gun at the three men. "Time's a wasting gentlemen. Please board your flight. The sooner we get started, the sooner this will be over."

The three men turned and looked at their boss. The Director shifted his feet, avoiding their eyes, then jerked his thumb to the commander of the armed guards. Sullenly, the CIA triggermen lowered their weapons and headed for the door. Gant stood aside as the three CIA men clambered on board the chopper, then he followed with Bailey and Neeley. The door was slid shut and they were airborne heading to Andrews Air Force Base to cross-load onto a waiting Combat Talon.

* * *

Emily got to her feet and slowly walked in a circle, reveling in the feeling of freedom. The leg that had been shackled felt like it could float in the air. There was just under a quarter inch of water left in the bottom of the tank and she got on all fours and lapped some of it, not even conscious of what she looked like doing this and the level to which she had been reduced.

Then she stood once more and slowly walked the outside of the tank, hands on the wood. Her initial feeling of elation began to drain out of her with each step as she felt how solid the boards were. She looked up at the lip of the tank and reached upward, her hands a good two and a half feet from the top. She squatted and jumped, barely lifting a foot off the ground in her weakened condition and when she landed, her knees buckled and she fell hard to the floor of the tank with a slight splash.

Emily lay there panting.

She'd escaped only the shackle but not the prison.

FINLEY STOOD WITH his arms crossed, staring down the dusty main street toward the rail line a quarter mile away on the other side of the ghost town. The water tank was visible just to the right, towering over the dilapidated train station. He was flanked by Forten and Payne, the two men carrying their duffle bags full of gear and looking somewhat tired after their recent exertions.

The town was small, the largest structure being the abandoned textile factory on the western edge. Along main street were single story brick buildings, the windows broken out. A church on the eastern side of the street dominated the entire area with its fifty-foot high bell steeple.

"She still alive?" Payne asked.

"Who cares?" Finley questioned in turn.

"Cranston wants proof of life before giving up the men he has," Forten said.

Finley turned and looked at him. "You think Cranston is coming alone?"

"Of course not," Forten replied. He slapped the side of his duffle bag, eliciting thud of metal on metal. "That's why we brought the goodies. But I do think he's bringing the men you want. And we want him. The rest—" he shrugged-- "we kill if they get in our way."

"So how do we give them proof of life?" Forten asked.

Finley gave a cold smile. "Oh, they'll have a chance to see her. The cache report I gave them has her right here in the middle of main street. So we're going to have a good old-fashioned showdown."

The three CIA men were ducks in row, seated next to each other on the starboard side of the plane, with Cranston flanking them on the right. Very unhappy ducks. Bailey had his pistol loosely held in one hand along the port side, but Gant didn't get the feeling there was much fight left in the three men. Of course, they might do as the elder of the Roberts' brother had done and do a dive, but that wasn't anything he felt concerned about since the back of the plane was sealed.

For a moment, Gant paused. The thought of the Roberts' brothers brought up an image of his own brother. He was surprised to realize that since he had started this mission he had not really thought much about his brother's death. Or his life. Gant glanced to his right where Neeley was seated next to him. He could feel the warmth of her body and her arm pressing against his.

As if sensing his thoughts, Neeley turned and looked at him, her dark eyes barely visible in the dimly lit cargo bay of the Combat Talon. She nodded, as if acknowledging something and Gant was surprised to find himself nodding back at her. She then inclined her head, indicating Doctor Golden, who, as usual, was immersed in her laptop, which was hooked to the plane's satellite communication system and via that, to the Cellar.

Gant turned to Bailey. "What do you have on the cache location?" He, Neeley, Golden and Bailey were wearing headsets on their own intercom loop.

"A ghost town," Bailey said succinctly. Something about that was significant enough to draw Golden's attention away from her computer for the moment.

"What did you say?" she asked.

"It's a ghost town," Bailey repeated. "Ms. Masterson forwarded me the data. Small town, northern Texas. Textile factory went out of business in the fifties, the town died out. No one lives there anymore and since it was on the end of a county line road no one drives through either. The rail line is on the south side of the town. Rarely used, maybe three, four times a day by freight trains, no passenger trains."

"Satellite imagery?" Gant asked.

Bailey shook his head. "Nope. We tend to put our satellites over other countries to spy, not our own."

"So we're going in blind," Neeley said, "and they know we're coming."

"We're going in to trade," Bailey said, indicating the three CIA men and Colonel Cranston.

"Right," Gant said, not bothering to hide the sarcasm.

"We have an FM frequency to contact Finley on, once we get in radio range," Bailey said.

"We need a plan," Gant said.

Bailey glanced at his watch. "We've got four hours flight time to the location. Plan away."

"What about back-up?" Neeley asked.

Bailey shook his head. "We're it other than aircraft and logistical support. Ms. Masterson believes—and Mister Nero concurs—that what happens today be kept as tightly held as possible."

Emily went to the exact center of her wooden prison, the bolt that her shackle had been chained to right between her feet. Slowly she looked around, trying to see what she had missed. It was still dark out, but there was a half moon and her eyes had adjusted to the moon and star light. Dawn was several hours off as near as she could guess.

The floor was solid. Too thick.

The planks surrounding her were also solid and thick.

The rim of the cistern was out of reach. Too high.

She couldn't go down.

She couldn't go to the side.

Emily looked up once more to the rim of her prison. It was the only way. She had to make up the gap between where she could reach and the top.

Emily shook her head, dizzy from the lack of food. This was not a complicated problem. Quite simple. She had limited supplies to work with. Just as she had had when she opened the shackle. Basically her body and her clothes.

Shoes. Skirt. Panties. The bra—well, not much left there. Blouse. Sweater.

If she piled them up—Emily laughed at the absurdity. She'd gain an inch maybe. She was hydrated but realizing the lack of food had lowered her IQ considerably.

An inch closer would do no good.

She slowly turned once more staring at the rim and came to a halt. Two of the boards came apart from each other ever so slightly near the top. She walked over to the wall and stared at the small notch near the top. Only about a half inch wide and two inches down. Still not close enough to reach.

Emily sat down and put her head in her hands, trying to get her brain working right. This was a problem. Problems could be solved.

And in the midst of her thinking she heard something.

Voices.

Emily opened her mouth to scream for help, then she paused. She could only catch a phrase here and there, but someone was talking about making sure everything was ready, which did not sound like a rescue team to her.

And then another voice spoke and she sat bolt upright. A voice she'd heard before. The voice that had left her chained to a tree. The voice that belonged to the man with the dead eyes.

Finley stood at the south end of main street with Forten and Payne. They wore body armor, had sub-machineguns slung over their shoulders and automatic pistols in thigh holsters. Forten held his sniper rifle in the crook of his arms. The night air was calm, a stillness that was very deep. Dawn was a couple of hours off.

The three men now echoed the stillness around them after Finley had ascertained that each had double-checked their positions. They were staring down the dusty main road of the town, as if expecting a posse to come riding in from the north.

Payne was the first one to look over his shoulder as a faint noise intruded from the east. They all turned and looked in that direction, watching the headlight of the freight train growing closer in concert with the noise. The train rumbled by, the cabin of the locomotive a bright glow, a single figure silhouetted, staring ahead into the darkness, never noticing the three men less than a hundred feet away. After a minute and a half the caboose rolled by, red lights glowing.

The sound of the train faded and silence once again reigned until Finley spoke. "Arm the charges."

Emily felt her heart skip a beat.

As the train had gone by, she'd tried to absorb the fact that 'voices' meant that her abductor wasn't alone. And now there were 'charges' to be armed? What the fuck was going on?

Someone was coming. For her. She knew it. That's what they, whoever the voices belonged to, were preparing for.

Her father.

"Take your positions."

She heard the voice clearly. They would be looking for her father. Not at the water tower.

Emily stared up at the small notch between the two boards. She knew it held the answer. She just couldn't drag it up out of her exhausted mind.

CHAPTER TWENTY-SEVEN

"PAYNE'S WIFE AND new husband were found dead," Golden announced.

Gant had his eyes closed, taking these last moments of rest, after having just laid out the best plan he could come up with given the circumstances. Golden's news was no surprise.

"The husband had been dead around three days," Golden continued. "The wife was killed less than six hours ago."

Neeley did the math. "So they killed her on the way out of Maine."

"It appears so. Jesus." Golden was obviously disgusted as she read the latest data from the Cellar. "The husband's body was tied to a chair in front of a bed. The wife was tied to the bed. So she had two and a half days tied there staring at his corpse."

"No shit," Gant snapped, coming out of his rest. "Are you just figuring out these guys are fucking nuts? When we hit the ground in Texas we all need to remember that. We get Emily and we take them out. No mercy."

Neeley nodded. Golden just stared at him. Bailey popped his gum. Across the way, the three CIA men and Cranston were dark figures that Gant could care less about at this point. They had started this mess. He was going to end it.

Golden continued reading the information from the Cellar. "A truck was found abandoned at the house. Forten and Payne's fingerprints were all over it."

"So they don't care about being identified any more," Gant said.

"Apparently not," Golden said.

"Wait a second," Neeley interrupted. "If they were in Main six hours ago, then we're ahead of them, right?"

Golden shook her head. "The police interviewed everyone in the area. Someone reported hearing a plane taking off, apparently a floatplane, from the lake behind the house about six hours ago."

"So it's going to be everyone in the town," Gant said.

"Finley didn't pick a ghost town by chance," Golden threw in.

"What do you have, Doctor?" Gant asked, looking for any piece of information that would give them an advantage going into what was certainly going to be an ambush.

"Horace Finley," Golden said looking at her computer. "I've been running his profile. Somebody should have caught this guy. Somehow his military records disappeared because I really don't have any data on him before he joined the DEA. No information on whatever childhood trauma formed him. But just the stuff he did on duty should have been a warning. He started State-side in the DEA. Working undercover in Atlanta. He was involved in three shootings in four years. Total of four kills."

"All kills, no wounded?" Neeley asked.

"All kills," Golden confirmed, "all his gun. All cleared by the shooting boards. But that's still a lot."

"OK, he's gun happy," Gant allowed.

Golden continued. "Then he volunteered to go undercover in Colombia, which from my experience in the FBI, might be considered insane behavior on its own."

"Or he's just an adrenaline junkie," Gant said. "I served with guys who constantly volunteered for dangerous tours of duty."

"Tours of duty in the Army are different from going undercover in Colombia for the DEA," Golden pointed out. "Finley not only went undercover, he went native. He married a Colombian woman and—"

Gant interrupted. "He should have lost his security clearance right then."

"The DEA thought it gave him better cover so they gave him a waiver for his clearance," Golden said. "He had a child with her. Guess where they lived."

Gant felt a chill settle in his stomach. "The village that was wiped out. That he tried to make the deal for. That he tried to protect."

"Right," Golden said. "And then his cover was given away by our friends across from us."

Gant rubbed his head. Working for the Cellar he had seen betrayal and double-crosses, but nothing like this. "That explains the family angle of the revenge. Finley probably thought that up. Do you think Finley can be reasoned with?" he asked Golden.

"'Reasoned with'?" Golden repeated. "He's crazy. That's not the clinical term but it sums it up."

"Can you talk to him, maybe enough to distract him, confuse him?" Gant pressed. "You're our negotiator. And you have what he wants." Gant pointed across at the CIA men and Cranston.

"Yes."

Gant took of the headset and walked across to Colonel Cranston. "What was your call sign in Colombia?"

"Falcon," Cranston said.

"And the team's?"

"Hammer."

Gant went back to his side of the plane and relayed that information to Golden.

"We're five minutes out from the link up point," Bailey announced. Even as he said it, Gant could feel the aircraft bank sharply and being to descend.

Gant stood once more. "Time to get ready."

Emily hadn't heard the voices for a while. Indeed, a profound silence had descended. Looking up she could see the faintest of light, indicating dawn was coming. This was her last day, Emily knew. Either her last day of captivity or the last day of her life.

She knew her father was coming for her. She was certain of it. And if he was coming he was bringing a lot of help. That was cause for optimism. The fact that there were more than one of the bad guys and the comment about the charges—not so good.

She stood near the side of the tank, looking up at the small notch. So close, yet out of reach.

She took a deep breath and tried to think. She could not simply stay here and wait for her father. Because that's what the evil men wanted her to do. She knew they had a plan. So she had to make one up.

Emily took her hand and pressed it against her forehead, pressing hard, as if by that act she could force inspiration to burst forth.

Work with what you have.

She could hear her father's voice. That's what he would tell her.

Emily stripped. She realized as she pulled her shirt off that her stomach was taut and flat, something she would have been proud of in any other circumstances. She was sure she'd be asked to dance now. Emily smiled for the first time—she was half-naked, standing in a water tank, held captive by crazy men, and she still thought about her weight.

She looked down at the red marks on her ankle from the shackle. She had defeated that. She could defeat this tank. She finished undressing.

She stared at all her possessions. Shirt. Shoes. Tattered remains of her bra. Skirt. Panties.

Combination. The word came to her.

The Combat Talon hit the dirt runway hard, buckling Gant's knees. While the plane was still rolling the back ramp cracked open, the lower portion leveling out while the top disappeared up into the darkness of the tail section. Bailey and Neeley had their weapons ready and began ushering the four prisoners toward the back of the plane.

Gant reached out and tapped Neeley's shoulder, halting her for a moment. He leaned close and had to yell to be heard above the roar of the plane's engines echoing in through the open tailgate. "I'm counting on you."

Neeley stared at him for a second, then nodded. "I'm counting on you too, Gant."

Then she was off the ramp with everyone else as the plane came to a brief stop. As soon as the last person was gone, the plane began moving again, the ramp coming back up. Gant's last glimpse was of Neeley, Bailey and Golden shepherding the four prisoners toward a waiting Blackhawk helicopter, then the ramp was shut and the plane was roaring down the dirt runway and back into the air.

"Six minutes," the crew chief yelled, holding up both hands with six fingers extended.

Gant turned to the pallet and grabbed the parachute off the top of it. He began to rig for the jump and the combat that was sure to follow.

As the Blackhawk lifted, Neeley watched the MC-130 take off at the far end of the runway. It was quickly gone into the dark sky and she turned her attention back to the inside of the chopper.

She shouted to be heard above the blades and engines. "You." She indicated the CIA Director of Operations. "You're number one." She pointed at the Chief of Direct Action. "Number Two." Then Paul Roberts. "Number three." And finally at Cranston. "Number four. When we touchdown and I yell your number, you get off the helicopter."

"Fuck you," the Director of Operations shouted back. "This is bullshit."

Bailey reached across the cargo bay and slapped the muzzle of his pistol across the man's face, drawing blood from his nose. "Wrong answer. You get off when your number is called or you die where you're sitting."

Neeley turned to Golden and indicated a headset. "Time for you to talk to them."

CHAPTER TWENTY-EIGHT

EMILY DUCKED AS the shoe almost hit her in the face as it fell back toward her. It was kept from hitting the floor of the tank by the sleeve of her shirt, which was tied through the strap. The other sleeve was in Emily's hand.

That had been her fifth attempt and she was surprised how tired her arm was from throwing and how hard she was breathing simply from tossing a shoe in the air. She took a few deep breaths, then looked up at the notch once more. She carefully tossed the shoe.

It bounced off the plank and back toward her once more.

"Fuck," Emily hissed.

Angry, she flung the shoe back at the notch, the sleeve in her hand ripping free. Emily froze as the shoe went over the top of the tank, her eyes focused on the shirt, fearing to see it disappear with the shoe.

But the shirt hung down the inside, the sleeve she'd lost within reach. She took it in her hand. The shirt was about three inches to the right of the notch. She tugged slightly, pulling to her left. The material moved an inch. She tugged again. Another inch. One more time and the shirt slid into the notch.

Holding her breath, Emily slowly pulled on the sleeve. The shirt slid smoothly through the notch until it suddenly came to a halt. Emily knew the shoe was just on the other side now. She allowed herself several shallow breaths.

Emily wrapped the sleeve around both hands and slowly shifted her weight from her feet to her arms. The shirt/shoe combination held as she put more and more weight on it. She felt the strain build in her arms as she held tighter and tighter. Hands shaking, she bent her knees and lifted her feet an inch off the ground.

It held.

She put her feet back on the ground and released the pressure as she caught her breath.

Now the question was: could she make the climb?

"HAMMER, THIS IS FALCON." Golden released the transmit button and Neeley leaned close to her.

"Say, 'over', when you're done sending."

Golden belatedly hit the transmit and barked: "Over."

All Neeley could hear was static on the FM channel that Bailey had been given by Finley. "Again," she said to Golden.

"Hammer, this is Falcon. Over."

The static was broken. "You're not Falcon, but that's all right, because I'm not Hammer." The voice was calm and matter-of-fact.

"Put Hammer on please," Golden said. "Over."

"Put Falcon on. I assume he's coming to get his little girl. After all, he's killed for her already."

"You don't need to talk to Colonel Cranston," Golden said. "You just need to see him. And the others. Over."

"Who are you?" Finley asked.

Neeley nodded. Golden was drawing him in, engaging him. The co-pilot in the front of the chopper held up five fingers, indicating they were five minutes from the town.

"My name is Doctor Golden. I'm a psychiatrist. Over."

There was a weird sound in reply and Neeley realized Finley was laughing. "You going to give me therapy, doc?"

"We want proof of life," Golden demanded. "Put Emily on. Over."

"Emily's not next to me either," Finley said. "We bought off on your proof of death at Fort Meade. Took your word for it. So take our word she's alive."

"Is she in the area?" Golden pressed.

"Oh, she's around," Finley said with a laugh.

The co-pilot held up four fingers. Neeley unbuckled her seat belt and grabbed a harness off a hook. She buckled it on as Golden continued to engage Finley in conversation. Neeley then tethered the harness to a bolt in the floor of the cargo bay. She opened up a long case and pulled out her sniper rifle. Then she slid over to the left side of the chopper and slid the door open, taking a seat on the floor, legs dangling. She tightened the tether to make sure the limit of her movement would keep her from sliding off, and then looked about the wind from the blades above her buffeting her skin.

The sun was rising in the east. It was the cusp between night and day. She switched frequencies tuning out Golden's psychobabble with Finley and tuning in the tactical frequency they'd agreed on.

"Gant?" She asked. "You there?"

Gant was standing at the edge of the open ramp, being whipped by the air swirling in the cargo bay. "I hear you," he replied. "Wait one. Over."

The light in the tail of the plane turned green and Gant stepped off the ramp, freefalling at ten thousand feet above the ground. He spread his arms and legs, arcing his back, and stabilized. He waited a few seconds, then grabbed the rip cord and opened his chute.

The opening shock pulled him upright and took his breath away. He reached up and grabbed the toggles, gaining control of the canopy. He checked the data board on top of his reserve chute and checked his altitude and location.

"Neeley? I'm airborne now. Eight thousand feet AGL and on track for the town."

"We're three minutes out," Neeley said. "Golden is talking to Finley. He said that Forten isn't with him. Nor is the girl."

"They're dispersed for an ambush," Gant said.

"Duh."

Gant smiled grimly. "See you on the ground."

"I hope so."

Emily had her feet against the wood and her hands tight around the shirt as she pulled herself up another couple of inches. Her arms felt like they would rip right out of their sockets, her muscles were vibrating in protest, but she slid one hand up a few inches, then the other, then her feet one at a time.

She was breathing hard but didn't care. Not much further. The top of the wood was close, damn close, but still out of reach. Emily was so tired, in so much pain, that not any one specific part of her body took precedence. It all hurt.

Two more inches. Emily held still panting, as she desperately glared at the lip of the tank. It looked close enough, but if she reached and missed.

She couldn't think about failure.

Then she heard a sound. Cloth tearing.

No time.

She bent her knees slightly, then pushed up as hard as she could as she let go of the shirt with her right hand and clawed for the top of the wood. Her fingers hooked over and she held on, even as the shirt in her left hand tore away. Ignoring the pain, she slammed her left hand onto the wood, scrabbling for the edge. Her fingers clawed over it and she was hanging by both hands.

"Fuck," she hissed. No way she could pull herself up to get a leg over. No way.

Then she heard the distinctive sound of a helicopter.

"Number one," Bailey called out.

The CIA's Director of Operations glared at him as the chopper's wheels touched down with a light bounce on the main street of the ghost town. Neeley shifted her attention back to the scope on the rifle. There was just enough light now to be able to see. She had the tactical frequency now in her left ear and Golden's freq with Finley in her right.

Bailey grabbed the Director and tossed him out of the chopper onto the broken tar of the street and the helicopter immediately lifted.

Golden's voice was matter of fact. "The Director of Operations is on the ground."

"What the fuck is that?" Finley snarled. "Chinese takeout?"

"First course," Golden said and her voice was so cold Neeley glanced at the woman sitting there with her laptop still open.

Gant was at five thousand feet and now could see the layout of the town. Rail-line to the south. Large factory building to the east. He also could see the chopper pulling back after making its deposit.

Neeley saw the Director of Operations start running, dashing toward the buildings on the left side of the street when his body was slammed hard to the tarmac. She shifted the rifle, knowing the bullet had to have come from the other side of the street and further away.

* * *

Emily heard the shot. She pulled upward with all her strength and swung her right leg in an arc toward the top. Her chin reached the top, her heel hooked over it and she continued with the momentum.

Her calf slid over the top, her thigh. Her hands bled as she pulled with all her strength and then she was on top, straddling the top of the wood planks. Emily leaned forward, placing her head down on the thin wood and breathe deeply, not daring yet to see what her next challenge was.

She looked down and saw that at the same distance down on the outside was a foot wide ring of wood, then a fifteen-foot drop to the ground.

Gant saw the body go down but had not seen the origin of the shot. He had the toggles pulled in tight, slowing his descent as much as possible. The slanting rays of the rising sun cast very long shadows, making observation difficult.

"At least give me a gun," the Chief of Direct Actions pleaded as the Blackhawk banked back toward the town.

Neeley glanced over her shoulder. Bailey looked like he hadn't even heard the man. Golden clicked the transmit button on the radio. "You got one. We want proof of life. Where is Emily Cranston?"

"We're not even at fifty percent yet," Finley replied.

"We're not asking you to give up Emily yet," Golden reasoned. "Just proof of life."

Neeley spoke into the tactical frequency. "Pilot, hold us in position."

The Blackhawk flared to a steady hover.

"We're not coming in," Golden said, "until we hear from Emily. We've got the Chief of Direct Action to be let off next."

"You don't have a choice," Finley replied. "Give me the DCA."

Gant had lost a thousand feet of altitude while Golden fought for proof of life. He'd been tempted to cut in and tell her to cut the bullshit—the girl was either alive or she wasn't. But then he could tell she'd already realized that as the Blackhawk came in for another landing, this time to the west side of town.

* * *

"I'm not going," the DCA flatly announced.

Bailey popped his gum and shot the DCA in his right thigh, reached forward as the man screamed and writhed in pain, and threw him out the right side of the helicopter even before it touched down. The man landed in the dust and the chopper was gaining altitude again.

Neeley wasn't watching the DCA. Her focus was on the town.

Gant, on the other hand, *was* watching the DCA. He saw the man roll, try to stand, leg buckle, try to stand again, sink to his knees.

Then get shot. Low, in his gut, making him shudder and double-over as if punched.

"Ground level, close," Gant called to Neeley over the radio.

"Fuck," Neeley replied. "Different shooter. I didn't see the muzzle flash and the angle is too divergent."

"He's still alive." Gant saw the DCA was now crawling, trying to get to a drainage ditch that lined the dirt road. A dark red trail of blood followed his body.

Gant angled his parachute, to the south side of the town away from where the chopper was, toward the crawling man.

"I've got him," he hissed as he saw a figure in the western shadows of an abandoned gas station creeping closer to shoot again, out of sight of the chopper.

Gant turned his chute in that direction, let go of the toggles and brought his rifle up to bear.

Emily had checked the shirt and saw that the noise she had heard was the shoulder seam nearest the shoe anchor had begun to split. So she tied the shoe to the other sleeve. Then she hooked it in the notch, the opposite of the way she had done it before.

She took several deep breaths and then began to crawl off the top of the wooden planks to climb down to the outer ring. She had both hands on the shirt and one leg pressed against the side of the tank. The other leg was still hooked over the top of the tank.

She unhooked that leg, gripping tight on the shirt.

Her strength wasn't enough as her grip failed and shirt slid through her fingers and she plummeted down, slamming onto the wood ring. She almost slid off but managed to back against the tank, trying to regain her wind and not fall off.

As she took a deep breath, a stabbing pain brutally informed her that she had broken at least one if not two ribs during the fall. As she lay there gasping she saw the strangest sight: a parachutist, floating by, heading toward the town, holding a rifle in his hands and trying to aim it.

Neeley saw the DCA's body get slammed by several more bullets, knocking it backward to sprawl face-up in the street.

"Gant?" she called out over the radio as the Blackhawk hovered.

Hanging under a canopy at the discretion of the wind and gravity was not the most stable platform Gant had ever used to try to shoot someone. In fact, he was realizing it was an impossible platform as he was rapidly losing altitude and the un-guided chute kept turning with the wind.

"Fuck it," he muttered, letting the rifle drop down to hang on its sling while he grabbed the toggles, dumped air, and flew straight toward the man standing in the shadow who had just fired three more rounds into the DCA.

Gant was about eighty feet off the ground when he felt the snap of a supersonic round whip close by, coming from his right. He twisted his head in that direction even as he dumped more air and the only thing he saw at his level was the church steeple, which made perfect sense.

"We got a sniper in the steeple," Gant got out as another bullet whipped by and the man on the ground turned and looked up, surprise filling his face as he spotted Gant screaming down toward him underneath his canopy. The man began to bring up his sub-machinegun.

No time for niceties at thirty feet altitude. Gant's hands raced from the toggles to the quick releases on his shoulders. His thumbs looped through the metal loops as the man brought his gun to bear.

Gant popped the releases at fifteen feet altitude just as the man fired. The burst of rounds flew over Gant's head as he disconnected from the canopy and free-fell to the ground. Gant hit hard, tumbled forward and jumped to his feet less than a yard from the man. Gant grabbed the barrel of the sub-machinegun and pushed it away from his body as the man fired another burst.

The hot barrel seared into Gant's flesh but he didn't let go as smashed his other fist into the man's face, staggering him backward. The man dropped the weapon and grabbed Gant by the throat and right away Gant knew he was facing Caleigh Roberts' killer as the mechanical hand began to compress his throat.

* * *

Neeley slid the sniper rifle toward Bailey who was still covering the two remaining prisoners. She got to her feet and moved to the small crew chief window behind the pilot where the M-2 .50 caliber machinegun was mounted. As she did so, she heard the pilot curse as there was a splintering of the cockpit glass just in front of him.

"We got ground fire," the pilot screamed. "From the steeple."

"Hold position," Neeley ordered as she grabbed the handles of the machinegun. "I'm taking care of it." She held the handles at chest level and aimed the large barrel of the machinegun toward the steeple. Her thumbs pressed down on the butterfly trigger and the gun roared into life, spitting huge .50 caliber rounds out, every fourth one being a tracer.

The strings of red tracers arced from the gun and hit the steeple at the base. Neeley 'walked' the rounds up the building, just the way Gant—Tony Gant—had taught her to do on numerous firing ranges. The large bullets tore away chunks of the light wood framework of the steeple.

She saw a muzzle flash in the belfry and adjusted. The rounds ripped into the lightly constructed building like miniature sledgehammers. She kept her thumb pressed down as the large barrel began to smoke from the hundreds of rounds going through it as she systematically destroyed the steeple and the sniper inside it.

Gant could faintly hear the firing of a heavy machinegun in the distance, but of more immediate concern to him was a lack of oxygen. He was seeing stars as his brain began to shut down and the hand around his throat increased pressure despite his attempts to pull it off with his right hand.

Gant lifted his left leg, grabbed the slim knife out of the ankle sheath with his left hand. He slammed the point into Payne's throat and was rewarded with a spray of blood that completely blinded him. Payne went to his knees, the prosthetic hand pulling Gant down also. As Payne fell over backward dead, the hand still maintained the same pressure, the mechanical sensors receiving no change in nerve messages from the dead arm it was attached.

Gant floundered about like a dying fish, jammed the knife into the mechanical hand, trying to cut something.

Then it all went dark.

CHAPTER TWENTY-NINE

"BACK US OFF," Neeley ordered the pilots. The barrel of the .50 caliber machinegun was red hot. The steeple was now nothing more than an abbreviated stump on the top of the church itself.

"Gant?" she called out on the tactical frequency. "Gant? Do you hear me, damn it?"

There was no reply. She looked at Golden. "Contact Finley."

"Hammer this is Falcon."

"Tell me why I shouldn't kill this bitch right now?" Finley snarled in reply.

"Because you still want Paul Roberts and Cranston," Golden said.

"Fuck Cranston. That was Forten's thing. And you just appear to have made mince meat of him."

"What about Payne?" Golden asked.

"What about him?"

"Doesn't he want Cranston?"

There was a moment of silence.

"Cranston and Roberts. Right on main street. Then you back that fucking chopper away or your girl ends up like Forten."

Neeley nodded when Golden looked at her. "All right," Golden said. "We're coming in."

"Gant?" Neeley called out on the tactical frequency. "Where the hell are you?"

* * *

219

Someone was tearing at his throat. That was the first conscious thought Gant had. He tried to reach up and defend himself, but whoever it was, batted his hands away and kept jerking his throat from side to side.

Then suddenly he felt nothing on his throat and blessed oxygen pouring in as he gasped for breath.

Gant blinked, blinded by the light, only seeing a silhouette over him. A person. Long hair. He shook his head, ears ringing as his brain tried to come back up to speed.

A half-naked girl. Dirty, grimy, haggard. And in her hands was the prosthesis that had been choking Gant. It all came rushing back to him as he took deep, steady breaths. He sat up and stared at the girl, who stared back at him with a half-wild look in her eyes.

Gant unbuckled his combat harness and pulled off his fatigue shirt and offered it to her. She eyed it warily for a second, then took it and slipped it over her shoulders.

And then she began to cry. Huge wracking sobs.

Gant reached forward and pulled her into his chest. "It'll be all right, Emily," he whispered, even though he knew it was a lie.

"Gant?" Neeley glanced at Golden and Bailey who were as mystified by Gant's last transmission as she was. "You ok?"

"Emily's with me," Gant said in a hoarse voice.

"Pull up," Neeley yelled to the pilot as they were about to touch down on main street.

The chopper shuddered as the pilot gave it power. They swooped over the destroyed steeple and Neeley could see spatters of blood and what appeared to a severed arm among the ruins.

"What the hell are you doing?" Finley's voice came over the FM freq.

Golden raised her eyebrows at Neeley, indicating she wasn't sure how to reply. Neeley switched her transmit frequency to the same one Golden was on. "The game has changed, asshole."

"Who the fuck is this?" Finley demanded.

"There's a fifty-fifty chance I'm the person who is going to kill you," Neeley said.

"I've got the girl. Back off. Give me Roberts and Cranston."

"You got nothing," Neeley said.

"Give them to me or she dies now," Finley warned.

"Let me check with my partner." Then she turned off the transmitter.

* * *

Gant had his breath back although it hurt to talk. Emily Cranston was still crying, wrapped in his shirt, her arms tight across her chest. He was scanning the immediate area, knowing they still had Finley out there somewhere. He'd heard Neeley's exchange with the man over the tactical frequency and considered the situation.

"Where did they have you?" Gant asked Emily.

She sniffled and raised her head up slightly. "The water tower by the rail tracks. Inside."

Gant remembered seeing it on his way down. He had no doubt that Finley was somewhere relatively close to the tower.

"How did you get out?" he asked.

"I used my bra wire to undo the shackle, then my shoe and shirt to climb over the top, then I climbed the ladder down. I saw you pass by with your parachute and followed."

Gant stared at the girl, amazed at what she had accomplished. He keyed the radio to talk to Neeley. "I've got Emily and she's ok. She was being held in the old water tank near the railroad tracks. Do you see it?"

"Roger that."

"I bet Finley is somewhere close to there," Gant said. "I got a suggestion."

"Go ahead."

The only expression Bailey showed when Neeley relayed Gant's suggestion was a slight rise in his eyebrows, then he nodded. "All right."

Bailey turned to Cranston and Roberts. "Finley is out there. He was holding your daughter in the old water tower. We've taken out Forten and Payne." He leaned over and opened a plastic case and removed two pistols. "You get these. Then you take out Finley."

Neeley reached over and cut the men's flex cuffs after ordering the chopper to set down on the near side of town at the end of the main street. "Finley," she said into the boom mike.

"I'm waiting."

"We're dropping Roberts and Cranston off at the end of main street. Let the girl go."

"When I see them," Finley said. "And I want you and that chopper and fucking machinegun to back way off."

"No problem," Neeley said.

The Blackhawk's wheels touched down and Bailey gestured for the two to get off. As soon as they were out, he tossed the guns out and the chopper took off once more.

* * *

"Stay here," Gant told Emily. They were in the back store room of what used to be a diner. They'd heard the chopper come in relatively close and Gant had considered taking her to it, but decided against it as it appeared Finley still thought she was in the water tower and that was a big advantage.

Emily nodded and sat down in an old rickety chair. Gant went through the open door to the front part of the store, staying in the shadows. He then crawled over to one of the booths and slid in, peering out the window. He could see Roberts and Cranston standing in the main street arguing, pistols in their hands.

Gant could well imagine what the fight was about: Roberts would want to save himself and Cranston would want to save Emily and face down the man behind her kidnapping.

The arguing ended when a voice yelled down the street. "This way."

Gant twisted his head, but he couldn't see who had called out, although he knew it had to be Finley. Glancing back, he could see Cranston and Roberts split up, one to each side of the street, keeping close to the buildings, weapons at the ready as they headed down toward the rail line at the end of the street.

"That's far enough."

Gant turned his head to the right and saw a man standing in the middle of the street, a sub-machinegun in one hand, a small black box in his other.

"Got this rigged with a dead man's switch," Finley yelled. "Shoot me, I let go of it—then the girl is dead."

Gant felt a presence behind him and saw that Emily had crawled out of the back. She slithered into the other side of the booth across from him and looked out at the showdown. "You have to save my father," Emily said.

Gant's instinct was to say no—all three of the men out there had played a dirty hand and innocents had suffered because of it. But Emily—she was staring at him and he knew that he owed her. Her ability to escape from her shackle and from that tower was the wild card that had tipped this entire thing against Finley.

"Drop your weapons," Finley ordered both Cranston and Roberts.

The two reluctantly put their pistols on the ground.

"How does it feel to be helpless?" Finley took a couple steps closer to the two.

"Please," Emily said. "Or I'll walk out that door."

Gant cursed to himself. "All right."

Gant stood and walked to the front door of the diner.

"I should make you suffer," Finley yelled. "Just like I suffered. Like all those you betrayed suffered."

Gant opened the door. "Oh, just shut up."

Finley spun, weapon at the ready. "Who the hell are you?"

Gant brought his own sub-machinegun up. "I'm from the Cellar."

"Fucking Cellar," Finley said with a nod. "Heard of it. Where the hell were you guys when these assholes were fucking me over? Fucking the sniper team over?"

When Golden's son disappeared, Gant thought. Perhaps Nero had been getting too old for the job. "I'm here now."

"Little fucking late," Finley said. "It's over now. I take them out, you take me out, it's done."

"That's fine by me, but Emily would like to keep her father alive," Gant said.

Finley laughed. "Tough shit on Emily."

Emily's voice came from behind Gant. "No, tough shit on you."

Finley looked stunned for a second, then, surprisingly, he laughed. "Very industrious of you Ms. Cranston."

"So go ahead and blow up the water tank," Gant said. "We could all use a show. And then we cut you down where you stand."

"I'll give you a show," Finley said. "But I recommend you hold off on the shooting. You see—" he held the transmitter up—"there are *two* buttons on this. The first, well, don't need that anymore." He let up a finger holding a button.

Everyone cringed as the water tower exploded. All four legs were blasted away and it began to topple over away from them when a secondary blast underneath the bottom of the tank went off shattering the woods into thousands of pieces.

Gant's ears were ringing and a few stray pieces of wood sprinkled down around him out of the sky but he kept his attention on Finley. His earlier confidence had faded. The targets' plans had always prepared for contingencies and he had a feeling Finley was going to unveil the last one.

Cranston had picked up his pistol and was bringing it up to bear on Finley.

"Hold it," Gant called out to him.

"Good call, Mister Cellar," Finley said, wiggling the box and the forefinger still pressed down on a button. "I've got a card up my sleeve."

"Fuck," Gant muttered to himself as he suddenly saw what he'd missed from the very beginning. "Where is he?"

"Very sharp, Mister Cellar," Finley said approvingly.

Cranston turned and looked at Gant. "What the hell is going on?"

Gant took a step closer to Finley, still not lowering his weapon. "Where is he?"

Finley pointed with the transmitter. "Right there. Inside. Along with five pounds of explosives."

Gant followed the gesture. A wooden coffin was leaning upright against the side of a building less than thirty feet from Finley. He walked over to the coffin and threw open the front.

A young boy was tied inside, gagged, eyes wide in fear, the interior of the coffin lined with C-4 charges as Finley had said.

Gant had never seen him before but he knew right away he was looking at Jimmy Golden.

CHAPTER THIRTY

"GANT?" NEELEY'S VOICE was in his ear. "What the fuck is going on?"

He knew that she—and Golden and Bailey—had heard everything he'd said. He imagined they were quite confused by getting only one half the dialogue.

"That's Doctor Golden's son you're holding there, right Finley?" Gant called out.

"Smart, Mister Cellar," Finley said. "He was the first target and he'll be the last casualty. And you can take your throat mike off and throw it in the street."

Gant did as he ordered and could only hope that the other three in the chopper reacted in the right way because things were going to get very messy, very soon.

"So, first things first," Finley said. He shifted the sub-machinegun toward Roberts. "Gave me up to the Cartel pretty easily, didn't you?"

"You—" Roberts began, but he was cut off as Finley fired a three rounds burst. The bullets tore into Roberts' legs, knocking him to the ground where he writhed in pain. Gant and Cranston remained perfectly still, both aware of the dead man's switch that Finley held.

Roberts tried to bring his pistol up to bear and Finley lowered his sub-machinegun and smiled, glancing from Gant to Cranston.

Gant cursed as he aimed at Roberts but Cranston was faster to the trigger. Cranston's round took the top of Roberts' head off, spraying the street with blood. Cranston turned to Finley. "I'm the last one. Me for the boy. He's innocent. And Doctor Golden had nothing to do with what happened to you guys."

"There are no innocents," Finley said.

"Let the boy go," Gant said.

"Where's his mother?" Finley asked. "Close, right? On the chopper? We knew she'd be brought in. Once we checked out Cranston. We knew he'd run to a woman for help. We even figured on Roberts letting his daughter die. We weren't so certain with the good Colonel here."

Cranston threw his sub-machinegun down to the ground. "I've killed for you like you asked me to. And I'm ready to die now. Let the boy go."

Bailey had to almost sit on top of Golden to keep her from jumping out of the chopper. She'd become hysterical the moment she found out her son was in the town. Neeley didn't have time to deal with the woman's histrionics. As soon as Gant threw away his mike, she'd opened the door and run toward town, leaving Bailey to handle Golden.

The sniper rifle felt heavy in her hand as she sprinted toward the edge of town. She heard a short burst of sub-machinegun fire but didn't pause. Whatever was playing out there was nothing she could do about it until she got a clear line of sight.

She reached the back of the row of stores facing main street and looked about. A ladder led to the roof of one of the single-story buildings and she ran over to it. She clambered up and slid over onto the roof on her belly. She low-crawled to the foot high rampart at the front.

Then she carefully eased her head up until she could see.

It took her a couple of seconds to figure out what she was observing: Roberts was dead in the middle of the street. Cranston was un-armed, pleading with Finley. And Gant was the third point of the triangle, standing next to a coffin with the boy in it, still armed, but not aiming his weapon at anyone.

Neeley slid the sniper rifle up and looked through the scope, examining the coffin. She saw the quarter pound charges lining the inside of it, linked together with detonating cord and knew if it went off, there wouldn't be anything left of Jimmy Golden or anyone within fifty feet.

She checked out the transmitter in Finley's hand. A dead-man's switch, which meant shooting it or him was out of the question. The only thing keeping the charges from going off was the pressure of his finger on the switch.

Neeley wished she still had communication with Gant. Her receiver was useless without him—that's when she smiled and shifted the rifle back to the coffin.

* * *

"Go join your daughter," Gant ordered Cranston.

"I'll kill the boy," Finley warned. "I want Cranston over here."

"And you'll still kill the boy," Gant said calmly. He kept his face impassive as he noted the red dot that was sliding along the edge of the coffin.

"Emily," Cranston called out. "I have to do this. I have to save the boy."

The red dot became steady and Gant tensed.

"Daddy, please," Emily cried out from behind Gant.

Gant heard the shot and swung up his sub-machinegun even as he tensed his body for the explosion.

Which didn't happen as Neeley's shot shattered the receiver hooked to the fuse inside the coffin. Finley was surprised for a second and that was all Gant needed to level his gun and fire a quick burst, stitching a neat line of bullet holes across Finley's chest.

He died staring at the transmitter in his hand as if it had betrayed him.

CHAPTER THIRTY-ONE

GANT SAT NEXT to Neeley in the back of the MC-130 Combat Talon as it flew east. Bailey was on the satellite radio, talking with Ms. Masterson and Nero back in the Cellar, debriefing the mission. Across the way, Colonel Masterson sat with his daughter's head resting on his thigh as she slept with the unconsciousness of sheer exhaustion. Next to them, Golden held her son tight in her arms. The medic on the plane said the drug he had been given would wear off in the next few hours.

"Well," Neeley said.

Gant glanced at her. "That was a good shot."

"If I'd missed—"

"I'd be dead. Along with the boy. And Finley. I trusted you to make it."

"A lot of dead people," Neeley noted.

"Yep."

Gant noted that Neeley seemed troubled. "You don't know Masterson very well, do you?"

Neeley shook her head. "No."

"I've known Nero many years and worked for him," Gant said.

They rode in silence for a while. "Well?" Neeley finally said, putting enough twist on it to let Gant know she was asking him.

And he knew what she was asking. He leaned close to her, not that those across the way could hear above the rumble of the engines. "I think Nero knew what was going on from the beginning. And so did Masterson. I think they had a very good idea when Jimmy Golden was snatched that it wasn't a child molester or random. And then when everything started to happen, they called us to follow because they wanted this whole thing to blow up. They not only wanted the targets—Finley and the SF team. They wanted the CIA guys and the others cleaned out.

"And it worked," Gant continued. "A lot of bad people who betrayed people are dead."

"And some innocents."

"Yes." Gant took a deep breath. "But that wasn't our fault and it wasn't the Cellar's fault. Nero and Masterson probably knew something stank to high heaven down south over what happened to Finley and the SF team. You had the Director of Operations and the Chief of Direct Action for the CIA involved, for God's sake. That's pretty fucking high level. So they let this whole thing play out to get to the truth. I agree with what they did. It was the only way in a world that's pretty dirty and dark."

"At least we got Emily and Jimmy back," Neeley said.

"At least," Gant agreed. He paused.

"What?" Neeley asked.

"I wonder if we're going to be asked to take out Colonel Cranston," Gant finally said with a glance across the plane. "The original plan was that he was to be sanctioned."

"Hannah isn't Nero," Neeley noted.

Gant shrugged. "No, I suppose she isn't."

Bailey came walking over. "Where do you guys want to be dropped off?"

"West Virginia," Neeley said without hesitation.

"Pritchard's?" Bailey asked Gant. "Oh wait." He grabbed his stainless steel briefcase. "This was sent to you." He opened it and pulled out a cigar case. Gant smiled as he recognized the case he'd given Goodwine what seemed like ages ago. He took it and unscrewed the metal end. A cigar slid out. Gant realized it was a fine Cuban and he nodded. The Gullah had their own contacts with the smugglers who worked the coast. A piece of paper was wrapped around it.

Gant read the words: *Mus tek cyear a de root fa heal de tree.*

He looked up at Bailey. "Where's my brother buried?"

"His cabin in Vermont."

"I want to go there." Then he turned to Neeley. "And then ask Jesse if it's ok if I come for a visit? I'd like to see her. And Bobbie."

Neeley smiled. "I'd be glad to."

THE TIME PATROL

BOOK FOUR
READ AN EXCERPT BELOW

WHEN IT CHANGED

WHEN IT CHANGED, Roland, stone cold killer, otherwise nice guy, and weapons man for the Nightstalkers, had the stock of a sniper rifle tucked tight in to his shoulder with a righteous target approaching and that made him happy. Neeley, a usually stone cold killer from the Cellar, was in overwatch, with her own sniper rifle, and she was acting wonky and that made Roland unhappy, since he liked her, and 'like' for Roland was the equivalent of rabid devotion in a well-trained attack dog. However, it all balanced out and mattered little since he was in combat mode and feelings were of no consequence to him in that mode. There was only the mission.

Roland was a man who could live and flourish in the here and now.

That's a rare, and valuable, trait.

It was going to get a lot more valuable.

It changed for Scout, now eighteen years old and almost two years past her first encounter, run-in, kerfuffle, whatever, involving the Nightstalkers, with a whiff of bacon. She'd only smelled real bacon outside the confines of her

BOB MAYER

home; never inside. Inside it was always fakon, vacon or one of the other imposters. If you gotta fake it, Scout had always reasoned, ever since she was old enough to reason, which had been pretty dang young, then isn't imitation the sincerest form of flattery and one should go with the original? Her rail-thin Mother, who counted each calorie as if they were mortal sins, did not see things that way.

Thus the mystery of the odor permeating the house.

For a moment Scout lie in bed wondering if perhaps it was wafting in from the old house next door, the one with the barn where she stabled her horse, Comanche. Out of the old stone chimney. People with a barn and a stone chimney had to eat bacon.

But in this relatively new house with its fake gas fireplace, with Scout's Mother ruling the kitchen, with the aroma of honest-to-goodness real bacon filling the air, Scout questioned reality.

That's a good trait, one the Nightstalkers had found valuable in the past and would need in the future.

If there was to be one.

It changed for Nada, team sergeant of the Nightstalkers, the most experienced member of the team, a man who'd stared death in the eye and French-kissed the grim reaper (figuratively, although stranger things have happened on Nightstalker' missions), with the irritating voices singing the *It's a Small World* whiny tune echoing in his head as his niece Zoey tried to spin their teacup faster and faster.

Definitely down a rabbit hole of dubious merit.

They'd gone from hell to a deeper hell, was Nada's estimation, walking from *It's A Small World* to *The Mad Hatter's Tea Party*. He was not the type of person Disneyland had been designed for and he was a bit disappointed Zoey was attacking each new ride with such zest. Of course she was just a kid, but still. He expected better of someone who shared his bloodline.

As they spun about, Nada wondered how small the world really was?

And why did Disneyland bother him so much and on a much deeper level than irritating songs?

Little did he know, he was about to find out the answers to both.

And the answers were not good.

Very much so.

* * *

232

It changed at Area 51 deep inside the sprawling complex set in the middle of Nowhere, Nevada, because many problems on the cutting edge of science, physics, the weird and the wonderful, started at Area 51. But this time not in the labs where scientists tested the outer boundaries of man's knowledge, occasionally traveling from genius to stupid at light speed (literally sometimes) and requiring the Nightstalkers to clean up their messes, but in the repository of the results of all those tests and so much more: the Archives. If the Ark of the Covenant was indeed found by some Indiana Jones type character, it would have been stored here and it would have fit right in with many of the other weird and wonderful and frightening items gathered from around the world and hidden away deep under the sort-of-secret-but-definitely-most-secure facility in the Continental United States.

Even though the CIA had acknowledged the place existed (it was on Google Earth now for frak's sake), that didn't mean they were holding an open house any time soon.

It changed with Ivar, or rather the sudden lack thereof, of Ivar. Which, considering Ivar's recent history and what had happened during the *'fun in North Carolina'*, might not be as strange as it seems.

But Ivar, and Doc, who was with Ivar, at least initially, were both physicists, and they understood the law of entropy (or thought they did) and knew when something was taken away, something was returned in kind (or thought they knew).

At least a distorted law of entropy, which Doc would come up with later. Sort of.

If there was a later.

It changed at the Ranch, outside of Area 51, on the other side of "Extraterrestrial Highway", but still pretty much Nowhere, Nevada, known to only a few as the headquarters of the Nightstalkers, in such a small way, that it was only because Eagle had a hippocampus twice that of a London cabbie and the resultant phenomenal memory, that it was noticed at all. Noticing didn't mean awareness though.

Which meant Eagle was going to have to learn something new.

If he was given the time.

It changed for Moms by figuratively traveling into her past, both in place and time. She was already in the place, having made the drive of tears back home. She was sitting on the front porch of the abandoned shotgun shack where she'd grown up in the middle of Nowhere, Kansas. Interstate 80 was to the south, across the flat plains, but so far away that no sound traveled from the eighteen-wheelers racing across the middle of the country.

There was no other house in sight, just slightly undulating miles and miles of fields, and despite all the years since she'd left, Moms still had a sick feeling in the pit of her stomach. It had started when she'd entered Kansas and grown stronger every mile she drew closer to 'home'. The house was empty, long deserted. Her younger brothers never came out here, smarter than she was, understanding some memories only brought pain.

It seemed Moms was a masochist, going back to her roots in order to remember.

But sometimes, going into the past is necessary in order to move forward.

There are variations on that, such as changing the present in order to move forward, which Moms was soon to be discover.

It had changed for Foreman, closing in on 70 years of service, in February 1945 in an area called the Devils Sea, off the coast of Japan, in the waning days of World War II. The event was after he and his pilot were forced to ditch because of engine trouble. Minutes later the rest of their squadron simply vanished into a strange mist in that enigmatic part of the world. No trace of the other planes or crews were ever found.

Then it was reinforced in December of that same year, the war finally over, on the other side of the world, when he begged off a mission because of the same premonition he'd had before the Devils Sea flight, and watched Flight 19 disappear from the radar in an area called the Bermuda Triangle.

He'd determined then and there, that he had to know the Truth.

So he'd gone from the Marine Corps, into the short-lived pre-cursor to the CIA, the Central Intelligence Group in 1946, then morphed with it into the CIA, where he moved upward, and, much more importantly inward, into the darkness of the most covert parts of various branches whose letters and designations changed over the years, but their missions grew more and more obscure, to the point where he'd outlived and outserved all his contemporaries so no one in the present was quite sure who exactly he worked for any more or what his mission was.

If he worked for anyone at all.

Not that anyone really cared.

They should.

He was now known as the Crazy Old Man in the covert bowels of the Pentagon and by some other names, associated with bowel movements.

How crazy he was, some people were about to discover.

ABOUT BOB MAYER

Bob Mayer is a *New York Times* bestselling author, a graduate of West Point, a former Green Beret (including commanding an A-Team), and the feeder of two yellow Labs, most famously Cool Gus. He's had over sixty books published, including the #1 bestselling series Area 51, Atlantis, and the Green Berets. Born in the Bronx and having traveled the world (usually not the tourist spots), he now lives peacefully with his wife and his Labs at Write on the River, Tennessee.

For more information about Bob Mayer and all his books please go to http://coolgus.com.

You can also follow him on Twitter: @Bob_Mayer.
Or on Facebook https://www.facebook.com/authorbobmayer.

Please join his newsletter where he gives away free books in all formats and also gives readers an opportunity to receive Advanced Reader Copies. Your email will not be given to anyone. You can join here: http://oi.vresp.com/?fid=e5f94ee30d

Another great way to make sure you don't miss any new release is to follow Bob on Amazon. You can go to Amazon.com and search Bob Mayer and go to his Author Page, or you can use this link: http://www.amazon.com/Bob-Mayer/e/B000AQ1SUK/.

Nothing but good times ahead!

Made in the USA
Columbia, SC
30 January 2018